Marianne Moves On

Cover design by Carol Tennant

Dedication

Once again, I'm dedicating this book to my beloved husband, Gordon. Previously, I thanked him for the size 12 applied for motivation when needed. Well, now I thank him for his size 13. He says things spread out as he gets older. They sure do. And I speak from experience.

Marianne Moves On

Barbara Schnell

CHAPTER 1

1989: I Leave Home

During my senior year in college, my mom announced over dinner that she'd set up a date for me with a local farmer's son. "He's a good worker; he'll inherit a big farm. His dad is a good customer and the family's Catholic. He'd make a good husband."

"Mom!" I exclaimed in exasperation. "Quit setting me up with your friends' kids!"

"If I didn't set you up, you wouldn't have any dates at all," Mom retorted.

"That's because you won't let me go out with anybody on campus," I protested.

"We know what happened to Aggie M. That won't happen to you," Mom said darkly.

"Let Marianne alone," my dad interrupted. "Marianne will be just fine. She can always stay home and take care of her parents. She'll be a great help to us in our old age." He smiled at me benignly. He obviously thought he was helping.

I smiled back weakly—and firmly resolved to leave home as soon as possible.

Some background:

I was the youngest kid in my immediate family—and the second girl. The oldest, my brother, Matt, was the heir apparent and the apple of my mother's eye. He was tall like my dad but had dark hair like my mom's before she'd gone gray. Next came my sister, Agnes Marie—Aggie M to us. Aggie M was petite and dark like my mom and had her porcelain skin. She also had blue eyes that glinted like my mom's. Mom accepted Aggie M because daughters could marry useful connections that would be good for business. But one daughter was enough. I think I was the reason my mother gave up alcohol. As a conscientious Catholic she probably practiced the rhythm method of birth control—or 'poke and hope' as it was known around my hometown of Brookings, South Dakota. Not that she'd ever discussed it with me; I'm just guessing—plus I never found any birth control apparatus or prescriptions in my surreptitious searches. But something threw her system out of whack and I arrived. I was tall and blond, like my dad, and had blue eyes like the rest of the family. Mom said I looked just like my dad except his eyes were dreamy. She said my eyes were more watchful—if that wasn't a redundant comment to make about eyes.

I'm not sure how my father felt about us. I'm not even sure he made the connection between intercourse and conception. He was pretty vague about things. He let Mom run the house, the kids, and the business. She was the queen and he was a drone.

It took me years of eavesdropping, snooping, and observing to figure out how they ever got together.

My mother, Mary Agnes, came from Northern Ireland when she was eighteen. Apparently, she came from a farming family where the farm was left to the oldest son. Since she didn't stand to inherit any money from her family and her employment prospects were dim because of her religion, she scraped together enough money for a plane ticket to New York City, the Promised Land. My mother was the left fist of God—or maybe the left tonsil. She hadn't hit me since I was ten and mouthed off to her but if I did anything she didn't approve of, she'd glare at me with her mad Irish eyes. If I persisted in misbehaving, she'd start yelling. She had a gift with language; she could flay you alive with sulfurous words. She'd lost most of her Irish accent but when she was angry, she sounded like she was straight out of the Old Sod. Fervent in her faith, she made sure we'd all be eligible for heaven. Black was black, white was white, and gray was a sub-section of black.

My dad, Alfred Matthew Fuchs Jr., was a South Dakota native whose family owned a hardware store in Brookings and had illusions of grandeur. Grandpa Fuchs predicted that his only child would accomplish great things in the world, so he insisted 'my boy Al' get an Ivy League degree in law. My dad attended Columbia, but his only interests were novels and my mom who worked at a small restaurant. Grandpa died early from a heart attack on the golf course and Grandma requested my father's presence to take over the hardware store. My dad never expressed disappointment at his interrupted schooling. From comments he dropped I think he was relieved. But I gathered that Grandma was less than thrilled when my father appeared with a young Irish bride on his arm—and a pregnant one at that.

Mom redeemed herself in Grandma's eyes when she produced a Fuchs heir, brother Matt—or Alfred Matthew Fuchs III, poor bastard. She turned into a heroine when she had my sister. I was only twelve when Grandma died—but I knew even then that she was completely dependent on my mother. She may never have liked Mom, but she needed her. So did my dad. From other eavesdropped conversations I concluded that, although my dad was the titular owner of the family business, he wasn't very diligent about managing it. He wrote bad novels and poetry during business hours and often closed up completely to play golf with his buddies if Mom didn't watch him.

The business was the sole support of the family and we all lived in Grandma's big house—which must have gotten old fast. I think Mom started working in the store just to get away from Grandma but eventually she took over management from Dad. After crossing an ocean by herself and settling in a foreign country, running a business in a mid-size town didn't scare her at all. And after Grandma died, Mom took over the big house among the gentry. Mom had arrived! But she wouldn't tolerate a spoiled child—except Dad, of course. All of us kids grew up in nail bins and paint cans. The only person allowed to screw off was Dad. But that was only fair; he'd provided the inheritance.

Big brother Matt, five years my senior, lived up to Mom's expectations. He was an altar boy, captain of his high school basketball team, and on the Dean's List at South Dakota State University. He married a local beauty queen whose father was Mom's lawyer. He completed an MBA before settling down to raise his children and run the business with Mom.

Older sister Aggie M started out living up to all Mom's expectations. She was in band and chorus until high school when she switched to cheerleading and musicals. As homecoming queen, she brought honor to the Fuchs name and went on to South Dakota State University with both my parents' blessings. That's where everything went kerflooey. Aggie M discovered beer in her freshman year and spent most of her time on academic probation. Mom put her in a sorority, hoping that peer pressure would tame her, but her sorority sisters were just as ditzy as she was. Her party time was cut short when she got pregnant. Aggie M's boyfriend was the heir of the local screen-door manufacturer--and Catholic!--so the marriage, outside of being unavoidable to all parties, was acceptable. Aggie M cheerfully dropped out of college and raised her family.

Nobody knew what to do with me when I came along. I was tall like the men in the family, not short, dark, and cute like the women. I played baseball and basketball with my brother until he left for college then I played softball and basketball on the high school girls' teams. I loved it. Mom muttered that I'd grow up to be a lesbian, but Dad came to most of the games and even took the whole team out for ice cream a few times. He patted me on my sweaty shoulder when we won a basketball championship, one of the few times I remember any physical contact with him. He seemed more comfortable with my sports uniforms than the ruffled dresses Mom insisted I wear. She desperately tried to counter my tomboy image until even she could see I looked ridiculous in the sort of clothes she and Aggie M wore. It was like putting a bow on a St. Bernard.

More acceptable occupations were my creative writing class and working on the school paper. Like Aggie M, I was in the school music program. Unlike Aggie M, I stayed in the band. I was the tall, gawky ugly duckling, the accidental birth—or the afterbirth, as Aggie M liked to taunt.

And while my mother bemoaned my differences from Aggie M, she assumed I would still make Aggie M's mistakes. She'd allowed Aggie M to live on campus and look what had happened! Liquor, parties, pregnancy! Not for Marianne! I had to be home from dates by 11:00—both in high school and college. I wasn't allowed to live in the dorm; I had to live at home where Mom could keep an eye on me. She also decided I'd major in English so I could teach when I graduated. She allowed me to select my own minor—communications—as long as I took a summer business course of typing, shorthand, and bookkeeping; all valuable fallback skills, she said. I didn't argue. She was right.

But I did argue about living at home for my college years.

"I don't see why I'm getting punished. Aggie M got pregnant, not me!" I would argue more or less hotly depending on my mood--and my mother's forbearance--over those long four years. "I'm missing out on everything!" I'd wail.

"You're not missing anything important," Mom would return shortly.

"How would you know? You never went to college," I muttered.

"And that's why I'm not going to let you ruin the opportunity I've provided for you," Mom said. "Aggie M didn't need an education; her looks would always see her right. But you need to be able to make a living."

I think she meant well but she still gave me an inferiority complex. As I entered my final college years, I plotted how to get out from under Mom's controlling thumb. I knew I had to go somewhere a long way off...but where? After watching the news one evening, the answer came: Los Angeles. I wanted excitement and apparently L.A. had the corner on the market. From what I saw on TV something was always going on—not necessarily good but nothing like safe, little old Brookings.

Of course, I still had to get through college while not losing my mind. I recruited my brother to help me lobby for a midnight curfew. After a spirited skirmish, Mom admitted that Matt was probably right (not me!); I could probably be trusted to stay out an hour later. An overnight with some girlfriends was possible. Mom also let me take her car so I could go to movies (bars) and student meetings (parties) with girlfriends. Life was still restrictive but at least I got out of the house. And slumber parties were short paroles. I got to hear about normal life. The girls' talk was all about sex and other adult pastimes so I had little to contribute but I would listen avidly. I finally accepted a blind date out of desperation. He was the friend of the boyfriend of a girlfriend, but he passed muster with Mom. She thought he was safe after she interrogated him. He took me to a few movies and I finally lost my virginity to him just to see what everybody was talking about...which apparently wasn't much. It was more embarrassing than anything else. I wasn't sure what to do—obviously passion didn't enter into the act—so I just lay there like a lox hoping he'd hit the elusive G spot I'd read about. I don't think he knew where it was either. After it was over, I worried. What if I'd gotten pregnant? He fell in love with me and kept calling and Mom got nosy and hopeful. It was a dreadful experience all around. When my period finally came, I said a prayer of thanks and told the guy I didn't think we had a future together. I certainly wasn't going to sweat through a month like that again and birth control in my house was impossible.

After that I decided that sex was probably like Scotch; I hadn't liked that the first time I tried it either. I'd developed a taste for it after I'd experimented with better brands. I'd tried plain wrap when I lost my virginity; I'd wait until I could get Johnny Walker Black. I joined some intramural sports teams to burn off calories and frustration.

Of course, Mom started worrying about me being a lesbian again and started setting me up with sons of her friends (earnest young Catholic men) and sons of customers (young farmers and manufacturers). Mom saw me as a workhorse, not a show pony.

I dutifully went on those wretched dates, studied hard, and played lots of softball and basketball until I graduated. Happy day! Now my life could start.

Which presented me with a whole new list of problems. What would I do for money? Mom told me I could work at the store until I "settled down" or went to grad school. While I appreciated the offer—which wasn't disinterested on Mom's part; she could pay me peanuts since I was living at home—and although I'd learn a lot about business, I had other plans. I needed a skill to make a living in Los Angeles and I wasn't sure being a clerk in a hardware store would pay well enough. When Matt's father-in-law offered me a job as a legal secretary, I jumped at it. I'd get some training, save some money, and be marketable in the Big City. I endured living at home and Mom's ridiculous matchmaking attempts for a year until Dad—I think trying to help me out—repeated his mantra one last time: "Marianne doesn't need to get married. She'll stay home and take care of her old folks." He smiled at me kindly as he said it.

Oh God. I announced that I was leaving home for Los Angeles.

My dad said, "Oh?"

My mom said, "Don't be ridiculous. That city's Sodom."

She refused to even entertain the idea until brother Matt took my part. "Let her find out how tough it is out there. She's lived such a sheltered life she'll be back in a year and be happy to settle down," he said in an after-Mass tete-a-tete with Mom (I was lurking in the hall). "Besides, I think the adventure would be good for her."

We finally talked Mom into the idea, but she argued about everything. When I found a contact for an apartment in LA, Mom insisted on interviewing the landlord. Mr. Friesman was related to a local family and had a garage apartment for rent behind his Los Angeles home. He was looking for a reliable tenant and I needed a place to live. It seemed like a match made in heaven, but Mom didn't like him.

"He seems flighty," was Mom's assessment after the phone conversation. "And he's charging too much. Four hundred dollars for a garage apartment? Something funny's going on."

"Mom, rents are more in Los Angeles than they are here."

"That's more than I paid in New York," Mom objected.

"You had one room not an apartment. And it was thirty years ago," I pointed out. Mom humphed and muttered something about brothels.

I found the names of some law firms from phone books at the University library and scheduled appointments with five of them.

"Law firms," Mom sniffed. "If you stayed home, I'd send you to grad school."

"If I stayed home, I'd lose my mind," I muttered.

"What?" asked Mom sharply.

"Nothing," I mumbled. I was too much of a coward to be too snotty to Mom. She was small but she scared me to death. But I came close when Mom announced she was coming to Los Angeles with me.

"You've never been that far away alone," she said. "I won't sleep a wink knowing you're on the road by yourself. Besides, I've got some cousins I haven't seen in years living around there. I could visit them. Maybe they could put you up somewhere. They'd be better than that Mr. Friesman."

"Mom," I said as reasonably as I could, "I'm twenty-three. It's time I was on my own. The car works fine. And if I did get into trouble there's nothing you could do to help me anyway. And you certainly can't dump me on people I've never met. Maybe you should talk to Matt again?"

Mom still muttered that family was supposed to help you, Matt couldn't cut through her hard-headedness, and I was starting to panic when Dad spoke up on my behalf. "She's a big, strong, healthy girl," he said. "She could probably beat up any man that tried to jump her."

Thanks Dad. I think.

Mom finally gave up on the idea of coming with me, mainly because Aggie M was pregnant again and she actually wanted Mom around. But Mom lectured while I packed her old Ford Tempo—a college graduation present from the folks. Mom got a Cadillac to replace it. I was happy to get the Tempo. I was afraid my dad would give me one of the Studebakers he collected and lovingly restored. I'd had to drive one of his old Studebaker station wagons in high school. He bought it from a bar called The Office and its slogan, "Come to where the action is", was painted on both sides. Of course, me and my friends were all pretty virginal so the football players would point and laugh as we drove past. It got to the point where nobody would ride with me in what my peers facetiously called the Action Wagon. The experience scarred me for life. I was relieved when Mom got a new car and gave me her Tempo instead of being offered one of Dad's treasures. Actually, I don't think he could bear to part with one.

The day of departure finally came and on a fine June morning in 1989 the whole family congregated in the driveway to see me off.

"You stay in Holiday Inns on the way," Mom instructed. "They're still pretty safe, I think. And don't take up with strangers. I don't want you disappearing in the desert someplace. And don't forget to call every night. If I don't get a call, I'm going to report you to the Highway Patrol."

"I will, Mom," I said, impatient, ready to be off. I hugged my brother, sister, and in-laws before turning to my Dad. He looked panicked. I don't think he knew whether to hug me or shake my hand, so I quickly gave him a short hug before he short-circuited from indecision. Then I turned to Mom, steeling myself for one last argument.

"I don't know why you have to go," Mom started querulously.

"I know," I said shortly. Now that the time had come to go, I was getting scared. I needed to leave before Mom succeeded in shaking my resolve.

Mom sensed my weakness and her eyes narrowed. "You can still stay home," she said, "or at least wait until I can come with you…"

"I better get going," I interrupted, briefly hugged her, and got into my car.

Mom tapped on the window as I started the ignition. I rolled down the window and she said, "Now you be sure to call tonight."

"I will," I promised.

"And you make sure you join a church right away," she added.

"The hell I will," I muttered to myself as I rolled the window back up. I'd had enough suppression, oppression, and repression to last me a lifetime, but I waved, backed out of the driveway, put the car in drive, and took off. In the rear-view mirror I saw my family standing together, waving, although they were blurring through my sudden tears. Funny, I thought I'd be a lot happier starting my big adventure.

CHAPTER 2

The Big City

I sniffled for at least an hour before I pulled into a rest stop and had a good sob. Which surprised me; I thought I'd be overjoyed to leave. I perked up when I pulled back onto the interstate and turned on the radio. Some rock & roll cheered me right up. I sang about my independence and freedom. I stopped for lunch after a couple of hours and resentfully ate the sandwiches Mom had packed for me. If I hadn't been trained not to waste anything, I'd have thrown them out. Then I got back on the road and sang my way to the Holiday Inn in Grand Island, Nebraska. I'd promised Mom I'd stop there, and I checked in, dutifully called Mom, then went down to the pool. The idea was to grandly sun myself like someone on a magazine cover. But I was too shy to flaunt myself in a bathing suit. I covered myself in towels and slunk to a chair as far from the screaming kids and their chatty mothers as I could get. I didn't even put sunscreen on, I didn't want anyone looking at me. I eased myself into the pool but was promptly hit in the head by a beachball to the amusement of the brats. This was not the sophisticated scene I'd hoped for, so I layered myself in towels again and scuttled back to my room. I skipped dinner—I was still full of sandwiches— then sat on the bed and watched TV. I was bored and starting to feel slightly homesick which was unacceptable. I'd worked too hard to fly the nest. I decided to try for sophistication again at the hotel lounge. I changed into a nice skirt (rather short but I was being a grown-up) and blouse, put on heavier than usual make-up (see 'sophistication' note), carefully combed my hair, and walked to the bar.

I seated myself on a stool and ordered a scotch & soda. The bartender didn't say anything to me when I ordered. He just raised an eyebrow which was disconcerting. What was his problem? I was polite; I hadn't done anything odd. He was silent as he put my drink in front of me and ignored my attempt to pay him. I was mystified. Nebraska wasn't far from South Dakota. The rules couldn't be that different, could they? I was diffidently sipping my drink through the straw when a strange man moved down the bar and sat next to me. I peeked at him out of the corner of my eye. He was chubby, balding, and in a rumpled gray suit. I glanced around the room. We were the only customers. Why was he sitting so close? I looked at the bartender for help, but he was smiling sardonically.

The man next to me looked me up and down and said, "How much?"

I found the situation creepy, but my mother raised me to be polite. "The drink you mean?" I replied. "I don't know. I haven't gotten the bill yet."

The man exchanged a look with the bartender. "That's taken care of," he said. "So how much?"

"For what?" I asked.

"Wait, are you a cop?" he returned.

"No," I said, baffled. Then I realized what he was talking about; I'd seen stuff like this on TV.

"You think I'm a prostitute?" I asked in horror.

"Aren't you?" he returned.

I looked from the man to the bartender who was standing with his arms crossed, looking skeptical.

"No, I'm not," I said, uncertain what to say but knowing I had to get out of that bar. I gaped at the bartender who was starting to look sympathetic.

"Ahh, beat it," he said.

I grabbed my purse and fled. I looked over my shoulder periodically to make sure I wasn't being followed back to my room. I had my key ready and unlocked the door quickly. I didn't feel safe even after I locked the door, so I put the desk chair under the handle. I wasn't sure if I did it right, I'd never had to do it before, but it made me feel more secure. Then I turned on the TV and huddled on the bed with all the lights on. Grand Island, Nebraska was obviously too much for me. How was I going to handle a city like Los Angeles? But I couldn't quit now. My mother would never let me live it down. I finally fell asleep.

I left the hotel early the next day, hoping that perverts slept in. I was in such a hurry to get away I skipped breakfast.

The rest of the trip was uneventful. I kept my eyes down and avoided conversation when I stopped for gas. I ordered fast food from drive-throughs and ate in my car. I found family hotels and stayed in my room. I called my mother every night now, not just because I'd promised that I would, but because I was lonely and scared. And I made great time; I'd have no problem making my scheduled interviews.

I was relieved when I finally got to the Los Angeles County line. I was almost there! I didn't realize how big Los Angeles County was; I drove and drove and drove and the traffic kept going slower and slower and slower. By the time I saw the skyline of Los Angeles itself I was creeping along at 10 miles an hour. It was only 4 in the afternoon! What could be causing this? After 45 minutes of beep and creep I passed a three-car accident. It seemed that everybody had to slow down and get a good gawk. *There better've been a head bouncing down the road to justify all this staring*, I snarled to myself, but traffic opened up a little after that. Now the problem was I'd never driven on such narrow lanes before. I got trapped between two trucks and felt like a zit. I was also terrified that I'd miss my exit; I couldn't even see the signs. I finally found the exit I needed west of downtown from the directions Mr. Friesman gave me. I got off without smashing into anybody, thank God, found Sunset Blvd. and proceeded to Maltman Ave. I turned left, drove up the hill, and checked the address. Yup, this was it. I parked outside a two-story craftsman that was in need of a paint job. I combed my hair before stepping out of and locking my car. I trudged up the steps and tentatively rang the bell. A small dog started yapping and didn't stop even when a woman wearing a painter's smock came to the door. Her dark hair was pulled back in a severe bun and she wore bright red lipstick.

"Yes?" she asked coolly.

"Hi, are you Mrs. Friesman? I'm Marianne Fuchs," I said nervously with a diffident smile. "I talked to your husband about renting the apartment?" I said more loudly over the barking dog.

"Oh, yeah," the woman said. "Just a sec. Let me get the key."

She closed the door in my face, leaving me standing on the porch. I wasn't quite sure what to do. In South Dakota I'd've been invited inside and asked if I wanted a glass of water or something. I was nonplussed by the rudeness, but I didn't have anywhere else to go so I just stood there. I knew she was returning when I heard the little dog barking again. She opened the door, picked up the dog, and said, "Follow me."

She led me around the house to a large building that I was pretty sure had once been a barn and was now a garage. I followed her to a stairway around the side of the converted garage and we went upstairs. She handed me the dog and unlocked the door. She motioned for her dog back and gestured inside. "This is it."

I brushed my hands off—the little dog was shedding badly and had weeping eyes—and peered into the single room. My mother had thought I'd paid too much for the apartment, but I'd argued that it was furnished and obviously worth it. Now I wasn't so sure. The Friesmans' taste ran to early garage sale. There was a faded overstuffed chair, a daybed, a scarred dresser, and a small table in the kitchen area with two rickety chairs. The kitchen area was a corner with a tiny sink, refrigerator, and apartment-sized stove surrounded by cheap cupboards. The opposite corner was a framed-in bathroom with a shower, sink, and toilet. There was no closet. The one lighting fixture hanging from the ceiling served the entire room. This is not what I'd been expecting, and I didn't know what to say. Fortunately, I heard the phone ring in the house.

"I gotta get that," Mrs. Friesman said shortly, and she took the key out of the lock. "This is my key. Come over to the house and I'll give you a copy."

I nodded and turned back to my garret. It was stifling so I opened the two windows--I'd already paid first and last months' rent, I felt entitled--and sighed in relief at the cross-breeze. I went back to the landing to check out the view. At least that was impressive. Well, I guess I'd have to make do for a while. At least my mother wasn't here. And speaking of my mother, I'd have to call her to tell her I'd arrived. I was intimidated by Mrs. Friesman's dismissive attitude, but I had to get my key anyway. Maybe she'd let me make a collect phone call. I trudged down the steps back to the front of the house and knocked on the door again. The dog started barking—again—and Mrs. Friesman opened the door and looked at me coolly—again.

"I came for the key," I started diffidently over the yapping dog.

Mrs. Friesman nodded, jerked her head indicating I should follow her—I hoped--and walked down the hall. I edged around the dog and trailed after her. She led me to the kitchen and rummaged in a drawer for the key.

"I was wondering where I could park," I asked uncomfortably while she dug. "I have to unload my car."

She looked up, startled I think, that I had the temerity to talk. I was a little surprised myself. My only excuse was exhaustion and desperation. "What do you drive?" she asked.

"A Ford Tempo."

She made a moue of distaste. "Oh, I don't think there's room by the garage," she said slowly. "I don't want our cars blocked in. You'll have to park on the street. But I guess it would be okay if you wanted to unload your stuff. Just don't leave your car there for long."

Gee, thanks, I thought sarcastically. I was really beginning to develop a dislike for Mrs. Friesman. But I was in no position to say anything. I had another favor to ask. "Do you mind if I call my mother? She'll want to know I got here safe. I'll call collect," I added hurriedly.

Mrs. Friesman glanced up quickly with a key in her hand. She looked like I'd asked to cook her dog for dinner. "I'll call collect," I repeated slowly.

"I guess," she said petulantly. "Here's the key. There's the phone. Don't take too long."

She hung around long enough to make sure I'd reversed the charges then scooped up her dog and left the room. Thank God. Mom answered the phone on the third ring. "It's me, Mom," I said. "I made it."

"Oh good!" Mom exclaimed. "Well, what's the apartment like? What're the Friesmans like?"

"The apartment is fine, and I just met Mrs. Friesman. She seems nice," I lied looking around to see if Mrs. Friesman was listening. "Listen, this is a collect call, so I want to keep it short. I'll call again when I get my own phone." I wasn't sure how I was going to go about doing that with Mrs. Friesman's unhelpful attitude, but I'd have to come up with something.

"Well, you be careful out there. I watch the news. It's Sodom."

"Nah, it's Gomorrah. Sodom's across the street," I retorted impatiently, taking advantage of the distance to be sassy. "Don't worry if you don't hear from me for a few weeks. I don't know how long it'll take to get a phone."

"I expect another collect call in five days, young lady. You find a phone, or I'll have the police track you down," Mom threatened.

I promised I would and hung up. I left the house without saying anything to Mrs. Friesman and moved my car near the garage staircase. I didn't have much to take upstairs; just my clothes, a clock/radio, bedding, towels, a box of books, and some dishes. Mrs. Friesman was peering out her back window after my last trip, so I took the hint and parked my car on the street. I was tired but antsy; it was Thursday night and I had to eat anyway. I washed my face and put on the same skirt and blouse I'd worn in Grand Island—maybe I'd looked sophisticated and that was why the creep had mistaken me for a hooker. I hope it wasn't because

I looked like a dumb hick. I drove down to Sunset Blvd. and grinned. I was on Sunset Blvd.! Wow. I found a restaurant called the Bright Spot. It looked like a converted Denny's and had parking out front. I parked my sensible Tempo and walked into the restaurant. People stared—with reason. Not only did I not look like a hooker, I looked like a first-grader in a hipster hangout. I was the only one not in the uniform of T-shirt, jeans, and sandals. Well, I was wearing sandals, but I wore pantyhose with them. I thought about turning around and going back to the apartment to change but I was hungry. I slunk to an empty booth and buried my nose in the menu. The gum-chewing, pink-haired punk waitress took my order after smirking at me. *Let her smirk*, I thought, *we'll see who smirks when she sees her tip*. I ate my burger and fries and drove back to the apartment. I'd need to unpack some jeans before I went anywhere else.

I had to park about a block away from the Friesmans'. Somebody must have been having a party; the whole street was parked in. I was walking up the driveway, carrying a lamp that I'd left in the trunk, when a man poked his head out the backdoor of the house. He was tall but running to fat with thinning blond hair and bright blue eyes. He looked like a good South Dakotan.

"Are you Marianne?" he called out. "I'm Mark Friesman." He hurried out to shake my hand. "Sorry I wasn't here when you arrived. Did you have any trouble getting settled?"

Only with your wife, I thought sourly but shook his hand and assured him I'd gotten in just fine and was returning from having supper.

He looked around. "Where's your car?" he asked. "You didn't take the bus, did you?"

"No, I parked on the street about a block away. Mrs. Friesman told me there wasn't room for my car here," I replied.

Mr. Friesman made a face. "She's having a bad day. There's plenty of room back here. Go get your car and park it next to the steps. It won't be in anybody's way. Go on now. I'll wait here for you. You can leave the lamp with me. No point carrying it around."

I got my car and parked it where he directed, next to the apartment stairs. When I tried to take the lamp away from him, he said, "Oh no, more than happy to carry it up for you." He was right behind me on the steps and for the first time that night I was glad I was wearing pantyhose and a slip. He followed me into the apartment, asking about the weather back in South Dakota as he sat at the kitchenette table. He explained that he'd been raised on a farm outside of Yankton but had gotten an engineering degree at South Dakota State University before getting an MBA at Stanford. That's where he'd met his wife. He talked and talked and talked. I didn't know how to get rid of him. He finally ran out of things to say but didn't seem to want to leave. He stared around at the apartment. "So, do you have everything you need?" he asked.

"For now," I said. "I'll probably have to buy a clothes rack, but I can do that tomorrow."

"I didn't think about a closet," he said thoughtfully. "If you can wait until this weekend, I can frame in a closet area for you."

"Sure, that'd be fine," I said anxious for him to leave. These Friesmans were the most uncomfortable people!

He finally rose slowly. "Well, if there's anything else I can do, let me know. My wife said you called your mother already, so you don't need to worry about that."

Oh yeah, the phone! Maybe there was a way to avoid asking Mrs. Friesman for any favors. "Could you ask your wife if I could use your phone to call the phone company?"

He looked at me shrewdly. "Tell you what, come over to the house tomorrow morning at about nine and make your call. I'll leave for work a little late. And I'll leave you my work number as a contact number in case anyone needs to find you. How's that?"

I was wondering how people could contact me if I got a job, so I smiled in relief and he left. I brushed my teeth, stripped down to a T-shirt, and crawled into my freshly made bed. I plugged in my lamp on a small table next to the daybed, found a radio station I liked, and pulled a paperback out of a box. I read for a while before turning off the lamp and radio. I stared up into the darkness. My adventure was not starting out anything like I'd thought it would.

CHAPTER 3

I Get a Job and a Closet and Skip Church

I made my phone call under the watchful eyes (an apologetic Mr. Friesman and a resentful Mrs. Friesman--what was with these people?!) of my landlords. The phone company said they could schedule my telephone installation after they got my check for the deposit. The tone of the representative seemed to imply that he was doing me a favor. Maybe by his lights he was. I promised to have the check in the mail and turned to the Friesmans. "I guess it'll be a while," I said, smiling ruefully.

"No problem!" said Mr. Friesman heartily. "Here's my work number if anybody needs to get in touch with you."

I accepted the piece of paper under Mrs. Frieman's frowning glance. "Thanks. Well, I've got some job interviews today. Guess I better go get ready."

I made my way out the back door as Mr. Friesman called after me, "Good luck on the interviews. Don't forget to give them my number."

I felt more than saw Mrs. Friesman's glare. What in the world had I done to make the woman hate me so much? I'd worry about that later. Right now, I had to figure out how to get to my interviews.

According to my city map two of my interviews were in an area called Century City and three were in downtown Los Angeles. I had one interview today in Century City and one downtown. The rest of the interviews were scheduled for next week. Century City didn't look that far away but I'd learned my lesson about driving time coming into town. I'd leave lots of time to get there. Thank God I did. It took me an hour to drive the fifteen miles. The office was impressive, and the people were nice enough, but the commute time convinced me I'd have to find someplace closer to home to work. I drove directly downtown for lunch before the second interview. Parking cost me $20 which made my South Dakota soul cringe. And lunch! I ate in the same building as the law firm and ordered the cheapest salad on the menu which was still $10. I'd need a job in a hurry to survive in Los Angeles. The interview was pretty much a copy of the morning's effort. No commitments were made, and I left Mr. Friesman's number. The weekend yawned in front of me.

But it was Friday night, my first Friday night in the Big City! In my lonely single bed in Brookings I'd imagined going clubbing, living the life I'd seen on TV. I got a take-out sandwich and ate it sitting on the steps outside my apartment overlooking the city. Mr. Friesman pulled up as I was finishing.

"How'd the job hunt go?" he called out as he got out of his car.

"Two down, three to go," I said after I hastily swallowed.

"Well, good luck," he said and turned to walk in the house. He abruptly turned back to me. "Say, how about we build that closet tomorrow?"

"Sure," I said with a shrug. It's not like I had anything better to do.

"Great!" He seemed delighted. "Get in your work clothes and be ready to go to the lumberyard tomorrow at nine. Okay? It'll be fun!"

"Yeah," I said weakly. Whoopee. It'd be like hanging out with my dad. But I needed a closet and, like I said, what else did I have to do?

I took a walk around the neighborhood before giving up for the night. It seemed to be an area of sharp contrasts. At the top of the hill where I now lived the homes were spacious and comfortable. As I walked things went literally downhill. Sunset Blvd. was a major thoroughfare, so the traffic was bumper-to-bumper. The concrete walls separating the homes from the street were covered in graffiti—most of it just names but some popular Anglo-Saxon vulgarities were included. I frowned in distaste and climbed back to the residential section, tripping over tree roots that had heaved up over the concrete sidewalk. Things were a lot neater in Brookings, but I had to admit that the surroundings were different and that's what I'd wanted. My impression of the city was improved by the vegetation. There were so many flowers and palm trees! The royal palms alone reassured me that I hadn't made a big mistake. I went back to the garage apartment to listen to the radio and read my book. I tried to ignore the yelling I heard drifting from the main house.

I was dressed in jeans and a T-shirt and waiting on the steps by nine the next morning. Mr. Friesman came out of the house, looking thunderous. He slammed the door before he saw me on the steps. Then he grinned shamefacedly. "Door got away from me," he muttered then he brightened. "Ready to go to work?" I nodded. "Good. I'll take some measurements. No point in going to the lumberyard until I know what I need for the job."

I unlocked the apartment again and followed him inside. We discussed how many rods and shelves I'd need. Then we talked about how much room the closet should take up. I didn't have many clothes, so he decided to make it six by three feet. Good enough.

Mr. Friesman brushed his hands off briskly and said, "Let me get the pickup out. Can't haul lumber in a BMW."

I followed him downstairs and waited while he slid the barn door back, started and backed up the pickup. When he yelled at me to close the door I did and slid into the passenger side of the pickup when he pointed to it. It was just like hanging out with brother Matt. I felt at home for the first time since I'd gotten to L.A. We drove to a lumberyard in the Valley (the Valley! I was going to the Valley! Honestly, it's much less impressive than it sounds) and discussed building strategy. He bought two by fours, plywood, a large dowel, nails...everything needed to build a closet. He even included a sliding mirror door. "So you can see how pretty you are," he said, smiling. I smiled back, convinced he was just being kind.

We drove back, unloaded, and spent the day measuring, cutting, and nailing. He was a good carpenter and whistled as he worked. I made a sandwich run at noon but that was the only time we stopped. At five Mrs. Friesman, carrying that wretched dog as usual, screa...called from the back door that he had to stop; they had a dinner to attend. He straightened and frowned.

"Guess we'll have to finish up tomorrow," he said.

"You go ahead," I said. "I can clean up here."

"Great." He started to leave then turned back. "I know you'll want to go to church tomorrow so we can start when you get back." I started to demur; I wasn't going to go to church my first weekend in Los Angeles! But he misunderstood my hesitation. "I know you don't know where the churches are so you can come with me to the Presbyterian Church down on Hyperion. It's about time I started going to church again. The wife doesn't approve of organized religion, but I miss it."

"I wouldn't want to get you in trouble with your wife," I started, eager for any excuse but he waved me off.

"No, she's had her way long enough. I won't make her go but she can't stop me."

"But I was raised Catholic," I argued weakly.

"That's fine," he said. "We'll find a Catholic Church and I can drop you off. We can go to breakfast afterward."

I seemed to be stuck. "Oh, the Presbyterian service will be fine," I assented. Mr. Friesman beamed and trotted off. I pouted a bit as I swept up. I consoled myself that at least it wasn't a Catholic service. My mother would have a fit if she knew.

So, I went to the Presbyterian service in my sensible skirt and blouse. Mr. Friesman sang lustily and seemed to thoroughly enjoy himself. We had pancakes at a coffee shop down the road before going back to work on the closet. Mr. Friesman was relaxed all day. He sang along to pop tunes on the radio while assembling the closet. He finished by screwing in the sliding mirrored door. He was whistling as he gathered up his tools, seeming at peace with the world. His demeanor changed completely when a loud "Mark" came from the foot of the steps. He straightened and his face went tense. "Up here," he yelled back.

Mrs. Friesman stomped up the steps. I was surprised not to see the little dog in her arms. She briefly looked at the finished closet, looked up and down at my sweaty self in my jeans and T-shirt, then glared at him.

"Don't you think you've spent enough time up here?" she asked poisonously.

"Not now, not here," returned Mr. Friesman. He carried his tools out and asked over his shoulder, "Can I leave the cleanup to you?"

"Sure," I said, glad that Mrs. Friesman followed him out. I had no idea what she was so mad at him about. But it wasn't my business; I wished they'd keep me out of their difficulties. Even through the closed door I could hear the garage and back doors slam as I swept up. The yelling didn't start until I started moving my clothes into the new closet. I turned the radio up and tuned them out. I went to bed early to be ready for more interviews. My first weekend in Los Angeles hadn't been anything like I'd expected. I might as well have been helping my brother out at home. I was not pleased.

I didn't have any contact with either Friesman over the next few days. I went to my final three interviews. The entertainment firm in Century City initially titillated me but it was clear that me in my sensible skirt and blouse wasn't glamorous enough for them. Who knew you had to look like a fashion model to type? I consoled myself that I didn't want to drive that far anyway. The last two interviews downtown were more promising. As a matter of fact, they both made offers. The money was much more than I could ever have anticipated, and the benefits and parking were similar. I wasn't sure which offer to take. I was on my way out of the second firm when I passed the bulletin board. There was a signup sheet for the women's softball team. I could play softball without my mom making me feel terrible! That was tempting but maybe the other firm had a team, too. I was considering calling the other firm to check when two employees walked down the hall talking animatedly—but only one caught my eye. He was tall with longish ash-blond hair and an aggressive nose. His sharp blue eyes took me in, and he followed the brief inspection with an easy go-to-hell grin before he went back to his business conversation. I felt a jolt and gulped. The decision was suddenly easy. I went right back to the Human Resources Department and announced I'd love to work for Dewey, Beatham & Howe. I signed my tax and insurance forms and got my employee parking pass. I was told to report to the steno pool until I got assigned to an attorney. I would be at work at 9 am sharp the following Monday. I put my name on the softball signup sheet on the way out, glad that I'd remembered to pack my glove. I thought about stopping at a bar to have a glass of wine in celebration until I remembered my unfortunate experience at the Grand Island hotel. I stopped at a grocery store and got some wine and munchies. I sat on the steps outside my garage apartment and sipped wine as I watched the clouds glow in the sunset. One thing I'd discovered about Los Angeles; it had the most spectacular sunsets in the world.

So. I had a few days until I started work. What should I do? Disneyland? I didn't feel comfortable going by myself. Museums were probably safe. And maybe I could go to the beach! I'd get out the Triple A guidebook I'd gotten in preparation for the trip. I'd study that tonight.

I'd gone inside to find my guidebook and have one more glass of wine when I heard steps. The door was open, so Mr. Friesman gave it a quick knock. "Okay, if I come in?" he asked.

"Sure," I said, surprised. Now what?

"I got a call from the phone company today. I'm your contact number, remember? They told me they could be here tomorrow to install the phone if you're free. I told them to come ahead; somebody would be here to let them in. I hope that was all right?"

"That's great," I said, surprised. Finally, something was going right!

Mr. Friesman noticed my glass of wine. "Celebrating or commiserating?" he asked.

"Celebrating," I said with a grin. "I got a job today." He smiled and stood there, waiting. "Would you like some wine?" I asked politely.

"Sure. Glad to help you celebrate. So, who are you working for?"

As I got another glass, I told him I would start in the steno pool at DB&H ("They're a reputable firm," he assured me) and that I'd signed up for the softball team.

"I loved playing sports when I was your age," he said wistfully. "My firm has a team, but Charlotte says I spend too much time at work as it is."

"Charlotte? Is that your wife's name?" I asked.

"She didn't tell you?" he returned, surprised. I shrugged. "Of course, she wouldn't," he muttered. Mr. Friesman stared around moodily. Suddenly he said, "You don't have a TV!"

"Not yet," I said. "Maybe after I get paid..."

"Doesn't it get boring up here?" he asked.

"Well, I have my radio and some books," I said. "I'll have to find a library pretty soon to get more."

"Listen, we have an extra TV in the spare room. You can use that until you can afford to get one." I tried to demur; I didn't want Mrs. Friesman mad about anything else until I could figure out how to make peace with her. Mr. Friesman held up his palm. "I won't take 'no' for an answer. There's no reason you can't use it for a while. We even had cable installed up here. All you have to do is plug it in."

Cable? Wow. Mom wouldn't allow us to have cable. She always said TV rotted your mind and if we didn't find anything on the free stations to watch, we could read a book. Her attitude gave me a healthy love of reading but also a desperate desire to find out what I was missing.

"Okay," I agreed. "Should I come down and get it?"

"No," he said hurriedly. "Charlotte isn't having a very good day." (He'd said that before; I wondered what it really meant.) "Pour me some wine and I'll be right back."

I watched him hurry out. I was wondering if he'd be met with yelling, but I didn't hear a thing—not even the little dog. After a few minutes he hurried back out with a small color television in

his arms. He puffed up the stairs, put the TV on the dresser--
"This isn't very stable," he commented with a frown--and
plugged it in. After checking everything out he sat back at the
kitchen table and clicked to an HBO movie. "I haven't seen this,
have you?" he asked excitedly. When I shook my head 'no' he
said, "Great! Let's watch it together."

So, we did. He only went home when I told him I should
probably go to bed. I had to be ready for the telephone person the
next day. He was a nice man and I appreciated everything he'd
done for me, but I was afraid he was going to become a problem.
But I had HBO! I watched a porn movie. It was creepy but my
mother would have had a fit. And at least I could say I'd seen
one.

The phone man showed up at about eleven the next morning
and the whole process took him fifteen minutes. All he had to do
was plug in the phone he brought with him and make sure the
line was live. "Why didn't you tell me you had a phone jack
already installed? We'd have just sent you a phone and new
number and turned on the service."

I apologized and said I hadn't known that's all I had to do. He
was unfriendly and annoyed, but I hadn't done anything
deliberately. Los Angeles people were going to take a lot of
getting used to. But it left me with the next few days free as a
bird.

With nothing to do.

I went to the grocery store to stock up on food. I wouldn't get
paid for a few weeks, so I had to conserve money. Eating at
home was a lot cheaper than going out so I bought a few weeks'
worth of ramen noodles. I also bought cereal and milk to wash it
down. When I got home, I looked at my remaining cash ruefully.
My first item of business tomorrow would be to open a checking
account and transfer the money from my account in Brookings.

I spent the next morning running errands. I found a bank on
Sunset Blvd. a few blocks from where I lived and opened an
account there. I got a library card from a library in Silver Lake. It
was cleaner than the library on Sunset and seemed to have better
selection of books. I also took time to look up movie theaters in
the Yellow Pages there. I decided to go to the AMC theater in

Burbank because I'd never been to Burbank before. I mapped out the route and managed to find my way through the freeway maze. I paid for my ticket and popcorn with my credit card, aghast at the price. I'd been so pleased at my future salary. Things cost so much out here I'd have to be careful just to get by. I didn't even enjoy the movie all that much. I took a stroll around the theater district and wandered through the shopping mall. I found some store brands that I was familiar with which was a relief. I'd already discovered my South Dakota wardrobe wouldn't work out here. I looked countrified compared to everybody else. Nothing much I could do about it now. I'd have to wait until I got paid.

I found the Pacific Ocean the next day. I was learning my way around the city on the freeway system. I was also getting used to the narrow lanes and the speed. I sat on the beach in my jeans and T-shirt. I'd worn my one-piece bathing suit under my clothes but when I got to Venice Beach the sight of the bikini-clad beauties intimidated me. At home I was in good shape after all my years of sports. Out here, I looked big and clunky. A wave of homesickness washed over me. Maybe Mom had been right about me moving out here. I went home to call her.

I hadn't called as soon as I got a phone because that would have made me seem obedient. Now I needed something familiar even if it was just to hear, "I told you so." When Mom picked up the line, she didn't give me a chance to give her the satisfaction of saying she was probably right.

"Why did you call now? It's not after seven! It'll cost too much! Give me your new number, quick, then hang up. Call me back this weekend when the rates are cheap!"

Rattled, I did as she said and hung up. I'd forgotten about the rates, so she was right to cut me off, but she didn't need to be so abrupt about it. Anger replaced depression. I didn't want to sit in my apartment and brood, so I drove down to a charming lake in the middle of the city and trotted around it until I felt calm enough to slow down and appreciate my surroundings. A sign said the flowers in the lake were lotuses. I'd never seen a lotus before. I found a park bench and enjoyed the palm trees and exotic flowers.

Thank God Mom had responded as she had. She might have talked me into going home and I knew I couldn't—not yet. Moving to a new area couldn't be easy for anybody. I should look at the positives: I had a job and a place to live. I'd make friends and find a place for myself. It would all work out for the best.

I hoped.

I went home and watched TV and ate noodles. The next few days I visited museums in Pasadena and on Wilshire Blvd. I'd save the amusement parks until I made a friend to go with. I didn't see Mr. Friesman again until Saturday night when he asked if I wanted to go to church with him again. I didn't but he seemed so hopeful I hated to disappoint him. I spent the rest of Sunday doing laundry and getting my wardrobe ready for the next day. I had a hard time falling asleep; I had a bad case of butterflies.

CHAPTER 4

I Start Work and Make a Friend

On Monday morning I dressed carefully in another blouse and skirt ensemble. I chose the fanciest blouse I had; it buttoned all the way up and had a nice bow. I wanted to make a good impression on my first day. I left early so I could be at my desk bright and early. I found an appropriate place to park and rode the elevator with the other wage slaves to DB&H. I stopped at Human Resources and the assistant ushered me to the steno pool. A woman not much older than me was seated in the nearest cubicle to the door. She glanced up from filing her nails to look at me--and smirk. She had one of those huge New York hairdos, a low-cut knit top showing an enormous amount of cleavage, and a tiny skirt. At least it looked tiny because her crossed legs hiked it up to the stratosphere of her thighs. And the feet beneath that enormous length of leg wore four-inch heels. Four-inch heels! How could she even walk in those things without messing up her ankles? She returned my less than flattering appraisal with one of her own. She obviously thought my demure skirt and blouse with sensible two-inch heels dowdy. And under her derisive gaze I felt like a shy country cousin.

"This is Cindy, one of our longest-term pool stenos," the HR assistant waved toward her. "Cindy, this is Marianne. She's a new hire."

I smiled politely and Cindy raised a penciled eyebrow at the assistant. "I'll get my own desk soon," she said in some sort of East Coast accent.

The assistant smiled slightly, turned her back to Cindy and crossed her eyes at me before directing me to a desk across the room. "You'll get overload work from assistants who are shared by four associates. And you might get called to temp for a sick or vacationing assistant. The assignments change every day. Just wait for something to come in. Other people work here so you won't get lonely or bored." I guess she thought that was instruction enough because she waved and walked out leaving me with Cindy. I smiled at her uncertainly.

"Don't get the idea I'm staying here for much longer," Cindy said belligerently apropos to nothing.

"Okay," I returned not sure if she was picking a fight or what. She glared at me briefly, turned to her desk drawer to get a piece of gum, deliberately unwrapped it and popped it in her mouth, then turned back to me and re-crossed her legs provocatively.

"I got the inside track to one of the senior partners," she said importantly. "I'll get twice the salary when I get that job."

"That's nice," I said. Fortunately, two other stenos, another young woman and a young man, came in. They introduced themselves as Sandy and Justin and we shook hands. I was relieved that they dressed much more sedately than Cindy. They weren't as conservative as I was, but they didn't look like streetwalkers either. They were new to Los Angeles like I was although they hadn't come as far; they were both from the San Francisco area which sounded really cool to me. Justin had graduated from Berkeley and Sandy came down from Fremont with her brother. They seemed just as fascinated by me when I told them I was from South Dakota.

"Gnarly," Justin breathed. "I bet winters are killer there."

I agreed that they were, and we all smiled until Cindy snidely called out, "Do they all dress like nuns?"

I didn't know what to make of Cindy. What had I done to offend her? But I didn't get a chance to pursue it. A messenger arrived with work for all of us. Sandy showed me what to do and I got busy. It was the sort of work I'd been used to, and I've always been a fast typist, so I got through my pile in short order. Justin seemed to be having trouble, so I took some of his work, too.

"Thanks," he said shamefacedly. "I'm not much good at this. I'm just temping until I get my video game developed. Hey, and don't listen to Cindy. She's been here forever and she's bitter."

"I heard that," Cindy cawed from across the room. "You just wait; I'll be out of here in a week."

"Yeah, when you get fired," Justin breathed. Sandy overheard and smothered a giggle. The three of us exchanged conspiratorial glances and got back to work. For lunch we got sandwiches at a shop downstairs and ate at our desks. We talked about our backgrounds and I was thinking I could be friends with them when an elegant woman in her mid-thirties strode into our room.

"Hey, kids, I need someone to fill in for Forrest Elliot. His assistant just walked out and he's preparing for a huge trial. Any takers?"

I thought the other three would jump at the chance to get out of the pool, but they remained silent. Even Cindy. I wasn't sure if it was appropriate for me to volunteer first, I was the newbie after all. I was trying to come to a decision when the attractive woman grinned at me and said, "How about you? You look like you can handle yourself."

"If nobody else wants to. Sure," I said. "Do I have to tell Human Resources?"

"We'll do that on the way up," the woman said. "Grab your purse, you won't be coming back today."

I picked up my stuff, waved at Sandy and Justin, and followed the woman out. She was half-way down the hall before I caught up to her, so I got a good chance to check her out from the rear. Frosted hair, expensive suit, great legs, and great shoes. I felt the bow under my chin blow up to clown size and turn neon. And I tucked the purse I'd bought at Target under my arm as soon as possible. I obediently followed her to Human

Resources where I heard I'd be working for Mr. Elliot for at least the week. Then the woman led me to the elevator where we went up, up, up.

"I'm Jackie Spencer," she introduced herself as we rode.

I tried to move my purse surreptitiously as I offered my hand to shake. She noticed with an amused smile and I blushed. "I'm Marianne Fuchs," I mumbled shyly and spelled my name for her at her request.

She smiled briefly and asked, "Are you new to the firm?"

"I'm new to everything," I admitted.

"I figured," Jackie said.

"Why? Do I look that awful?" I asked in dismay.

"No, you look decent. And you're nice. Midwesterner?"

"South Dakota," I admitted.

"Well, don't lose the niceness. It's a pleasant change."

We arrived at the top floor and as I followed Jackie I tried not to gawk at the views as we walked past the receptionist's desk. I gawked at the expensive art on the walls instead. The offices we passed had huge desks. This was a far cry from the steno pool. I stayed close to Jackie as she explained the situation.

"Forrest is a brilliant lawyer but he's rude and impatient. He can't keep a secretary because he's abusive. I'm telling you this because he'll probably pitch a fit somewhere along the way and I want you to be prepared. Don't take it personally and don't worry that you'll be fired. If this doesn't work out, you'll just go back to the pool. Your station will be next to mine and I don't have to take his crap because my boss doesn't want to lose me. I'll run interference for you as much as I can. Just try to put up with him."

"Okay," I said weakly. What in the world was I getting into?

Jackie noticed my nervousness. "I've got two magic words for you when somebody gives you a hard time. Just don't say them out loud to your boss. He's paying you a lot of money to give you a hard time." She stopped.

"What are they?" I prodded.

She paused briefly then bared her teeth and said explosively, "That's enough!" She smiled. "Even if you don't say it out loud it stiffens your spine. At least it does mine. But say it with feeling."

I blinked and grinned. Jackie winked, stopped at a door, tapped, and announced, "Forrest? I've got your new assistant. Try not to be a total jerk, okay?"

Mr. Elliot looked up to see me peeking over Jackie's shoulder. He looked me up and down and I returned the favor. His eyes narrowed at my skirt, blouse, and sensible shoes. My eyes widened as I took in what had to be a three-thousand-dollar suit and perfectly polished Allen Edmond shoes. He had thick black hair and wore horn-rimmed glasses. "What's your name?" he asked shortly as he stood up and offered a hand to shake— Jackie raised a perfectly penciled eyebrow at that. I shook his hand firmly and noticed that he had to be at least six feet four inches tall. And he was skeletally thin. His hand was raw-boned, and his nails were bitten.

"Marianne Fuchs," I returned bravely.

"Hmm, how do you spell that?" he asked. He nodded briefly when I did and concluded, "Jackie will show you what to do."

I was dismissed.

Jackie showed me to my desk and explained the work that needed to be done. It was pretty much the sort of work I'd done in Brookings except the numbers were much, much larger. Jackie was able to answer all my questions about the differing statutes between the states and I sailed through my work. I gained confidence with every day and was surprised how fast the week went. When Friday afternoon came, I straightened everything on the desk. Then I asked Jackie if I should go to Human Resources or just show up at the pool on Monday.

She looked me in surprise. "Didn't Forrest speak to you yet? I think he wants to keep you on if you're agreeable."

"He didn't say a word to me," I said. "He hasn't said two words to me all week."

Jackie shook her head and stood up. "Let's get this settled," she said and crossed to Mr. Elliot's office. She knocked, opened the door before getting an answer which got a frown from Mr. Elliot, and said, "Forrest, did you want to speak to Marianne?"

"Oh, sure, send her in," he said. He gestured me into a chair and looked at Jackie. "Thank you, I'll take it from here. Close the door."

Mr. Elliot and I stared at each other after Jackie left. I waited for him to open the conversation. He just looked at me.

"Well," he said finally, "how was the week?"

"Fine," I said. "I hope my work was satisfactory."

"It was," he said slowly. "Tell me about yourself."

"What do you want to know?"

"Well, start with where you're from." He glanced at my blouse when he said that.

So, I told him that I graduated from South Dakota State University with an English degree. I came to Los Angeles to see the world. He nodded along. I thought he might tell me something about himself after my dissertation, but he just rubbed his eyes under his glasses wearily.

"I suppose Jackie told you about the permanent position as my assistant?" he asked.

"She mentioned something about it," I evaded.

"You're too young for the job but your work this week was acceptable, and you show up on time. You follow directions, you don't take long lunches, and you don't spend the day talking to your boyfriend on the phone."

I didn't know what to say to that. That I didn't even have a boyfriend? I decided to keep my mouth shut.

"Do you know what the job pays?" he asked.

I shook my head. He named a figure and I blinked. "Does that interest you?"

"Yes," I said eagerly. It was almost half again what I started at. With that kind of money maybe I could buy a suit like Jackie's. Maybe two. If I knew where to find them.

He took his glasses off and tossed them on the desk. "Then the job's yours if you want it."

"Great!" I said with a grin.

"That's all," he said. "Be here Monday at the same time."

I gave Jackie a big thumbs up when I left his office. "I got the job!" I told her excitedly.

She smiled. "Good. See you Monday."

I hummed as I drove home. I'd have something to tell Mom when I called tomorrow.

Saturday started well. I found a laundromat and washed my clothes, sheets, and towels. I read a book while I waited because the soap opera the manager had on the TV was in Spanish. Not a big deal; I'd just find a laundromat that showed shows in English next time. I treated myself to lunch out because I knew I'd have a bigger paycheck soon. I just had a burger, but it was a change from ramen noodles. I'd have to be careful; a steady diet of burgers would put on weight I didn't need. I was too heavy compared to the women I'd seen out here as it was.

I also treated myself to a movie. I was still horrified at the price—it cost twice what a movie cost in Brookings—so I didn't buy any popcorn or pop. But it kept me away from my apartment. See, I was trying to avoid Mr. Friesman. I didn't want to go to church with him anymore.

I didn't see anyone when I pulled up the driveway next to my garage apartment. I grabbed my laundry from the trunk of the car and tried to sneak up the stairs without being noticed. No such luck. Mr. Friesman stuck his head out his back door and called out to me, "Hey, you ready for church again tomorrow?"

I slumped. "Oh, I don't want to cause you any trouble. I'd be happy to sleep in tomorrow. You go ahead without me."

"Nonsense," Mr. Friesman said jovially. "It's good for both of us. And your mother would kill me if I let you skip church. Remember, I'm a South Dakota boy, too. We go to church; that's what we do."

"Okay," I agreed weakly. He was my landlord. Would he throw me out on the street if I said 'no'? I didn't have anywhere to go. And I'd been raised to obey my elders. I didn't know how to handle this situation and I didn't have anyone to ask. I spent that evening at the grocery store buying fruit and salad vegetables for the following week and stewing over the problem.

Mr. Friesman and I sang hymns with the Presbyterians again. I prayed for guidance but apparently God didn't recognize importuning in a Protestant church from a lapsed Catholic because I didn't get any insights. Mr. Friesman insisted on buying breakfast afterward.

35

"Mr. Friesman, I can't," I objected. "That's imposing too much."

"Nonsense," Mr. Friesman repeated. "And call me Mark. Mr. Friesman makes me think of my father."

"Oh, I can't do that," I said. He wouldn't take 'no' for an answer, so I didn't call him anything except 'You'. I was feeling trapped.

He did most of the talking over breakfast at the diner. He told me about his upbringing in South Dakota. "My hometown was a lot smaller than Brookings," he assured me. "I thought I was living in a big city when I got to South Dakota State University."

I smiled at that.

He smiled back. "You can imagine how I felt when I got to California." I nodded ruefully. "You probably feel the same way in Los Angeles," he concluded. I nodded again and stuffed some pancakes in my mouth. "Yeah, I was pretty lost when I got to Palo Alto," he continued and stared off into space. "I would have latched on to anyone who was nice to me. As a matter of fact, I did. That's where I met Charlotte. She was confident, pretty…I never really saw what she wanted in me."

He stopped his vocal reverie when he noticed me staring as I chewed my pancakes. I probably didn't look very intelligent at the moment, so he said, "It's not important." Then he talked about his father. I finished my food long before he did because he spent so much time reminiscing. He finally cleaned his plate. "I haven't talked that much in ages," he said with some surprise. "You're a good listener, Marianne."

He paid the check and we finally went home. I thought a nap would be nice, but I had to go through one more ordeal. Mrs. Friesman trudged up my stairs and knocked on my door.

"Yoo hoo, Marianne, I need a favor," she called out.

I reluctantly answered the door. "Yes?" I asked politely.

"Since you seem to be such good friends with my husband, I told him I was sure you'd be happy to do me a favor, too," she started poisonously.

Oh no. I was in hell.

"He's taking me to a party of some of my friends this afternoon and we need someone to walk my dog for me," she said and held up her moth-eaten, rheumy-eyed little poodle who yapped once at me. "Maybe you want to take her around the block now, so you'll be used to each other? Hmmm?"

She, too, was my landlord and I didn't know how to say 'no', so I nodded resignedly. She smirked in a satisfied way, handed me a bag, the dog, the leash, and my instructions. I was to wait until Poopsie 'made', pick it up in the bag, and bring Poopsie home. This apparently was my punishment for spending too much time with her husband. I wanted to tell her that going to church wasn't my idea, or breakfast either, but I didn't know how to express the thought without the situation sounding even weirder than it was.

I walked that bad-natured, smelly little dog around the block and picked up her poop. I didn't know how I'd gotten in the middle of what was apparently a troubled marriage and I didn't know how to get out of it.

CHAPTER 5

I Play Softball and Get Insulted

Fortunately, my new position at work kept me away from my apartment. Mr. Elliot's team was in the last stages of going to trial, so I worked fourteen hours a day helping him get ready. I didn't object to the long hours because I was getting overtime. That would pay for a new wardrobe, hopefully, as long as I didn't get demoted. Jackie was the assistant of the Senior Partner, Mr. Brady, who oversaw everything at the firm, so I spent most of my time with her asking questions and making sure I didn't screw up. I kept waiting for Mr. Elliot to go bananas about something, but he never did; he was terse when he spoke to me but wasn't offensive. As a matter of fact, he was easier to work for than my mother. As long as I followed instructions and didn't screw up, he left me alone. Unlike my mother, he didn't comment on my appearance or rail at me because he didn't approve of the direction my life was taking. In quiet moments, I reflected that working for a nut case like my mother had prepared me for an exacting boss but there were few quiet moments.

We didn't have much time for lunch, so we ate at our desks. Jackie told me tantalizing tidbits about her life. She was single and in her mid-30s and alluded darkly to an affair that soured her on men generally. She didn't get specific and from her tone it sounded like it was better to let the matter drop.

I got up the nerve to ask her about her clothes. "I feel like a little kid in these skirts and blouses," I complained. "Where do you get your suits?"

Jackie smiled. "You look age appropriate in your clothes," she assured me. "You'd look a little silly in clothes like mine. But after the trial I'll help you shop if you like."

"That'd be great," I said. "I can't buy anything until I get paid anyway. I don't want to run up my credit card."

"Smart," Jackie commented and started talking about the case. I glowed in the approval of my mentor.

I allowed myself one distraction while I was working. Actually, it wasn't my choice to have the distraction. The tall, blond, good-looking young man who'd caught my eye when I originally took this job appeared.

"Who's that?" I finally asked Jackie, jerking my chin toward the young man.

"One of the messengers," she said dismissively. "He's a law student interning over the summer. I can introduce you if you like."

"Oh no," I demurred, shyness setting in. Jackie shrugged and returned to her work.

I followed the young man out of the corner of my eye but ducked when he glanced my way. I don't know if he caught me watching or not.

Mr. Elliot finally went to trial and my hours went back to normal. I still didn't spend much time at my apartment because the softball team had started practice. And I had excuses ready when Mr. Friesman suggested we go to church. I'd told Jackie about my difficulties with the Friesmans and she suggested I lie. My mother would have been horrified but, as Jackie pointed out, sometimes a little white lie was better than going to war. At least until I had a back-up plan.

"But wouldn't your mother object if you skip church?" Mr. Friesman complained when I said I couldn't go with him.

"She'd be mad that I was going to a Presbyterian service," I said truthfully. Then I lied. "I'll be going to a Catholic mass from now on." I'd probably go to a movie, but he didn't need to know that.

"Maybe we could at least meet for breakfast afterward?" he suggested wistfully.

"I'll probably still have to go in to work. We're prepping for a trial. Or go to softball practice," I parried. He finally gave up— for the time being.

And it wasn't a complete lie—except we had softball practice on Wednesday evenings after work. The games were on the weekend. And it was fun.

The law firm sponsored the women's team and Mandy, a paralegal, was the organizer. She told me she'd graduated from Harvard in prelaw, was working as a paralegal until she got accepted into one of the prestigious schools, didn't matter which coast it was on, and that she was a lesbian. She was quite aggressive on that point. "That's nice," I returned, not sure how to respond. Was I supposed to tell her I wasn't? She continued, "Yeah, half the team is out so sexuality is no big deal." She looked at me expectantly.

"Good," I commented neutrally.

Women's softball consists of ten players, not nine, so we needed a short center fielder. After several practices it was easy to see who'd played before; the four lesbians who played the outfield positions were power hitters and Mandy was the pitcher. I was assigned as shortstop although I hadn't specified any sexual tendencies—I let my ability speak for itself. The other women were not only not lesbians, they'd never played before. But they were enthusiastic. Sandy, the girl from the steno pool I'd met the first day, promised to practice with her brother every day if we'd let her play first base. "My brother even lent me his mitt," she caroled as she proudly held out her glove.

She was as good as the other newbies, so Mandy let her have the position. I commented to Sandy that it was nice to see her again and she congratulated me on my promotion and said she was glad I was on the team, too. "I didn't even know you were a lesbian," she said.

"I'm not," I said. "I played in South Dakota. Are you gay?"

"No, but don't tell Mandy," she returned, looking around nervously. "She might throw me off the team."

"I doubt if she cares," I said, smiling.

"Maybe. Say, could you could give me some pointers?" she asked. "My brother's not very patient."

I agreed to help where I could, and we got ready to practice. We had a game coming up and we needed to get serious. "We're in the D league," Mandy lectured. "That's the lowest because we're new. The team we're playing is new, too, but they're sponsored by a lesbian bar, so you know they're going to be good. We've got our work cut out for us."

We assumed our assigned positions and Mandy hit grounders to us. Boy, the lesbians took the game seriously! But I think they took everything seriously. As I got to know them, I found out that they were all trying to get into prestigious law schools. And I'd bet on them getting exactly what they wanted. I wished I could be that focused about something. They were smart, interesting, rather humorless, and damn good ball players. At least I could stay with them on the playing field. I may not have been a lesbian, but I knew what I was doing as a shortstop. I even got a compliment from one of the power hitters.

"Nice moves, kid," she yelled after I'd stopped a short hop and fired to Sandy on first—who missed.

"Thanks," I yelled to the outfielder and, "Sorry!" I yelled to Sandy who was chasing the ball. I went home sweaty and happy and wondering how we'd do at our first game the coming Saturday.

I was optimistic as I warmed up for our first game. I was surprised to see some of the lawyers from the firm in the stands. I looked at Mandy questioningly and she said, "The firm paid for our entry fee. They had to; they paid for the men's team. I think the guys just want to laugh at us. Let's show 'em we can play."

I nodded in agreement and waved at Jackie who'd appeared and sat next to one of the partners. I was amused at her attire. She was wearing chinos and had a cardigan sweater over her shoulders. I wondered if she ever wore jeans and sweatshirts and figured she probably didn't. She waved back and immediately started talking to the partner.

Mandy, as team captain, met with the umpire and the opposing team captain. Mandy called the coin in the air and won the toss. We got last at bats. Then she gathered us around for a brief pep talk. "Don't worry too much about this game," she instructed. "Just do your best. We'll be able to tell our strengths and weaknesses and learn what we have to work on. Everybody's hand in the middle." We all reached in, layering our hands, Mandy yelled, "Team!" and we broke up the circle. I'd never heard anybody yell "Team!" before. Everybody I'd played with yelled the name of the team. Maybe I'd suggest we give ourselves a name--after we'd learned our strengths and weaknesses, of course.

I trotted out to my spot on the infield and was startled at the size of the young woman taking practice swings. She had to be at least six feet tall. And I'd never seen such a muscular woman before. I hoped Mandy was a good pitcher. If this woman connected, she'd knock the ball out of the park. I flexed my knees and punched my glove. I was distracted by Sandy who started yelling, "No batter, no batter!" in a high soprano. It was like being hazed by Minnie Mouse and I started laughing. I shook my head to clear my mind and focused on the hitter. It's a good thing I did. The amazon hit a line drive right to me. I got my glove up before it broke my nose. One out. So far so good.

Sandy continued her high-pitched chatter and the next hitter popped out to the short center. Mandy managed to strike out the third hitter and we all trotted in, relieved that we'd stopped the top of the order. Maybe it wouldn't be a blowout.

Mandy led off and almost got her head taken off by the opposing pitcher. I'd never seen a pitcher try to bean anybody in softball before. These women were more bloodthirsty about their game than South Dakotans were. I frowned unhappily but didn't say anything. That would have been rude.

Mandy got to first on a bobbled catch by the second baseman—woman?—and one of our power hitters got a double. Then it was my turn. Mandy's instruction was to try just to get on: "Don't try anything fancy." Then another outfielder would try to bring us all home. I selected a bat and took a practice swing at the plate.

"Don't worry about Suzy Creamcheese," the catcher bawled to the pitcher, in a deep voice. "She can't hit nothin'! Easy out, easy out!"

What a horrible thing to say! Especially to a woman with a bat in her hand! "I'll show you an easy out," I muttered to her and focused on the pitcher. The catcher shouldn't have made me mad; I got a double, bringing in two runs.

"Way to go," sang Sandy in her sweet voice from the bench.

I relaxed after that. I didn't know if we'd win but I'd be okay.

Until the fourth inning. I was scooping up a grounder when I got body-slammed by one of the six-foot powerhouses from the other side. I managed to hang onto the ball, but she almost knocked me out. The umpire, an elderly man, called a time-out and gave the bruiser a lecture on sportsmanship and acting 'like a lady'. From her expression I could tell that being a lady wasn't high on her list of aspirations. She nodded meekly at the umpire when he finished his little speech and smirked at me when his back was turned. I glared back at her, refusing to be intimidated.

Things got dirtier after that. Our second baseman, a newbie, got spiked by a sliding opponent. I got up enough nerve to protest to the umpire that spikes were supposed to be illegal in softball. The ump took our protest to the opposing team captain who said they hadn't known, and they didn't have any other footwear. She tried smiling sweetly as she said this bare-faced lie, but the kindly old umpire took it at face value.

"Remember to wear the proper shoes next time," he instructed. "And be careful not to hurt anyone today. We're all out here to have fun."

He was going to let this pass?! Mandy and I exchanged incredulous looks. Mandy recovered first. "Let's win this thing," she growled at the rest of us.

And we did. We didn't worry about being nice or "ladylike" anymore. The bigger women slammed onto bases. Mandy brushed back all their best hitters. She wasn't even trying to pretend that the ball got away from her. The poor umpire seemed flummoxed by all the near misses. He kept bleating about "young ladies" and "not embarrassing your mothers". I don't think he spent a lot of time around women in their 20s. Things probably had changed a lot in forty years.

The fans even got involved. The supporters of the other team decided I was "Suzy Creamcheese" and they yelled the name at me derisively every time I came up to bat--which only served to inspire me. I don't remember ever hitting that well. I scored a run every time I was at bat. "Ol' Suzy here is cleaning your clock, huh," I commented to their second baseman after hitting another double. And I gave her the same smile I'd seen my mother give to a customer who hadn't paid their bill for six months and wanted more credit. Apparently, it was just as curdling to the second baseman as it had been to the moocher.

In the sixth inning I was in my position watching the bruiser with the spikes step up to the plate. She waved her bat and stuck her butt out in what my dad called the Stan Musial stance, whoever that was. She had a large derriere, so the stance was memorable. I heard a voice yell out, "Nice ass, lady!" and some giggling from the stands. It came from the good-looking blond messenger I'd noticed in the office. He and his friends acted like they'd been drinking. The bruiser blushed (who would have thought that she could blush?) and tucked her butt in self-consciously. I'd have felt sorry for her if she hadn't been such a jerk. As it was, I just thought, *She's got it coming*, and slapped my glove. *Now* the umpire got upset and charged over to the stands to lecture the messenger. Apparently, this was a situation he understood. I heard him say something about treating these young women like ladies (seriously?) and if that wasn't possible, he would have to request that the young men leave. That seemed to quiet the fans down and the game went on without event until the last inning. Our soprano first baseman kept up her infield chatter about 'no batter, no batter'. It was so sweet and ridiculous that everybody started to laugh every time she opened her mouth. I was thinking maybe someone should suggest that she try to bring her voice down an octave or two when I saw poor Sandy catch a line drive with her cheek bone. She went down in a heap. We all ran over to her to see if we needed to call an ambulance, but she just kept apologizing for missing the ball. Her eye was swelling to alarming dimensions, but she said she was okay; she wanted to finish the game. Maybe she couldn't catch but she had guts. At least she stopped her infield chatter for the rest of the game. We won by four runs and didn't mind when the other team wouldn't shake hands despite all the admonishments by the umpire. He shook his head at their bad behavior.

Sandy even came to the bar for a beer with us after the game. The bartender took one look at her and offered a small bag of ice to put on her eye—which, not being a complete idiot, she accepted.

Our team took over the back of the bar and was joined by some of the firm lawyers who congratulated us on our first win. "You did better than the men's team," commented one of the partners and he bought four pitchers of beer to celebrate. The blond messenger and his cronies joined our group, too, and helped themselves to our beer--not that they needed any more. I noticed that Jackie didn't come.

I had a great time celebrating with 'the girls'. We toasted each other and we all laughed when Mandy yelled out, "And here's to Suzy Creamcheese! She knocked in more runs than any of us!" I stood up and curtsied. Apparently, I now had a nickname. I guess it could've been worse.

I was about three beers in when I noticed that the girl sitting in the chair next to mine had moved and been replaced by the blond messenger. He took a long slurp of beer and leaned in to talk to me. He seemed to have trouble focusing his blue eyes—which weren't steely anymore, just bleary--and keeping his balance. He put his hand on my thigh to catch himself. It was July so I was wearing shorts. I thought he'd move his hand, but he smiled genially and ran his hand up my leg. Then he looked at me seriously. "You have the nubs," he announced.

I shoved his hand off my leg and stood up to leave. "That's enough," I said shortly. Jackie was right! Those two little words stiffened my spine.

He seemed to be having difficulty following the conversation. "I was wondering if you wanted to come home with me," he said, sounding confused.

Was he offering me a ride, something he was in no position to do, or was he propositioning me? Neither option was acceptable. What a jerk! He was probably one of those frat boys who picked up not-very-attractive girls, had sex with them, and then made fun of them. Well, I may not be the most sophisticated, gorgeous girl on the planet, but I could spot a creep when I saw one. This was one country girl he wouldn't so easily take advantage of. I tried to act worldly as I raised an eyebrow and answered in what I thought was a crushing tone of voice, "I don't think so."

He nodded and said, "Just thought I'd ask." Then he lurched off.

At first, I was disappointed; in my fantasies I'd imagined him as my Johnny Walker Black. Then I snorted in disgust; he was just another beer. It was time for me to go home so I left.

CHAPTER 6

I Learn Blondie's Name

Sunday morning, I went to a movie to get out of the apartment. I appreciated the fact that early movies were cheaper, and the popcorn was fresh. This was my kind of church. Mr. Friesman caught me coming home and tried to talk me into going to breakfast with him.

"Why don't you take Mrs. Friesman?" I asked lamely.

"She doesn't like pancakes. She says she has to cut down on carbs."

"Oh," I returned and tried to think of an argument to avoid breakfast. I couldn't tell him I was full of popcorn.

"Why don't you want to go to breakfast with me?" Mr. Friesman asked, interrupting my musing.

I took a deep breath, snarled *That's enough!* with feeling to myself for courage, and started, "I don't think your wife likes you spending so much time with me."

He waved that off. "She doesn't care. It gets me out of her hair. Besides, you're just a kid."

I took another deep breath. "Mr. Friesman, I'm not a kid; I'm twenty-three years old. And I don't need carbohydrates either. I'm on a diet. And your wife does object. She's been making comments. She could make things very hard for me. I don't need that, Mr. Friesman."

Mr. Friesman looked disappointed. "I thought we were friends. It was nice having somebody from back home to talk to."

"Yes, it was nice, but you need to straighten things out with your wife. Because it's very clear to me she doesn't like us spending so much time together. You have to at least include her."

"I tried but she's not interested," he said disconsolately.

"Well, I don't know what else I can do," I said honestly. "I think you should only spend time with me when she's included. It just doesn't look good. My mother wouldn't like this at all."

That clinched it. He sighed and accepted my decision. I watched him turn to go into his house and saw Mrs. Friesman staring at me from her back window, eyes narrowed, nasty little yapping dog in her arms. Poopsie seemed to be vocalizing the dislike radiating from her.

That's enough, I thought at both of them. Thank God for Jackie and her magic words. I straightened my spine and climbed the stairs to my apartment. I spent the rest of the day regretting not getting pancakes. I was really tired of ramen noodles.

I was busy at work the next week. Mr. Elliot was back in trial and I was constantly chasing down documentation and files that had to go to the courthouse. Messengers were in and out all day and I didn't pay any attention to them—until the blond nub-announcing jerk showed up. I'd been digging through a bottom drawer on my hands and knees to get the file I wanted when I abruptly turned and saw him. My jaw dropped and he ducked his head in embarrassment. "Are you here for this?" I asked shortly and offered the file. He nodded and took it from me. He turned to go as I stood and brushed off my skirt.

He abruptly turned back and said, "I guess I should apologize. I shouldn't have said what I did. You know, the nub thing?"

"I know. You shouldn't have touched me either," I said shortly.

"Yeah. Sorry."

I shrugged and sat in my desk chair, waiting for him to leave. He just stood there so I started arranging things on my desk, pointedly ignoring him. He still didn't leave. "Yes?" I finally said.

He stuck his hand out. "My name's Jeff Foster," he said. I reluctantly shook his hand. It was hot and sweaty. "And you're Marianne," he announced.

"I know," I retorted and jerked my hand free, tempted to wipe it on my skirt.

"Iwaswonderingifyouwantedtogoforcoffeesometime," he said in a rush.

Was he kidding? "I don't really have time right now," I said, not wanting to be too rude. I had to work with this guy, after all.

"Maybe later," he amended hopefully.

"Maybe," I said shortly. "Listen, I have to get back to work…"

"Yeah, me too," he said. "I'll see you around?"

"Sure."

I was baffled as I watched him walk off, so I wandered over to Jackie's desk to report the encounter. She laughed. "Sounds like he has a crush on you," she said.

"Really?" I said dubiously. That certainly was a different take on the situation. So, I told her what he'd done at the bar. "That's not a crush, that's creepy," I declared.

"You just proved my point," she insisted. "He had to get drunk to talk to you. If he were ten years younger, he probably would have thrown a rock at you. You're lucky he just grabbed your thigh."

"Hmmmm," I mused. "I figured he was a player. Aren't guys that good-looking up to their eyeballs in willing women?"

"A player wouldn't be that gauche," Jackie assured me.

"But why me?" I asked looking down at my sensible skirt and blouse. "It's not like I'm a sex symbol or anything."

"Oh c'mon. Even I've noticed that you've slimmed down. Maybe it's time for some new clothes if you don't like the ones you've got."

I brightened. "You can tell? I've dropped five pounds in the last month. Five more pounds and I'll be ready to shop."

"Let me know when," Jackie said and went back to work.

I smiled to myself on my way back to my desk. Eating at home was working! In another month I'd be down another size. And I'd have enough money saved for some seriously neat clothes. Just had to get there.

I stuck to my plan. I only played softball on Saturdays, so I started running every morning before work…and lost weight even faster. Jeff Foster showed up to our games, but he never came to the parties afterwards. Once he waved at me diffidently when I was in the field, but I couldn't wave back; I was avoiding the spikes of a particularly aggressive base runner. Geez, sometimes those women were so competitive. And how come they were still wearing spikes?! *That's enough!* I thought to myself, and the next time I came to bat I got a triple. I almost knocked the third baseman out of her spikes when I slid in. I could be aggressive, too. My mother would have been horrified.

Another month passed and I asked Jackie if she had time to advise me on clothes and we appealed to Mr. Elliot to let me have Friday afternoon off to go shopping. He was so aloof most of the time I sometimes thought he considered me an accessory that came with the desk.

Mr. Elliot considered the two supplicants across from him. "If it's for work, I don't want anything too high or too low," he instructed.

"Okay." I didn't argue. I was buying clothes for the office and he was my boss.

We skipped lunch and Jackie drove us to Nordstrom's in Glendale. She walked me past the Junior Miss section and went upstairs to where the adults shopped. We agreed that I'd probably look best in simple, classic things; clothes that would look professional for work but could easily be dressed up with accessories.

Jackie selected some man-tailored shirts to replace my girlish blouses. And they were silk! I'd have to have them dry-cleaned. I worried about the expense, but Jackie told me I'd probably get a raise once I'd passed the probation period. Mr. Elliot was pleased with my work. I blinked. How did she know all this stuff? But I didn't pursue it. I was trying on some wide-leg, high-waisted slacks. Jackie approved. Then I tried on some skirts, blazers, and another pair of slacks; all natural fabrics, not a speck of polyester in the bunch.

"You're not planning on losing any more weight, are you?" she asked as she slipped a finger around the waistband.

"Maybe a little more," I said. "Why? Don't you think I should?"

"No," Jackie returned. "People are going to think you're anorexic. You're thin enough."

That was a relief. I could eat again! I was happy until I saw the price tags on the clothes Jackie and I had selected. I wouldn't be able to eat out again until after I'd paid all this stuff off.

But we weren't done yet. I had to have some shoes and a new bag. I got an expensive pair of shoes that made my legs look long and elegant. Then Jackie eyed the purse I was carrying critically. "You got that at Kmart, didn't you," she stated.

"Target," I corrected diffidently.

"Hmm," Jackie said noncommittally and led me to the Coach store across the hall. I got a simple bag that matched my new shoes. I was horrified at the price, but Jackie told me I wouldn't have to get another one for years. "Good quality lasts," she assured me. "And a woman is known by her bag and shoes. You have to look expensive."

Well, I looked expensive all right. Two hours of shopping had wiped out the savings of the last few months. But I'd look like an adult instead of a tall, 13-year-old.

I grabbed all my bags. "Are we done? Do you want to have lunch or anything?"

"It's Friday afternoon. Let's go somewhere we can have wine."

We packed my bags in Jackie's Mercedes and drove a few blocks down to an Italian restaurant. I marveled that we drove the two blocks but didn't say anything. I was discovering that nobody walked anywhere in Southern California.

We ordered and Jackie told me what to do with my hair as we sipped our wine. "You've got to let your hair grow out," she told me. "That perm isn't a good look on you."

I touched my hair self-consciously. "It was my mom's idea. She said I had to do something to add body. My hair is so fine and thin."

Jackie eyed my hair judiciously. "It's fine but it's not thin," she said. "Frou frou isn't your style. You're tall and slim with great bone structure in your face. You need something simple and classic. You know, cool and sophisticated." She paused and asked delicately, "Is your mother different than you?"

"Oh my God! She is so different! She and my older sister are a lot shorter than me and they both have curly brunette hair. I always felt like a Clydesdale next to them. And Mom always tried to make me look like them."

"Maybe she didn't know any better," Jackie said charitably. "But we're going to get your look, not hers. I'll take you to the man who cuts my hair."

I smiled my gratitude. "But can we wait for a while?" I asked. "I'm kinda broke after all the new clothes."

"Of course. That perm needs to grow out anyway. We'll pull your hair back to give it a sleek look. And we can work on your make-up."

I looked at her in dismay. "What's wrong with it?"

"You should enhance, not cover," Jackie lectured gently.

I accepted the quiet criticism humbly and listened to her pointers. She said I used too much eyeliner. "You don't want to look like that girl in the steno pool, do you? What's her name?"

"Cindy," I supplied. "I look that bad?"

"No," Jackie hurried to reply. "But you're going in that direction."

Jackie concluded her comments and our food came. I picked at my salad as I tried to frame my next question without sounding too geeky. "So, this Jeff guy. Do you know him well?"

"No, he's just a summer messenger. He's in law school at UCLA. He'll probably be gone before long. He'll have to study. But Ted seems to think he's a decent sort. If Jeff asks you out it wouldn't hurt to go."

I dismissed the idea. I still didn't trust him. "Maybe," I said. "Who's Ted?"

"Mr. Brady. You know, our boss?" Jackie said with a slight smile.

"Oooh," I breathed. I'd always seen 'Theodore' on official papers. He was 'Ted' to Jackie? "So how does Mr. Brady know him?"

"He talks at student seminars all the time. UCLA is a regular stop. The firm is always looking for new recruits."

"Oh," I said. I stirred my fork in my salad before asking diffidently, "Do you date any of the lawyers in the firm?"

Jackie looked me right in the eye and said, "Yes. I date Ted. I have for years."

I looked at sleek, polished Jackie and thought about Mr. Brady. He had to be in his sixties and his expensive suits hung off his paunchy body. And hadn't I heard…

"I thought he was married," I said, confused.

"He is."

My Catholic soul almost exploded. "Oh, well, I'm sor…I didn't mean to pry…."

Jackie laughed. "Don't look so shocked. I bet I'd shock your mother, wouldn't I."

"Well, she's Catholic, you know…" I dithered. My mother would be horrified. But I didn't want to tell Jackie that. She'd been so kind I didn't want to offend her with negative judgements.

"So's my boss," Jackie said matter-of-factly. "That's why he can't get divorced. But I don't know if I'd marry him anyway. I like the freedom. And he pays me very well. I also get all the time off I need. I get all the benefits of a wife and none of the responsibility. The arrangement suits us both."

"You're a mistress," I exclaimed in delight. "That's so cool!"

Jackie shook her head at my gaucherie. "I guess. You want another glass of wine?"

I was dazed at the level of sophistication I'd found myself in. "Sure. Why not? I don't have any place to be."

"I do. But not until later. I have to pay my rent with my boss tonight."

"Wow," I breathed again, delighted with the wickedness of big city life. Maybe Mom had been right about Sodom. "Do you wear a negligee when he comes?"

"You read too many romance novels," Jackie laughed. Then she raised an eyebrow and added, "But sometimes I do." She laughed again at my goggled eyes and changed the subject. We gossiped about the cases we were working on until it was time to go.

She drove me back to the office and I bought some coffee before I went home. I spent the rest of Friday night reading bodice rippers. I wondered when and if I'd have the nerve to have an affair. But I still wasn't sold on Jeff Foster, no matter what Jackie said.

Softball season came to an end after Labor Day. We played the same team we started the season with. They still wore spikes, they still screamed insults, and we still beat them. Little Sandy on first base was particularly effective. She'd learned a lot this summer, including and especially, to keep her glove up. I wished she had a deeper voice but at least we'd gotten used to the Minnie Mouse in-field chatter.

The umpire gave a little speech to our team at the end of our last game. "It was such a pleasure to work with lovely young ladies like you," he said, glancing at the opposition in their spikes--hair and feet-- and pads—shin guards, not bras--and sighed.

Mandy and I exchanged smiles at the final comment. Poor man; the world was changing so rapidly. I could understand that he was having a hard time keeping up. I was, too. I wondered if we'd see him next season.

We went to the usual bar to celebrate with pitchers of beer, paid for by Mr. Brady. I was surprised to see him at the bar. I hadn't noticed him at the game. Probably because all my attention was taken by the sight of Jeff Foster in the stands. Who knew he was such a fan of softball?

I was on my second beer when Sandy left the chair next to me and Jeff quietly slid into the seat. I was wearing my shorts and didn't want a repeat of the 'nubs' incident so I edged away from him. He smiled ruefully and said, "Don't worry. I won't touch you. Your leg anyway."

"What else did you have in mind to touch?" I asked warily. "I can get one of the outfielders over here if you cause trouble."

"No, no, let them drink their beer. They earned it. I just wanted to talk," he protested.

I raised an eyebrow and edged my leg farther away—which wasn't far. I was crammed into the person next to me.

"I guess I should apologize again for last time," he added. "I shouldn't have grabbed your leg. Or commented that you hadn't shaved."

He was making things worse. I scowled at him. "Just shut up about me shaving my legs, okay? It's gross."

"Okay," he agreed hurriedly then seemed at a loss as to what to say next. He looked at me, looked around at other people when I frowned at him, looked back at me, then asked desperately, "Do you want another beer?" I pointedly lifted my full glass. "No, I guess you don't." Then he stared at me helplessly.

I wondered why he was so focused on my legs—shaved or unshaved--and why he was bothering me now. Jackie said he had a crush on me; that seemed a little far-fetched. But I was curious why he picked on me for his limb explorations.

"Why'd you do it?" I asked. "You know, grabbing my leg...and talking about my nubs?" I added in response to his confused look. "Were you making fun of me?"

"No, I was trying to impress you, I guess."

"Well, you impressed me all right," I said snidely.

"Yeah," he said unhappily. "Listen, can we start over? I'm really not that bad a guy."

There didn't seem to be any point in holding a grudge, so I said, "Sure."

We shook hands. Then Jeff asked, "Tell me, just so I don't mess things up in future; how do you pronounce your last name? I don't want to get into trouble again."

I smiled. "It's Fooks. German word for Fox. I really should change it to the English word, but Dad would have a fit. But thanks for asking. It can get awkward."

My stupid name finally came in handy. It broke the ice. Jeff helped himself to another beer and told me all about himself. He wasn't a rich man's kid, like I'd thought. His dad was a college professor at a Northern California university. His grandmother paid for some of his education and he worked part-time jobs to pay for the rest. Actually, his background sounded a lot like mine except he wasn't Catholic. "My family is Presbyterian. My mother wanted us to be Episcopalian, she thought they were a better class of people, but Grandma insisted we be raised Presbyterian. She usually gets her way," he explained.

He thought it was fascinating that I was from South Dakota. "I've never met anyone from there before."

"Probably none that would admit it," I smiled. "People can be a little snotty about the interior states out here. I guess they don't know any better."

We talked about what I'd seen and hadn't seen in Southern California. He was amazed that I hadn't been to Disneyland. "That's usually the first place people go!"

"I know," I said, shame-facedly, "but I didn't want to go by myself."

"Listen, if you're free next Saturday I'll take you myself," he declared.

I looked at him appraisingly. He seemed normal enough, but I still wasn't over the leg incursion. But Disneyland...I really wanted to see Disneyland. "Okay," I agreed. "But I'll pay my own way."

He looked a little surprised at that (also a little relieved) and I gave him my address and phone number. He told me he'd pick me up at nine so we could spend the entire day there and we clinked beers.

I was going to Disneyland!

CHAPTER 7

Disneyland!

Jeff showed up right at nine…on a motorcycle. I was sitting on the landing outside my door, sipping coffee, when he roared up the driveway and shut off the bike. My heart skipped when he took off his helmet and shook out that mop of blond hair. He looked up at me and my coffee and grinned that easy pirate smile. "I forgot to ask if you had a helmet," he called. I shook my head 'no'. "Oh, well, then do you have any more coffee? We have to talk this over."

"Sure. Come on up," I called back and led the way into my apartment, glad that I'd made my bed and the bathroom didn't have bras hanging all over it.

I poured him some coffee and we sat at my little kitchen table. "I don't have a car," Jeff explained as he sipped. "So, we have to take my bike except…"

"I don't have a helmet," I finished.

"Yeah, and the law is pretty strict about that out here. The ticket would cost a fortune. And thirty miles on a motorcycle…well, you really have to want to do it."

I suggested, "We could take my car."

Jeff brightened. "I was hoping you'd say that. Could I leave my bike here?"

"I don't think it'd be a problem. As long as you leave it in my spot and not block the other cars."

We finished our coffee, I locked up, and Jeff rolled his bike off to the side of the garage. Mr. Friesman came out to observe. Then he strolled over to inspect the motorcycle.

"Nice Yamaha," he commented.

Jeff beamed proudly. "Yeah, it's a cafed, two-stroke rice rocket. I got it used; they don't make 'em anymore," he said and patted the bike fondly.

"My mother called them organ-donor transportation. I wasn't allowed to have one when I was your age," Mr. Friesman said ruefully.

"Well, you don't live with your mother anymore," Jeff responded cheerfully.

"No-o-o," Mr. Friesman said slowly, "but I have responsibilities now. Can't take chances like that." He looked at me and said, "Don't you have a helmet? And gloves? The first place you land is on your hands if the bike goes down. You can't go if you don't have the proper equipment. And where are you going?"

Jeff looked put out at the interrogation, so I hurried to introduce them to each other. "Jeff, this is my landlord, Mr. Friesman. Jeff here worked with me at the law firm."

They shook hands politely although I thought Mr. Friesman looked like he was trying to bear down a little hard. Jeff smiled slightly and pressed back. This was getting ridiculous.

"Jeff is taking me to Disneyland. I've never been there before, and I've wanted to go since I was a little kid." I smiled brightly at them and they finally released each other. "We're taking my car," I continued babbling. "I hope it's okay if we leave Jeff's bike here."

"Who's driving?" Mr. Friesman asked.

"I suppose I am," I returned with a shrug.

"Do you know how to get there?" Jeff countered.

"Well, no, but you could tell me…"

"Why don't you let me drive? I know the easiest way to get there. It'd save time and stress for both of us."

I started to agree when Mr. Friesman interrupted, "Do you know if he's a safe driver, Marianne? It doesn't sound like you know much about this young man."

Mr. Friesman had a point, but he was starting to sound like my mother. "Oh, he can probably handle a Ford Tempo," I scoffed lightly. "Well, we better get on the road. I don't want to miss anything. Thanks for your concern. Bye now. Have a good day!"

I dug my cars keys out of my purse as I spoke, unlocked the passenger door, and threw the keys to Jeff. Then I climbed into the passenger seat, still talking, and Jeff unlocked the driver's side. Doors slammed, Jeff started the car, we strapped in, and backed out. I waved cheerfully at a disapproving Mr. Friesman as we left.

"What was that about?" Jeff asked as we drove down the street. "Is he always that nosy?"

"He's from South Dakota," I explained. "I guess he feels responsible for me. But it did seem a little weird, didn't it?"

Jeff nodded emphatically then changed the subject. "Hey, have you had breakfast?"

I shook my head. "Just coffee."

"Great! I mean, I haven't eaten either. I know a place for breakfast called Belisle's. It's just outside of Disneyland and it's sort of an institution."

I paid close attention to Jeff's driving. He took more chances than I did but he seemed to know what he was doing and where he was going. I relaxed and focused on my next problem; conversation. I thought finding something to talk about with Jeff would be difficult, but it wasn't. He talked about himself—which was fine. I listened and focused on his blue eyes and go-to-hell grin again. On the drive to the breakfast place he expanded on his family.

"My dad's a college professor up north at UC Davis," he explained.

"You mentioned that. Wow, a college professor," I said, impressed. "What's he teach?"

"Agricultural economics, but it's not that big a deal. My mom said being a teacher is for losers, but the benefits are great."

"What's your mother do?"

"She's a stay-at-home mom. So, with all of us gone she doesn't have a lot to do."

"She's not in much of a position to be calling anyone else a loser, is she?" I commented diffidently.

"Oh, that's just Mom."

"Hmmm," I murmured and changed the subject. "How many kids are in your family?"

"There's four of us. All boys. I'm second to the last. Mom said she always wanted a girl. I think that's why they had me. Then they gave it one last shot and had my brother. My mother gave up after that. How about you? Any brothers and sisters?"

I told him about Matt and Aggie M. "I don't think my mother wanted any more children after she had one of each. Matt and Aggie M are close in age, but I came along about three years after Aggie M. That's what happens when you put your faith in the rhythm method. Catholic, you know."

"Oh? You're Catholic?"

"Raised Catholic," I amended. "I'm not sure what I am. I don't agree with the 'woman as second-class citizen' teaching. Especially about birth control."

His ears pricked up. "You're on birth control?"

Uh oh. Sex. This was getting dangerous. "I don't believe in the Church's teaching on birth control," I corrected and changed the subject again. "So, what's this breakfast place you're taking me to?"

He went into a long, involved story about the waffles at this restaurant, how his family always stopped there on their way to Disneyland, and how his grandmother always paid for the trips.

"Why'd your grandmother pay?" I asked.

"She's the one in the family with the money," Jeff explained. "She and my grandfather had a big ranch outside of Sonoma. That's a town outside of San Francisco," he explained when I looked at him questioningly. "When Grandpa died Grandma sold out to a developer."

"Didn't your dad want to run a ranch?"

"No, he likes academia. So, Grandma kept all the money. Oh, she's generous. She's helping me pay for my JD/MBA. But

60

Mom thinks she should give my father more money right now. We have a nice enough house and car, but Mom insists she needs a housekeeper and Grandma won't pay for that. I don't think they like each other very much."

I had to agree with Grandma. I was raised to take care of yourself. You didn't have any right to anybody else's money unless you did something to earn it. I was diverted from my internal criticism of Jeff's mother when he started talking about school.

We finally pulled into the parking lot of Belisle's and Jeff handed me the keys. "Or should I just hang on to them?" he asked.

"No, I'll take them," I replied and put the keys in my purse. Jeff led the way into the restaurant which was half full.

"Good, there's room," he said in relief. "I didn't make reservations and this place used to be really popular."

After we were seated, I asked, "It's not popular anymore?"

"Well, the population's changing. I don't think the new residents like waffles as much. They probably prefer huevos rancheros."

I didn't know what huevos rancheros were, so I let the subject drop. The waitress took our waffle orders and left a pot of coffee. She hurried back with orange juice but then we were stuck with each other again.

"So, how'd you get into the legal profession?" Jeff finally asked after an awkward pause.

"Oh, I worked for our family attorney right out of college and it was the only thing I could do as a job when I came out here," I explained.

"What'd you major in and where?" Jeff asked.

"I went to South Dakota State University," I said a little defensively. I'd gotten so used to people making snide comments about the Midwest I think I was a little prickly.

"Never heard of it," Jeff said equitably. "What'd you major in?

"English," I admitted and hung my head.

"What'd you want to do with English?" Jess asked curiously.

"Nothing. It was my mother's idea. She wanted me to be a teacher."

"And you didn't?

"Maybe later. I don't know what I want to do. I guess she picked English because I like to read, and I used to write stories for myself." I sipped my coffee moodily. "She had my life all settled. I'd stay in South Dakota and get married and have babies…And maybe I'll do all of that. But it's a big world; I'd like to see some of it before I settle down to anything. I want to look around and see what my options are."

We talked about the types of things we liked to read. I talked more than Jeff because he concentrated on his huge plate of waffles. He listened as I discussed Dickens ("Never read anything except *Great Expectations* and that's because I had to in school," he admitted) and Jane Austen. Literature was my favorite subject, so I talked as he chewed.

I was halfway through my waffle when Jeff finished mopping up the last of his syrup. I wasn't used to so much food after my ramen diet and couldn't finish mine. I pushed my plate toward him. "Do you want the rest of my waffle?" I asked.

"Sure," he said and switched plates with me. I watched bemusedly as he finished up my waffle. He didn't have an ounce of fat on him; where did he put all that food?

We finished our coffee and he paid the check. "You're paying for gas," he pointed out. But he let me pay my own way into Disneyland.

I didn't want to act like a wide-eyed yokel in front of Jeff, but I couldn't help it; Disneyland is great! I'd been watching *Wonderful World of Disney* ever since I could remember—it was one of the few things Mom let me watch on TV—so I was enchanted. We walked past the train station into Main Street USA. I marveled at the animatronic Abraham Lincoln. We crossed back to the Tiki Room which I thought was charming.

"Really?" Jeff asked skeptically at my enthusiasm. "Me and my brothers called it the Tiki Tiki Tiki Tiki Tacky Room."

I was momentarily abashed at the comment but rallied. Nobody was going to spoil my enjoyment. "Well, I liked it," I said stoutly.

"This is America, that's your right," Jeff murmured. And he kept his mouth shut when I rhapsodized about the Swiss Family Robinson Treehouse and climbed all the way to the top.

"I remember this movie," I said breathlessly. "I had such a crush on the Kirk kid."

"I think he was gay," Jeff said then held up his hands in surrender when I scowled at him. "But I'm sure he was a cute kid."

Jeff ignored the hokey comments the guide made on the Jungle Ride, although he looked bored. Then he asked if we could stop for something to eat. "After that huge breakfast you're hungry?" I asked incredulously.

"I'm a growing boy," he grinned.

So, we went to a restaurant and he ordered an extremely expensive Monte Cristo. I had a Diet Coke. When his sandwich came, he asked me if I wanted a bite. I took one look at the deep-fat-fried sandwich and my stomach turned over. "Not now," I said. He happily snarfed it down.

Then we started to look for the serious rides. They were easy to spot; they were the ones with the long lines. We stood in line for forty-five minutes for Space Mountain. Jeff spent the time talking about pursuing a JD/MBA; the challenges he faced and his hopes for the future.

"I don't know if I'll go the business or the law route," he finished. "I thought it was nice to have options."

"You don't want to go into corporate law?" I asked. "That's where the money is."

"Maybe if I got a job with the firm," he agreed, "but I don't think I'd do well there. Right off the bat, that is. Except for my grandmother, I don't have any serious connections. So that's a long shot. I'll probably end up as a prosecutor with the District Attorney. I'll get to know people that way. And if I ever decide to go into politics it'd be invaluable."

"No interest in being a public defender?"

"That's for idealists. I think it's more important not to charge innocent people in the first place. Saves everybody a lot of time and money. No, I'm no do-gooder."

"What about the MBA?" I asked.

"Same problem. You need contacts and I don't have them. And I can't see being an analyst or marketer for the rest of my life. But I'll see what kind of offers I get. I'll probably get better ones from the business world."

He smiled that easy pirate smile. With his charm I didn't think he'd have any problem with his future.

We rode Space Mountain and didn't really talk until the next long line for the Haunted Mansion.

"Have you considered being a lawyer?" he asked conversationally.

"Me? Oh no," I pooh-poohed the suggestion.

"Why not? Elliot was telling the boss the other day that you're a find and seem to have a feel for the law."

"Oh, he said that because I get things done on time, and I don't lose things or screw up deadlines. That's being organized. After living with my mother, the law is a piece of cake."

"I think you're selling yourself short," Jeff said with a knowing look. "What do you do for fun?"

"Well, I used to play softball. I guess my main hobby is reading."

He asked me about the stories I'd mentioned writing. "They're angsty teenage poetry and some cruddy short stories," I laughed.

"I'd like to read them," Jeff said seriously.

I was startled by the request. No one had ever asked to read my stuff before except my teachers and they had to because it was their job.

"I used to play flute, too," I joked. "Do you want to hear me play?"

"Are you serious about music?"

"About as serious as I am about softball."

Thankfully we got on the ride and I enjoyed the special effects as much as the lack of interrogation. Jeff seemed to think he had to direct me into a career. I'd just gotten to Los Angeles! Give me a break!

That's how the day went. We'd wait in line, he'd talk about himself, pry into my life, we'd ride the ride, and move onto the next line. We took a break from the lines to eat over-priced food.

Well, Jeff would eat, and I'd watch him. I couldn't understand how he stayed so slim the way he poured calories into his system. Then we'd stand in another line. It was exhausting.

At the end of nine hours I'd had enough but Jeff assured me we had to stay for the Light Parade and the fireworks. So, we did. But first Jeff had to have ice cream and I had another disappointment.

I'd seen Disney characters interacting with customers all day but I was always on my way to a line or in a line so I couldn't talk to them. While we were sitting on a curb eating our ice cream cones Mickey Mouse walked close to us. Micky Mouse! I was star-struck. I waited for Mickey to turn my way but when he did, he just walked off. The damn rat wouldn't even shake my hand. Jeff howled and I sat disconsolately, licking dripping ice cream off my affronted hand.

We sat on the curb through the Light Parade and the fireworks--which were good—because my feet were shot. And I was dreading the drive home. My stomach was upset from too much rich food and I wasn't sure how the evening would end. Would he expect me to kiss him? Would he expect more? I wasn't ready for that. He was cute and charming, but I figured he was a player; and I wasn't going to be just another notch on what was probably a heavily notched belt. I dozed off on the ride home, so I guess I couldn't have been too worried. Or maybe I was that tired.

Jeff pulled into the driveway and we both got out of the car. Jeff was walking around the car to meet me, whether to kiss me or what I'll never know, when the back door of the main house slammed open and Mrs. Friesman came staggering out. She was drunk as a lord.

"Who told you you could leave that motorcycle here?" she screamed at Jeff. "This isn't a public parking lot!"

Jeff and I looked at each other, neither one of us knowing what to do. Mrs. Friesman came at us, still screaming. "It's bad enough I have to have that…that…Ford killing the grass," she howled, "but I don't need some biker trash hanging around." She stopped about twenty feet away from us to hang onto a tree. She was so drunk she'd probably have fallen if she hadn't.

"Should I go?" Jeff asked me uncertainly, warily watching Mrs. Friesman. "Maybe I better stay until you're upstairs."

Fortunately, Mr. Friesman came outside and corralled her. "It's okay," he said to Jeff. Then he turned his attention back to his wife. "I told him he could park there. Now come back inside. You're making a scene." He steered her back inside and closed the door on her before turning back to us. "Sorry about that," he called out. "It won't happen again." Then he followed her inside.

Jeff stared after him then asked me, "Has that happened before?"

"It's never been that bad," I said, staring at the main house. "Sorry that happened."

"Yeah, me too," Jeff said. "Well, guess I better get my bike out of here before she goes off again. Seriously, I'll wait until you're upstairs. You can lock her out, can't you?"

"Yeah, but I think Mr. Friesman will keep her under control," I assured him. I hoped so anyway.

Jeff was as good as his word; I got a warm feeling as he watched me climb the stairs into my garage apartment. He didn't start the bike until the door closed. When I heard him roar away, I decided he wasn't such a jerk after all.

It was a strange end to a long day. At least I didn't have to face the kissing problem. Although maybe that wouldn't have been such a bad thing. I was starting to see a Johnny Walker Black label circling Jeff's chest.

CHAPTER 8

Oh, Sweet Mystery of Life...

I was sitting at my tiny kitchen table, sipping coffee, and trying to figure out how to get in my car and drive to the grocery store without Mrs. Friesman tearing outside and screaming at me like a harpy on fire--or Mr. Friesman trying to get me to go to church with him--when I heard steps slowly creaking up the staircase. *Oh no*, I thought, *it's got to be a Friesman and I don't want to talk to either of them.* I grimaced when a tentative knock sounded. Damn, this wouldn't pass me by. I warily opened the door a crack on a shame-faced Mr. Friesman.

"Can I come in?" he asked.

I reluctantly opened the door wider and gestured him to the kitchen table.

"Coffee?" I asked with as much cheer as I could muster—which wasn't much—and poured him a cup when he nodded. I seated myself opposite him after he'd declined my offer of cream or sugar, took a sip of coffee, and waited for him to begin. He fidgeted a bit and peeked quickly at me from under his brows, maybe to check my mood. I cupped my hands around my mug and waited him out.

"I'd like to apologize for my wife's behavior," he plunged in finally. "She sometimes drinks too much and gets the craziest ideas in her head."

"I didn't think a motorcycle would be so bad," I said. "It sat where my car sits. It took up less room, so I don't see the problem."

"It wasn't the motorcycle. That just set things off. I don't know how to explain this," Mr. Friesman said with a sigh. I sipped my coffee as I waited for him to get his thoughts together. I hoped Mrs. Friesman didn't get some 'crazy idea' and end up on my landing with a butcher knife.

"She's been unhappy for a long time," Mr. Friesman began again. Then stopped again.

Visions of drunken crazy women were dancing in my head, so I prodded him. "About what?"

"She's been upset about her art. It doesn't seem to be taking off," Mr. Friesman said.

"What kind of art does she do?" I asked. I'd been curious about her paint-daubed smocks for weeks.

"She wants to be a painter." Another pause.

"And?"

"Well, she's been working on one painting for years. Ever since art school really."

"When did she graduate from art school?"

"Oh, she never graduated. She left school when we moved down here."

"When was that?" I said slowly and distinctly.

"About twelve years ago."

I looked at him skeptically. "One painting in twelve years?"

"Well, it was the painting she was working on in art school. She said her instructor really liked it and encouraged her to finish it. So, she keeps trying."

This was sounding weirder all the time. "How long was she in art school?"

"Two years," he replied. "But that was after four years at Stanford studying Contemporary Poetry."

"She got her degree in Literature? Why the switch to painting?"

"Oh, she never graduated from Stanford. She dropped out and started art school."

I was from working people. I'd never heard of such a thing. "Four years and no degree? Isn't Stanford expensive? Her parents must be really wealthy," I concluded.

Mr. Friesman shook his head unhappily. "No, she took out student loans."

"Who's paying those off?" I asked incredulously.

"Well, I am," Mr. Friesman admitted. "Which is one of the reasons we can't work on the house the way I'd planned. Money is a little tight. And she really hates the way the house is. She wants a chef's kitchen."

Finally, something I understood. "So, she's a chef," I said.

"No," Mr. Friesman said wryly. "She doesn't like to cook either. But she likes the idea of a chef's kitchen."

I was a simple country girl. This was too much for me. "I still don't understand why she got so mad yesterday."

"You two came home when we'd been fighting. She's been drinking too much lately, and I asked her to keep it to a glass of wine a day. She'd had an entire bottle yesterday and I worry about her health. And that led to a fight about money. And the fact that I don't make enough to pay for everything that needs to be done. That's why we rented out this apartment. To help pay for things. But she thinks having a tenant is tacky. I think that's part of the reason she's so rude to you. Anyway, I suggested that she get a job if she wanted more money, but she claims that she needs the time to paint. And I said," he hung his head, "and I know I shouldn't have, that she could have had fifty paintings done in the time she's been working on the one. So, she said I was the reason she drank too much, and she opened another bottle of wine. And that's when you two pulled in. I would have stopped her but there's not much I can do when she's like that. She has a terrible hangover this morning and I'm sure she's embarrassed about yesterday, that's why she's not here to apologize herself."

He hung his head briefly then peeked up to see how I was reacting. I stared at him. I had no idea how to respond to all this.

"I suppose it's the artistic temperament," I said lamely. "I'm not an artist so I can't really judge."

Mr. Friesman clutched at my comment eagerly. "That's what I keep telling myself. I'm not an artist so I suppose I should be more supportive. But it's hard. I sometimes think I should have married someone from my own background."

We both sat, nodding silently at the comment. I finally broke the silence. "How did you guys get together anyway?" I asked, curious.

"I was getting my MBA at Stanford and we met at a party. She was young and beautiful and exotic. I was right out of South Dakota; I'd never met anyone like her before. And she seemed so brave. Living the free life. We didn't spend much time together because I was working so hard on my degree but when I graduated and got a job here in Los Angeles, she offered to come with me. I was glad to take her up on it. Los Angeles scared me, and I thought we'd back each other up. But when my parents found out we were living together my mother blew up. So, we got married." He sat in silence.

I got us more coffee and after I'd seated myself, he burst out, "I've got one piece of advice for you. Don't let anyone make you do anything just because it's the way they live. Live your own life. Make sure you know what you're doing before you do it."

"I'm sorry," I offered lamely.

He shook himself. "I knew marriage was tough. I just didn't expect it to be this tough." He rose. "I better go. She thinks I spend too much time with you anyway" (I knew it!) "and I don't want to give her another reason to blow up. Thanks for the coffee."

I saw him to the door. "Thanks for the explanation."

"Yeah," he offered his hand. "I'm going to miss our breakfasts. And our talks. It was like being normal again. Sometimes I get homesick."

I shook his hand. "Well, I guess I'm normal, all right." I saw Mrs. Friesman glaring out the back screen and I pulled my hand back quickly. "I'll see you when my rent is due."

He nodded, trudged down the steps, and crossed the yard to meet his glaring wife.

What a cautionary tale. I knew I was right not to let Mom railroad me into marrying so early—especially with a comparative stranger. But it was something else I wouldn't tell my mother about on my weekly phone call. She'd be on the next plane out here trying to drag me back home.

Mr. Elliot lent me out to Jackie so I could help her on a case that 'Ted' would be taking to trial soon. Over lunch she quizzed me about Disneyland.

"It was fun," I shrugged.

"Fun? That's it?"

"Well, I liked the rides and all. It's really an amazing place. And I've always wanted to see it and I'm glad I have even though my feet were killing me by the end of the day. Oh, and Mickey wouldn't shake my hand. That really hurt my feelings. But the fireworks were nice."

Jackie looked at me blankly. "But what about Jeff? Do you like him?"

"He's all right," I hedged. "I'm not even sure it was a date. I think he was trying to make up for being a jerk. It was no big deal. I insisted on paying my own way."

"What's wrong with young women these days?" Jackie muttered to herself. Then she directed her gaze to me. "Did he even try to kiss you? That's pretty much a giveaway about how a man feels."

"He didn't get the chance," I retorted and related the story of Mrs. Friesman's meltdown in the driveway. "He decided to leave before she went even crazier than she already had. It was probably a good decision. But it was so awful I don't expect to hear from him again." I felt a little sad when I said that.

Jackie's mouth was hanging open. She snapped it shut when I cocked an eyebrow at her and asked, "Was her husband anywhere around when this was happening?"

"Oh sure. And he apologized for her behavior yesterday." And I told Jackie about *that* conversation. "You know, I'm beginning to think I should find somewhere else to live."

Jackie nodded emphatically. "I think you're right. This woman sounds ready to go off the deep end."

I sighed. "The problem is I don't have any money. My new clothes took most of my savings. I'll have to start again."

We ate quietly for a while until Jackie abruptly said, "See, that's one of the reasons I won't get married. I'm not saddled with some nut job and his debts. I'm not responsible for anyone else. And I'm not trapped. I get a nice dinner twice a week and predictable sex. That's enough for me. The rest of my life is mine." She took a rather savage bite out of her sandwich to punctuate her point.

"Maybe you're right," I agreed ruefully.

Well, I heard from Jeff again. He called the next day to invite me to a kegger with his classmates at UCLA. I offered to meet him at his place to avoid the Friesman situation and he agreed with relief. I wasn't worried about what to wear on what seemed to be a date; I knew how to dress to drink beer. That's pretty much the same all over the country. I debated on wearing my Reeboks or dressier shoes—this was UCLA, maybe the students didn't wear running shoes—but I didn't want to spill beer on nice shoes. Or have someone vomit on them. I wouldn't have been able to replace them. So, Reeboks it was. I showed up at Jeff's apartment in Westwood wearing jeans, a cotton sweater, and light jacket. His roommate opened the door.

"You must be Marianne. I'm Scott," said a tall, broad, ruddy-faced man about my age. "C'mon in."

I was ushered into a huge, messy, two-bedroom apartment with open floor plan. My gazed went from the fireplace in the living room to the granite counter-tops and top-of-the-line appliances in the kitchen with awe. "Jeff'll be out in a minute," Scott said. "You want a beer?"

I recovered quickly "Not right now," I smiled and sat in a lumpy chair after Scott whisked a shirt off it.

Scott flopped on the couch across from me. "Jeff tells me you two worked together."

I agreed that was so.

"And you're from South Dakota."

I admitted to that, too.

"I've never met anybody from South Dakota," Scott observed.

"I don't think anybody out here ever has," I returned. "We're pretty much like everybody else. Well, maybe a little quieter," I qualified.

"I'm from Los Angeles," Scott offered. "Palos Verdes actually. That's south of here."

"Ummm," I murmured, wondering where Jeff was.

"Yeah, Jeff and I have been roommates for the last year. I graduate at the end of this year. I guess you know Jeff still has another year because the double degree. I'm just getting an MBA."

"Do you have a job when you graduate?" I asked, "Or do you still have to find one?"

"My dad's an exec with Sony," Scott said nonchalantly. "He can probably get me something there."

"Must be nice," I said, not knowing what to talk about from there. Fortunately, Jeff came out of his room. "Hey, Marianne, ready to go?" he asked as he grabbed a jacket from a closet by the front door.

I stood quickly. "Sure."

"Then let's go."

I was a little surprised to see Scott grab a jacket and follow us. I looked at him in surprise and Jeff said quickly, "We're carpooling with Scott. Parking is tight on campus. You don't mind, do you?"

Well, at least I wouldn't have to worry about the kissing issue again. Would I ever know if we were on a date? Or were we just buddies? I mulled the question until Jeff directed me to Scott's Porsche. Wow, I'd never known anybody who owned such an expensive sports car. I pretended I wasn't impressed as I crawled onto Jeff's lap in the Porsche.

The kegger was fun in spite of not knowing anyone. I kept my consumption to two beers even though Scott kept trying to fill my red cup. He was pouring beer directly down his gullet from the tap, but nobody seemed to mind. Jeff stayed close even though conversation wasn't easy due to the noise. We left at midnight when the university personnel told us all to go home. Jeff drove the Porsche, so I had to sit on Scott's lap. Scott expressed no objections; he put his head back and snored the minute he sat down. Jeff dropped me off by my car and told me he'd call me. Then he parked and steered a sodden Scott up to the apartment. I wondered how he'd get Scott into bed; Scott was almost twice his size. I drove home alone. Mrs. Friesman was sitting in the dark, staring out. I only noticed her when I saw the moonlight shining off her wine glass. I shivered and hurried inside.

When Jackie and I dissected this meeting, neither one of us could tell if it was a date. We chalked it up to experience.

Jeff called again the following Tuesday. He invited me to a Saturday movie. As seemed safest, I drove over to Jeff's. He paid for the movie and we had a glass of wine afterwards. I was starting to feel more comfortable with him. And I appreciated those blue eyes and easy smile as he talked. That surprised me. I also appreciated the brief kiss he gave me when he dropped me off at my car.

And that's pretty much how things went. He'd call on Tuesday and we'd schedule something for the next Saturday. I guess it was the only time he had free. I didn't mind. I was working a lot of overtime and socking away every penny I possibly could so I could move. Things hadn't gotten any better at the Friesmans'. They both avoided me—and I avoided them right back—but I noticed dog poop on the first step of my stairway one morning. Did Poopsie relieve herself there or was Mrs. Friesman trying to make a point? At least it wasn't in a flaming paper bag.

After six weeks of chaste meetings--dates?--with Jeff, Jackie asked me what the hell was going on? I didn't have much to tell her.

"We kiss," I reported, "but that's it."

"How do you feel about him?"

"I like him," I said honestly. "I'm beginning to think he's not the player I thought he was."

"Maybe he has someone on the side," Jackie suggested with a frown.

"I thought that, too," I admitted. "But his roommate, Scott, teased him about me being his girlfriend and he didn't deny it. He just laughed—whatever that means. And I saw his workload. He doesn't have much free time. He invites me to the Friday night parties and sometimes I go but mostly we spend Saturdays together. And he's fun. I like him," I repeated.

"Do you think he's a repressed gay guy?"

"I wondered that, too. But last Saturday he took me to Griffith Park to show me the city lights and it got pretty hot and heavy. The car windows steamed up. I didn't know Los Angeles had enough humidity to fog up windows like that. But we got interrupted by a passing guard and I dropped him off at home. Scott was still up."

"You have your own place," Jackie pointed out.

"With the Friesmans watching my every move? What if Mrs. F went bat-shit crazy on him again? I'm twenty-three years old and it's almost as bad as living with my mother. Who, by the way, Mr. F would call if he thought I was doing something wrong."

"You could always go to a hotel," Jackie suggested.

"Only if he wanted to. And I'm not sure he does," I returned.

"It's puzzling," Jackie nodded. "Makes me glad I'm not young anymore."

Jeff and I went out for pizza after a movie the next Saturday and I decided to take the bull by the horns. I wanted to find out what was going on.

I waited until he took a sip of beer and blurted out, "What exactly are we doing anyway?"

Jeff put his beer down and picked up his slice of pizza. "Movie and a pizza," he said with a smile. "Don't you do that in South Dakota?"

"I mean, is this a date? Or are we just friends?"

"Both, I think," he returned, confused. "What are you asking?"

I was never flirty like Aggie M; I came from the bulldozer school of relationships...probably because I'd never had a steady one before. I plunged right in. "How come you've never tried to do more than...well, kiss me?"

"We tried in the parking lot of Griffith Park and that guard broke it up. Remember?"

"Yeah..."

"When exactly should I have tried anything more. And where?"

He had a point. "So, you'd try something if you could," I clarified.

"Well, yeah," he admitted.

"Does that mean I'm your girlfriend?"

"I suppose," Jeff said slowly. "I'm not seeing anyone else. Are you?"

"Don't really have time," I said.

"Does that mean I'm your boyfriend?"

"Maybe. I like you. I'd like to take the next step to see if that's good but..."

"When and where," Jeff finished for me.

"Yeah."

We both sat thoughtfully. Finally, Jeff said, "Thanksgiving's coming up and Scott said he's going out of town with his family. I'm going home but I can come back early, like on Saturday. I'll tell my folks I have a lot of work to do. And that's not a lie. But we'd have the apartment to ourselves. We could see how things work without Scott getting in the way and being weird."

"Yeah," I agreed, "and you wouldn't have to worry about tripping over dog poop the next morning at my place."

"Dog poop?"

"Long story. I'll tell you later." I mused for a minute then said, "You know, that sounds like a good plan. Let's do it."

We clinked beer bottles on the date. It wasn't romantic but it would give me a chance to run everything by Jackie. Hopefully, the romance would come.

I was finally going to explore my scotch theory. I hoped it was better than the one beer I'd had.

CHAPTER 9

At Last I've Found You

"Youth is wasted on the young," Jackie declared when I told her about the discussion and resolution. "Are you at least on birth control?"

When I shook my head 'no' she called her doctor and made an appointment. Then we discussed what form of birth control I should use. We decided I should start with a diaphragm since I didn't know if the relationship was going anywhere.

"It's not as reliable as the Pill but there's no point in putting all those extra hormones in your body until you're more active," Jackie decided for me. "But ask for a Pill prescription anyway. It might come in handy."

I nodded earnestly. It seemed like a good plan.

Jackie came with me to her OB/GYN's office. "He's an older man," she comforted me, "but he's kind and gentle. So, you don't have to be embarrassed to talk to him."

Jackie may have found him comforting but I felt like an idiot, sitting in my paper suit. Who wants to talk to your grandfather about sex? Of course, I would have felt like an idiot talking to any doctor about sex. I'd never been to a gynecologist before. Actually, I'd never spent much time with doctors at all. Oh, I had to have school vaccinations, of course, and I'd had a brief physical so I could play basketball on the school team but that was pretty much it. My mom didn't believe in spending money on doctors until there was something wrong. Fortunately, I'd been pretty healthy. One of my college friends suggested that maybe if Aggie M had had a regular doctor, she wouldn't have gotten pregnant—she'd have had access to birth control. But Aggie M could have gone to the college infirmary and she hadn't. Maybe she'd lived in fear of Mom, too, but I suspect she put her faith in a condom and look where that led. Better to be embarrassed talking to a grandfather than changing diapers before I was ready.

I was relieved when the doctor didn't dodder in and pat me on the head. He was a no-nonsense man, probably in his late-50s. His nurse followed him in. *She* was the one who patted me on the back and urged me to "slide your butt down and put your feet in the stirrups." I was glad I'd kept my socks on. I was feeling vulnerable enough without having cold feet, too.

I stared at the artwork on the ceiling and tried not to flinch when I felt the speculum. Someone, probably the nurse, had put up a picture of a cow in a field. I momentarily thought maybe a picture of a movie star might be interesting, or at least make the penetration happening at my other end more palatable. But I quickly dismissed that idea. Arousal was wildly inappropriate in this setting.

The doctor asked brisk questions about my general health as he palpated my breasts and the nurse wrote down my responses. I kept my focus on the cow. And that made me think of milking machines I'd seen on friends' fathers' farms. I almost broke out into a guffaw but managed to stifle it. The doctor looked at me sharply. "Am I hurting you?" he asked.

"No, no," I said quickly. "Just had an...itch."

The doctor finished his examination, told me to come to his office when I was dressed, and left. The nurse handed me a tissue to wipe up any blobs, patted me again, and followed the doctor out with my chart.

The doctor was more friendly when he was staring at my face, not my crotch. I realized that it must not be easy to meet a person for the first time and then start digging around in her privates. In any other situation like that, he'd probably be arrested. He gave me a little lecture about protecting my health, answered all questions, then gave me prescriptions for the diaphragm and the Pill. He finished by telling me to call the office anytime if I had questions or concerns, shook my hand, and wished me well. I could see why Jackie liked him. He wasn't judgmental or creepy. He seemed genuinely concerned about my well-being. He even came out to the waiting room to say 'hi' to Jackie when I told him she'd referred him and was sitting outside waiting for me. I was amazed when Jackie blushed a bit, seeming pleased at the special attention. I'd thought she was too sophisticated for blushing.

We went out for a glass of wine after I'd dropped off my diaphragm prescription to be filled (I'd save the Pill prescription for later—if I needed it). Jackie asked what else I needed to shop for.

"What else do I need?" I asked, puzzled.

"Lingerie maybe?"

"Lingerie? Oh, I don't know about lingerie. I wouldn't even know what to get."

"I'll go shopping with you if you like," Jackie offered.

But I declined. I couldn't handle a gynecologist and a lingerie store on the same afternoon. Jackie seemed disappointed. I think she was anticipating this more than I was.

"So, the big event is over Thanksgiving weekend, huh?" she asked after we'd exhausted the lingerie argument.

"Yeah," I agreed. "He's going home for Thanksgiving to be with his family but he's coming back that Saturday. We'll do it then."

"What are you doing for Thanksgiving?"

I shrugged. "Denny's, I guess."

"How about if we go to dinner together? Someplace decent. Ted will be with his wife and kids, so I usually treat myself to a nice meal. It's another reason to stay single. No slaving over a hot stove for an entire day. I get to relax."

Gee, that sounded cool and I eagerly agreed. I was especially glad that I'd made plans during my weekly phone call to my mother. She again suggested I call her long-lost relatives in Orange County and invite myself to their house.

"I'm sure they'd love to see you," she enthused.

"Oh no, Mom, I can't do that," I said. "I've never met them. Besides, I already have plans. I'm going to dinner with Jackie, my friend from work."

"Doesn't she have a family?" Mom asked suspiciously.

"She's a career woman," I evaded and switched the conversation to the birth of Aggie M's baby—a little girl. Mom happily switched topics and the call ended amicably.

I was glad I was doing something different with Jackie. This would be my first time away from home for Thanksgiving and I was feeling a little homesick.

I put on a 'nice' dress—I was finding my mother's voice always in my ear—and drove downtown to Jackie's condo. I didn't have to dodge either the Friesmans or Poopsie; they must have found someplace to go for Thanksgiving. I hadn't spoken to them except to pay my rent. Frankly, I'd found it a relief. I'd see Mrs. Friesman glaring at me when I came home sometimes but she hadn't bothered me since she'd gone ballistic. I still found dog droppings on my steps but the first time I'd stepped in it taught me to be careful.

Jackie's condo was in a downtown high-rise. I parked my car in the visitors' section and checked in with the doorman. He called up and reported that Jackie would be right down. I had a nice conversation with him while I waited. He was originally from Brooklyn and had come to Los Angeles to be an actor.

"Any luck?" I asked.

"Not so far," he returned.

"What do you think of L.A.?" I asked, curious about what a city person would think about a new city.

He paused thoughtfully and said, "Well, the weather's nice but Los Angeles is scary. Everybody here has gun-slinger eyes."

What great imagery! I tucked the comment away to share with Jeff.

The elevator door opened, and Jackie appeared, looking smartly turned out, as usual.

"I made a reservation at the Huntington Hotel in Pasadena. I hope that's okay," she stated briskly after greeting the doorman with a bright "Happy Thanksgiving!" Back to me, "Let's take my car." And she led me off to her Mercedes. I didn't know which paid better; being a mistress or an executive secretary.

I was glad we took her car instead of my Ford. I was intimidated by the grandeur of the hotel and meekly followed Jackie into the dining room, trying not to look too much like a country bumpkin.

We were seated at a table for two overlooking the grounds. From the way Jackie spoke to all the wait staff she must have been a regular. Jackie refused the menu and told the waiter that we were here for the buffet. "Don't worry about us," she assured him. "I know my way around the buffet."

The waiter smiled and told Jackie he'd have the champagne poured before we got back. Jackie led me to the buffet.

"Have anything you want," she told me grandly. "Our boss is picking up the tab."

"Really? Why?" I asked.

"I told him I was dining with you today and he said he was impressed with your work. So, this is his little treat."

Little? To my South Dakota soul a $75 meal wasn't little, but I was glad to find out I wouldn't have to dip into my savings to pay for some turkey.

I must say, the buffet was pretty good. Not as good as my grandmother's cooking had been but much better than my mom's. Mom always made the joke that an Irish seven-course meal was a six-pack and a potato, and her cooking reflected it. My mom was more interested in the front office than the kitchen.

The waiter kept refilling Jackie's glass as we ate. He finally must have gotten tired of making the rounds because he eventually left a bottle. Which Jackie finished by herself—I was too intimidated by my surroundings to drink much. I didn't want to lose control and put my elbow in the butter or some equally boorish thing. Jackie had no such reservations and pretty soon she was smiling beatifically and slurring her words a bit. Something my mother had asked me stuck in my head and in her current state of feeling no pain maybe Jackie wouldn't mind if I asked a personal question.

"Say, Jackie," I asked innocently, "how come you can spend time with me on Thanksgiving? Don't you have any family around?"

"Nope, thank God," she returned.

I smiled at her. "Why 'thank God'?"

"I didn't have much of a home life," she said with a shrug.

"Well, me neither," I said, "but I still had to show up for Thanksgiving. My mother would have killed me."

"I think you're probably being too hard on your mother," Jackie said and poured herself another glass of champagne. "At least she cares what happens to you. Didn't she help you through college?"

"Yeah, but I had to live at home. And she picked my major. I didn't have any freedom at all. I bet you were always free to do what you wanted."

Jackie smiled wryly. "Yeah, my mother let me do whatever I wanted. She set me completely free when I was fifteen. I ended up in the system."

"Where'd you go to college?" I asked.

"What makes you think I went to college?"

"But you're so smart!"

"Being smart and being formally educated don't necessarily go together," Jackie said. "You want to hear about my sordid past?"

"Well, if you don't mind sharing," I replied.

"I'm drunk enough," she returned equably. "And I think you're old enough to learn from my experience."

I accepted a cup of coffee from the waiter and Jackie sipped her champagne.

"I got married when I was seventeen to get out of the foster home I ended up in," she started.

"What was wrong with the foster home?" I asked, curious. I'd never known anyone who'd ended up in foster care.

"Same thing that was wrong with my mother's house," she returned with a slight smile. "The man of the house thought I was pretty."

"Did he try to…get fresh with you?" I asked as delicately as I could.

"I think the term you're looking for is rape," Jackie said.

"Oohhh," I said weakly.

"Don't look like that," Jackie said and took a healthy slug of champagne. "I never got raped. And I learned not to trust men…or most women either. My mother and the foster woman? Neither one looked out for me. They both blamed me because their men went after me."

After an uncomfortable pause I asked, "Who'd you marry?"

"A guy who delivered to the McDonald's I worked at. I had to get my mother to sign permission. That's the last time I ever spoke to her. And it's the only good turn she ever did me."

"How long did the marriage last?"

"Long enough for me to be of legal age. We moved from Ohio to Las Vegas for better jobs. I woke up one morning and he'd cleaned out our bank account and split. Fortunately, you can get a quickie divorce in Vegas so that wasn't a problem. And I worked nights so I could get my GED."

"Did you think of going on to college then?"

"No point. I'd connected with Ted. He sent me to secretarial school for a year and I went to work for him when I finished."

"Oohhh," was my only comment. God, I'd led such a sheltered existence! But I had more questions. "How'd you meet Mr. Brady?"

"He came into the bar I worked at in Vegas. And one thing led to another…"

"Were you a cocktail waitress?"

"I was a dancer," Jackie returned shortly then grinned at my expression. "Pick your jaw off the table. I wasn't a hooker. I made plenty of money dancing around a pole. And I had a body that wouldn't quit when I was your age. Ted came in with a bunch of other lawyers and we got to talking. He kept coming back, slipping $100 bills in my g-string, and we'd go out for coffee after my shift. After a week we made a deal. He'd pay for my condo and car and he could stay at my place whenever he got to Vegas. After six months he decided he wanted to see me more often, so he put me through secretarial school, and I went to work for him."

"Didn't it bother you that he was married?"

"Why should it?" Jackie challenged. "I didn't believe him when he told me his wife didn't understand him; I thought it was just a lie married men tell themselves to justify their behavior. But I've met his wife. She knows all about me and she doesn't care. She's Catholic, too, so divorce is out of the question. Besides, if she wanted a divorce, she'd lose everything. Haven't you figured out yet that these big-shot legal types control the courts and get what they want? I can have the condo as long as she gets the big house and the status. She gets him for the holidays to keep up appearances and if he wants sex, he comes to me."

I frowned, creeped out at the thought of old Mr. Brady in the sack. "Doesn't it bother you that he's so, well..."

She grinned at my distaste. "Old? No. It just means that the sex is few and far between these days. But we're good friends. We like to hang out together and watch movies. And he's a generous man. My condo is paid for as is my Mercedes. I'm the highest paid assistant in the firm and I'm worth every penny."

"But what happens when he retires?"

"I have enough in my portfolio; I could retire, too. But I'll probably go to another firm. Or start a secretarial service. I know everybody in town, and everybody knows I'm good. I'm too young to sit around doing nothing."

I frowned. "Don't you ever get lonely?"

Jackie snorted. "If I ever do, I'll get a cat. People are over-rated."

"But don't you ever want to like...settle down?"

"I've been married, remember? I never want to wake up again with no money."

She had a point. She was turning everything I'd been taught on its head.

Jackie laughed at my confusion. "I'll tell you what I'd do if I were your age. I'd grab that young student and take advantage of him. There's nothing like a beautiful young man. Just don't hand your life over to him. You're both too young for that kind of commitment."

"I don't know if I even want to grab him now," I murmured. "What if he picks law? He could do a lot of damage."

"I want you to have fun," Jackie clarified. "I just don't want you to ruin your life the way I did. Why do you think I insisted you get birth control? Can you afford to take care of a kid? I didn't think so. And I doubt you'd get an abortion, am I right? That's what I thought. Just remember to keep it light and protect your heart and health." She poured herself another glass of champagne. "So, tell me: what approach are you taking for the big event?"

"I hadn't gotten that far," I admitted, still unsettled by Jackie's take on life.

Jackie gave me sex advice as she finished the bottle of champagne by herself. I tuned her out and cogitated about Jeff. Would he be the sort of man who offered to 'keep' me? Eeewww. That was creepy. Besides, he didn't have any money.

Jackie was still advising, and I was still unsettled, as she paid the check and we left. I offered to drive Jackie home since she'd had so much wine. She hicced and thanked me. I carefully piloted the Mercedes back to her building and helped her up to her apartment—which was gorgeous. She smiled at me blissfully and wished me well on Saturday night. As I drove home, I tried to think of an excuse to cancel on Saturday. Jackie's dissertation had squelched any amorous thoughts I might have had about Jeff.

At least the Friesmans didn't bother me as I climbed to my apartment. Thank God for small favors.

I tried all day Friday to think of a good reason to cancel Saturday night. After watching the Friesmans in action and listening to Jackie, romance seemed dead in the world. Of course, this wasn't about romance, this was about developing a taste for fine scotch instead of beer. I'd go through with this if it killed me.

I inserted my diaphragm before I left my apartment. The directions said I was good to go for two to four hours. It took me half an hour to drive to Jeff's so that left me an hour and a half of security. I didn't waste time when I got to his place.

Jeff met me at the door with a big smile and a bottle of wine.

"Fine, fine," I muttered. "Bring it to the bedroom." And I stalked off. Better get this over with.

Jeff appeared with the wine and two glasses as I was assessing the situation. I'd avoided his bedroom until now, for obvious reasons. I stared at the bed.

"Would you like some wine?" Jeff asked tentatively, seeming to be a bit put off by my manner.

"Umhmm," I murmured, wondering which one of us should make the first move.

Jeff handed me a full glass and I tossed it off. "Okay, let's do this," I said with steely determination as I made the decision and started unbuttoning my shirt. It occurred to me that this was the second time in a week I'd undressed for a strange man. And I felt like I had at the crotch doctor's; this was unpleasant but necessary.

I finished undressing and sat on the bed, staring up at Jeff. His turn.

Jeff stared back, open-mouthed. Then he took a swig out of the wine bottle and quickly stripped. "Okay," he said, crawling across the bed.

Well, we did it within the two-hour time frame. Which is good because I hadn't brought any additional spermicide. I don't think either one of us enjoyed it particularly. I thought Jeff looked just as confused as I felt. Then it occurred to me: maybe I was beer instead of scotch.

"They say the first time is always kind of...well, not good," I offered weakly.

Jeff looked relieved. "I wasn't going to say anything..."

"So maybe we just need to practice."

"We can take our time, you know," Jeff pointed out. "We've got all day tomorrow, too."

"Well, actually..." I explained to Jeff about the spermicide directions.

Jeff listened intently. "If I understand correctly the directions said two to four hours. We've got at least two hours left. And there are drugstores around here, you know. We can buy more spermicide. Why didn't you bring some with you?" Then he started laughing. "God, I wondered why you were so business-like."

I was chagrined; it had never occurred to me to pack spermicide in my purse. "Well, I worry about pregnancy," I muttered. "And I don't have a lot of experience."

"We both need more practice," Jeff assured me.

So, we did. Practice, that is.

CHAPTER 10

Sex Is Everywhere!

J eff and I practiced every chance we got. I had a lot to learn and I figured Jeff could teach me. He said he wasn't the player I seemed to think he was.

"But you're so good-looking! All the girls at the firm would love to date you," I protested.

"I learned a long time ago not to shit where I eat," Jeff returned. "I've only had a few serious girlfriends and if you think I'm into one-night stands, you're wrong. Ask Scott about them. He's got herpes for life from a one-night stand. I'd rather go steady with my hand."

I was a little surprised by his confession. I thought all good-looking guys screwed around. Apparently, the media over-generalized. But maybe I wouldn't have to be embarrassed by my inexperience. He probably wouldn't know the difference. I filled my Pill prescription; it allowed for more spontaneity.

We did most of our practicing at his place. Jeff didn't want 'that crazy Mrs. Friesman' running out and jumping him. And I preferred Jeff's place because I was afraid Mr. Friesman would report me to my mother. He had her phone number on record as Next of Kin. Things were nuts enough with him; I didn't want to give him an excuse to call her.

I didn't stay overnight at first (see above about being ratted out to my mom) because I was a little creeped out by Scott. He'd watch us disappear into Jeff's bedroom and he was always waiting in the living room, leering, when we came out. After a particularly satisfying session late one Friday Jeff suggested I stay the night. I was tired and I figured it couldn't get any weirder. I just had to deal with Scott making inappropriate sexually laden comments as Jeff and I watched cartoons and ate Cocoa Puffs the next morning.

"Why doesn't he have a girlfriend?" I asked Jeff once.

"He says he's not ready to settle down," Jeff explained.

"But he's always here staring at us. Why doesn't he go out on a date or something?"

"I don't know. I never thought about it."

Jeff seemed to be oblivious.

Mr. Friesman accepted the story that I was spending time with Jackie. I had to tell him something when he asked. So, I didn't have to worry about the wrath of Mom. Mrs. Friesman never talked to me at all and the dog poop incidents became intermittent. Maybe she was happy I was gone.

And practice went on. It was getting really enjoyable; I was starting to think I was getting pretty good at it--although our repertoire needed expansion. I'd always found the information I wanted at the library, but I didn't think the city library would have the instruction I needed. So, I went to a bookstore. There was a whole section on human sexuality including that old standby *The Joy of Sex*. There was a copy of the *Kama Sutra*, but it looked a little complicated to me. Actually, it looked like naked people playing Twister--which explained why Mom wouldn't let us play it as kids. I went back to *The Joy of Sex*. The clerk smirked and I looked anywhere but at him, but I stood my ground and paid for my purchase. I was a little amazed that I didn't slink out with nothing but my embarrassment. I must be adjusting to adulthood.

I was also discovering that once you let sex in your life it's everywhere! One Friday when I got to Jeff's Scott asked Jeff and me if we'd come with him to a sex shop before we all went to dinner. He wanted to buy a joke present for a buddy. I was glad when Jeff agreed for both of us. I was curious; I'd never been to an adult toy store before. Brookings didn't have anything like that. Oh, Art's Smoke Shop on the corner reputedly had dirty magazines but I had no first-hand knowledge. My mother would have beaten me to death if I'd ever set foot in the place. And that was just magazines not sex toys.

I was shocked when I walked into the store. There was a whole counter of dildos of various sizes. I'd only seen two live penises before, so I thought the size of some of the dildoes was a little extreme. Maybe this was the sort of joke that Scott was looking for? But Jeff said 'no'. "People actually use these things," he said professorially.

"Really? How could anybody possibly fit them in? Do they normally have sex with elephants?"

Jeff told me to keep my voice down. People were looking at me.

I wandered over to the wall full of dirty magazines. The magazines had titles and were devoted to subjects I'd never dreamed existed. One was called *Big Black Tits*. And that's all it was: African American women with the largest breasts I'd ever seen. They must have had trouble sitting up without help. There was a magazine called *Pregnant Mommas*—I couldn't believe it but that's exactly what it was; hugely pregnant naked women. And some of the covers could have been used for a gynecological anatomy class. Of course, a medical class picture wouldn't have been completely hairless. "My God, Jeff, look at these things!" I exclaimed, pointing. Jeff came over and started to laugh. "Have you ever seen anything like this before?" I asked.

"No," Jeff said, walking down the aisle to get a better look at some of the covers. I glared at him with distaste and he snickered and veered off down another aisle.

I could feel my mouth starting to hang open again. I snapped it shut when I noticed a greasy little man huddled down the row. This was the sort of person I normally crossed the street to avoid. Why did Jeff pick this moment to desert me? I was looking around for Jeff when the greasy little man scurried off into the back of the store. I was still in my work clothes and the sight of me in my sensible skirt and trench coat must have unnerved him, thank God.

I checked out the other wares available then joined Jeff and Scott at the counter. Scott was paying for a squeeze toy woman whose boobs popped out when you pressed her stomach. Scott was delighted with it, but I frowned in distaste. "Who'd want that?"

"It's a joke," Scott protested. "My buddy will love it."

"Must be a guy thing," I commented doubtfully.

"Yeah, it is," Jeff agreed. Then he paid for some sort of lubricating gel. "It's supposed to increase sensation," he informed me.

"Anything for you?" the clerk asked me.

"No-o-o-o," I returned slowly, completely out of my depth in this store.

But I wasn't embarrassed. I think I was getting desensitized. Or I was in shock.

Scott howled about Little Suzy Creamcheese—geez, that nickname was going to follow me to my grave!--in the adult bookstore. "With a name like Fuchs you shouldn't be so squeamish!" he chortled. Scott had been making pointed jokes about my last name ever since he first heard it, which was getting really old. And I didn't think a working knowledge about adult sex toys was necessarily a sign of sophistication.

We all went for a burger and fries for dinner. I'd taken a slurp of my beer when Scott handed me a sack. I pulled out a book; the *Kama Sutra*.

"I thought you'd appreciate it," he said with a leer.

I riffled through the book and said to Jeff, "Looks like we're playing Twister tonight." Then I grinned at Scott and threw a french fry at him. He'd have to work harder to make me feel embarrassed. Little Suzy Creamcheese was learning to live in Los Angeles.

Of course, Scott took that as a challenge. He decided my sex education wasn't complete and he declared I needed to see an X-rated movie. Jeff frowned and said, "Really? Is this necessary?" But I was game. Scott suggested I wear my trench coat. I thought he wanted a repeat of the Little Suzy Creamcheese effect in the sex toy store. He laughed and said he wanted me to fit in.

So, the three of us went to an adult movie theater in Hollywood. I hadn't had much dinner because I like to have popcorn with my film but the popcorn available looked like it had been scraped off the floor from the previous night's show. I even refused a soda. If it didn't come out of a bottle or a can, I wasn't willing to chance it. From the appearance of the lobby it was clear a health inspector hadn't been around recently.

The three of us got seats in the middle of the theater.

"We can leave if you don't like this," Jeff whispered to me.

"Don't worry about me," I declared stoutly. "I'll probably never do this again so I might as well get the full experience."

Scott laughed again and Jeff frowned at him. I didn't see what the big deal was. It's not like I was a minor and I'd been exposed to HBO. I would probably survive some adult entertainment. Although five minutes into the movie I wasn't so sure.

I don't remember the name of the movie, but I don't think it mattered. Jeff said they were all interchangeable. I was used to dialogue and characterization—and Disney movies. A Disney princess may wear a corset over her breasts, but you never saw much skin. This movie was nothing but skin. I'd never seen so many naked boobs since my last communal shower after a basketball game. And none of those boobs came anywhere near the size of the specimens I was seeing on the screen. And to date, the only rampant penis I'd ever seen—I don't count my first sexual experience; it was dark, and I wasn't paying attention to that end of the guy—was Jeff's. The lead actor spent most of his time running around with an erection. He didn't have much dialogue and that was probably a good thing. I doubt he had much blood left in his brain to enable him to remember lines. And the really weird thing was when he ejaculated. He pulled out of the actress and squirted around the room! You couldn't have a guy like that around unless you wanted to repaint every time he came over—pun intended. The heroine squealed and breathed heavily. I didn't find the production even remotely erotic. I'd never seen a vagina up close and personal before. And

I'd certainly never seen pubic hair shaved so carefully. It looked like topiary framing the vagina. They're rather odd looking— vaginas, that is. But so are penises—all those veins hanging out. Scott and Jeff were watching everything intently, mouths hanging open, so I looked down our row to a guy sitting in a trench coat similar to mine. He was squirming with both hands hidden in his coat. Oh my God, I think he was masturbating. He turned his wet little eyes in my direction and caught me staring at him. He abruptly quit fidgeting, then quickly stood up and left. I lifted my hands from the armrests and stared at my seat in horror. Who'd been sitting in this seat before me and what had they been doing?

I leaned over to Jeff and whispered, "I've seen enough. We can go if you want to."

Jeff never took his eyes off the screen. He whispered back, "No, we can wait until the end."

I looked over at Scott expecting him to be waiting for me to wimp out on him so he could laugh at me. He didn't care about me at all. He was engrossed with the spectacle in front of him.

So, I gingerly settled back in my seat, resigned to seeing this tiresome thing to the end. It never got better. I could even do the dialogue by myself after a few minutes. It never changed: "Aarrgghh...I'm...coming!" The woman would writhe, and the man would squirt. It was stupid. But I was the only one who thought so. Of course, I was the only woman in the theater...

Scott howled at my comments about the squirting and the pubic topiary; I wasn't going to give him the satisfaction of sounding like a scandalized small-town girl—even though that's exactly what I was. I noticed that Jeff was particularly frisky that night. I wondered if Scott was listening and fidgeting under his covers. That thought creeped me out.

I'd been saturated with sex and I'd had enough. I was beginning to think Mom was right. Maybe this was Sodom.

I needed to find a more uplifting form of entertainment. The perfect opportunity presented itself before Christmas. Our law firm supported a local theater by buying a block of seats. Two were available for Friday night so Jeff and I decided we'd try to improve ourselves by a night of live theater. I thought about leaving the trench coat at home--it had so many bad associations for me at this point—but it was December. I needed the warmth.

The theater was downtown so Jeff met me at work. The theater was an art-house place, so I didn't worry about dressing up. I figured my work clothes would be sufficient. Jeff treated me to a small restaurant not far from the office. I told him we could go dutch—I'd gotten the tickets for free, after all—but he said dinner was his share of the evening's entertainment.

The restaurant was small but tasteful. I had chicken and a glass of wine. Then another. We had so much time before we had to be at the theater that we sat over coffee and talked. We'd been so immersed in sex we hadn't had much time to do that. Jeff told me about his classes and asked me if I was going home for Christmas.

"No," I returned. "I don't have any vacation time yet."

Then he asked me how life was with that 'crazy Friesman woman'.

"Sort of at a stalemate," I admitted. "Mr. Friesman doesn't talk to me much anymore, but Mrs. Friesman still seems to hate me."

"That's awful," Jeff sympathized. "When can you move?"

"I need to save some more money," I said. "From what I've heard of L.A. landlords I might have a hard time getting my security deposit back. And I don't know how bad things will get if I give them a month's notice and don't pay for the last month. And it's not like I can afford to disappear in the middle of the night. I need that security deposit back."

"Do you want me to talk to them?"

"That might make things worse. And really, what can you do?"

Jeff thought for a minute and made a surprising offer. "If it gets too bad you can always stay with me."

I was startled by that. I didn't think we had that kind of relationship. We were sex buddies, not real friends.

"Thanks for the offer but I don't think Scott would take kindly to another roommate. You ready to go?"

He was, so we got my car out of the parking lot and drove it ten blocks down to the theater—which struck me as an almost criminal waste of money. If we did this again, I'd wear my Reeboks and walk.

I pulled out the tickets as we approached the building. "What are we seeing?" Jeff asked.

"Something about Euridice," I read from the tickets. "Sounds like a Greek drama. At least I won't be drowning in sex. That's a relief."

Jeff grinned and we were ushered to seats four rows from the stage, right in the middle of the row. "These are great!" Jeff whispered.

"I think the firm contributes a lot of money," I whispered and settled back to be edified. Greek tragedy! This was the sort of sophisticated thing I'd come to the Big City for.

Well, this was not classical Greek tragedy. It seemed to be a contemporary sex farce. I never figured out why Orpheus and Euridice were the main characters. All the actors were miked, but the music soundtrack was so loud that I couldn't understand a word anyone was saying. I was startled when a chorus line of naked men did a Rockettes imitation. I was particularly amazed by the penis ring through the foreskin of the middle dancer. I'd never seen an uncircumcised man before--and certainly never one with a foreskin ring. I was mesmerized by the movement as the ring flashed and flopped from one leg to the other as he did high kicks. My head bobbed from side to side following the bouncing ring. It was like watching the world's smallest tennis match. But that wasn't the only bouncing penis. Orpheus' penis flopped around when the naked actor was attached to a spinning wheel. I didn't know if this was torture or we were playing a perverted game of *Price is Right*. Jeff and I exchanged appalled glances and I choked back a laugh at the confused look on his face. I had to stifle my giggles. We were so close to the actors they would have heard my laughter and that would have been rude; I almost popped a sinus.

The play was performed without an intermission. I noticed people on the aisles sneaking out, but we were dead center in those great seats and we couldn't just pick up and leave, much as we wanted to. So, we suffered through it. I wish I'd brought some aspirin; the decibel level was giving me a headache.

The miserable thing finally ended. When we made our way to the lobby the actor with the penis ring was mingling with the audience wearing a pink pinafore and combat boots. I was a long way from South Dakota.

After we left the building one of the other shell-shocked patrons looked at me in bewilderment as we waited to cross the street to the parking lot. "What in the world was that all about?" he asked.

"I have no idea," I assured him.

I drove back to the office so Jeff could get his motorcycle. "Thanks for dinner," I said as he got ready to leave.

"Do you want to come back to my place?" Jeff asked hopefully.

"Oh, I don't think so. I've had as much sex as I can handle right now," I returned with a slight shudder.

"We don't have to have sex. We could just, you know, hang out." I looked at him, puzzled. "I probably won't see you again until after Christmas. I have to go home for a few days; my folks expect it," he explained.

"Well, sure, they would," I agreed, still mystified.

"I want to give you something," Jeff clarified, "and I don't want to do it in the car."

"I didn't get you anything," I protested.

"That's fine, it's really nothing. I just...oh hell," he said as he reached into his pocket and pulled out a small, navy-blue, velvet box and handed it to me. "Merry Christmas!" he finished hurriedly. "You want to open it now?"

I opened the box to find a small locket. It was inexpensive but it was tasteful. I didn't know what to say. "It's lovely," I said slowly. "Thank you."

"Maybe we should talk about where this is going," Jeff said after a moment.

"This?" I repeated stupidly.

"Us," he clarified.

So, he thought we were an 'us'. Now I was really lost. Fortunately, a police car was prowling down the street. "I better go," I said quickly. "Merry Christmas!"

Jeff got out of the car and slammed the door. "You, too," I heard as I pulled away. After that silly play and Jeff's pronouncement I was completely discombobulated. This small-town girl had had too many shocks to her system. I ignored fresh dog poop as I hurried to the refuge of my garret.

CHAPTER 11

Christmas and Confessions

I was still unnerved about Jeff's question about 'us' so I talked to Jackie about it. First, I showed her the locket. "What is this?" I asked.

"It's a necklace," Jackie said reasonably, looking at me like I'd lost my mind.

"I know," I returned shortly. "Jeff gave it to me after the play."

"So, it's a Christmas present?" Jackie said searchingly. "Don't you give Christmas presents where you come from?"

"Yes," I responded witheringly. "But what is he going to expect?"

"A present back?" Jackie said, sounding lost.

"No!" I said exasperated. "Is he getting serious?"

"How would I know?" Jackie asked.

I related the rest of what Jeff had said. "I don't think I'm ready for an 'us' conversation," I continued. "I mean, we've only been going out for a couple months. Isn't this a little soon?"

Jackie shrugged.

"But he didn't say anything about love and if he were getting serious wouldn't he have said something about that?"

Jackie shrugged again and watched me stew sympathetically. "Why don't you ask him?" she finally asked.

"He's at his parents' place."

"Well, you could call him," Jackie suggested.

"I don't think this is something I want to talk about over the phone. I don't know what to say to him yet."

"When's he coming back to town?"

"We have a date for New Year's Eve. But I don't think I want to bring this up then. It'd probably ruin the whole evening."

"Guess you better call him and arrange a meeting before then if you can. I really think you're worrying over nothing. It's just a necklace. Don't let it become something it's not."

She was obviously bored by my little difficulties, so I let the subject drop.

"We need to talk," I announced when I called Jeff. At least I waited until after pleasantries had been exchanged. "Preferably before New Year's Eve."

Jeff sounded alarmed by my tone. "Is it serious?" he asked.

"I don't know," I said. "When are you coming back?"

"Right after Christmas," Jeff replied, and we agreed to meet for dinner when he got back. I wanted to meet in a public place just in case he went nuts like Mrs. Friesman. I had one crazy person after me; I didn't need another. And I was on my own. I didn't even have my mother as protection. After I'd made the date, I spent a lot of time staring at the little necklace in its innocent navy-blue velvet box.

And speaking of my mom, we had a rather strained Christmas call.

"Why aren't you coming home for Christmas?" she'd demanded.

"I don't have any vacation time yet. You know that," I countered.

"You could have asked for unpaid time. It's not right, you so far away. We've never had a Christmas without all the kids around. Your father doesn't know what to do with himself."

I suspected Dad missed playing golf over the winter more than me, but Mom was on a tear. I tried to point out that she had all her grandchildren around, so she really didn't need me. I snarkily mentioned that she'd certainly never appeared to appreciate my company before, but the intended guilt trip missed its mark. She was oblivious.

"I suppose you're spending Christmas with that older secretary who doesn't sound like she's any better than she should be," she sniped at the end.

I certainly wasn't going to listen to any criticism about Jackie; she'd been trying to re-enforce an ego my mother had tried to suppress—God knows why.

"I don't have any plans for Christmas," I returned snippily. "But if Jackie asks me to have dinner with her, I'll be glad to go. She's my best friend here. She's helped me at work, and she's helped me buy clothes…"

"What's wrong with the clothes you had?" Mom barked. "You're a secretary; what special clothes do you need?"

I thought about retorting that Los Angeles was a whole different world than South Dakota but I also knew that Mom knew that; she'd been around a lot more than I had. But, as usual, I backed down. I placated her and told her maybe I could come home next year when I had vacation time and more money. I got another lecture from her about being a good girl—I wonder what she'd have said if she could see the copy of the *Kama Sutra* Jeff and I were studying so assiduously—and to be on the lookout for the mail. "I sent you a check," she closed the conversation. "I don't like the sound of those Friesmans. I don't care that he grew up in South Dakota. That woman he married doesn't sound at all normal. I think you should leave as soon as you can."

Well, I had to agree with her on that. Mrs. Friesman was back to dropping dog doo on my step on a regular basis. That wasn't normal, was it?

I spent Christmas by myself, although without snow it didn't feel like Christmas at all. Jackie said she was going out of town and I didn't ask where or with whom. I thought about getting a little tree but decided that was too pathetic. I spent a lot of time at work racking up the overtime. The only time I spent at home was to sleep. Which was good. If I'd had to watch all the Christmas specials on TV, I'd probably have killed myself. I was horribly homesick. I even thought about calling Jeff but decided I better put that off until I could see his face. On Christmas Eve I found a church that had a wonderful choir. But I made sure it wasn't Catholic—one more futile act of rebellion. I enjoyed the music even though I was sure I was going to hell. I went to a movie on Christmas day. Then I had a burger. But I didn't enjoy it. I knew that two mean girls were making fun of me as I choked down my food, but the kind people were even worse; they feel sorry for you when you're alone at Christmas. I hate being an object of pity even if the motives are pure. I went home to dog poop on my step. It was a horrible Christmas.

And I still had to find out what was going on with Jeff. It was a confusing time.

When I was seated opposite Jeff at a sandwich place, I put the little blue box on the table between us. Jeff looked puzzled and asked, "Didn't you like it?"

"What's it mean?" I asked bluntly.

Jeff shrugged. "It's a Christmas present," he said. "I can exchange it if you'd rather have earrings or something. I kept the receipt."

"No, no," I dithered. "You said you wanted to talk about us. What's that mean?"

Jeff eyed me closely. "Well, you're my girlfriend. Aren't you?" he started.

"Wait a minute," I interrupted and raised the finger I'd been using to push the little box around on the table. "Are you getting serious?"

"Would that be so terrible? I like you. Do you like me?"

"Of course, I do," I assured him. "I have lots of fun with you."

"And the sex thing is okay too, isn't it?" Jeff pursued.

"Yeah," I agreed. "As a matter of fact, it's getting better. But then again I don't have much to compare it to."

Jeff looked alarmed. "Do you want to find somebody else? So you can compare?"

I took a minute to think about this. "No," I concluded. "I wouldn't feel comfortable doing the stuff we do with anybody else."

Jeff looked relieved. "Great," he enthused, "so what's the problem?"

I leaned back and stared at Jeff. "I'm wondering how serious you're getting. The last time I got intimate with a guy he assumed we were getting married and I'm nowhere near wanting to get married to anybody."

Jeff looked surprised. "Well, it's a little soon for me, too. But you do want to get married someday, don't you? Maybe not to me but to somebody?"

"I don't know," I admitted. "I just started living on my own. There's lots of stuff I want to do. I can't afford to settle down." Jeff looked unconvinced so I continued logically, "I've been watching people. You know, like the Friesmans? They're miserable together. Jackie's perfectly happy being a mistress. It's lots less hassle." I looked at Jeff expectantly, hoping he'd say something, but he just stared at me. "So, I guess I'm saying: I don't want you falling in love with me or anything like that." Jeff still said nothing, so I hurried on. "I'm not ready for marriage now and I may never be. I know that probably isn't what you wanted to hear so if you want your necklace back..." I pushed the little blue box on the table toward him regretfully. It was a pretty thing and it was my first present of jewelry.

Jeff pushed the box back at me. "Keep it. What am I going to do with it?" he asked, irritated. "So, you're breaking up with me?"

"No, not unless you want it that way. I just don't want you thinking about me long term. And that's not fair to you. So, if marriage is your goal maybe we should break things off before we get more involved than we are."

"Then it's not me you object to, it's the institution of marriage," Jeff said.

I nodded. "That's as good a way of putting it as any," I agreed.

"Well, I hadn't been thinking of marriage yet, so we agree on that," Jeff informed me.

"And the necklace isn't like a promissory note or anything," I concluded, relieved.

"No," Jeff said. "It's just a necklace."

"Oh good," I said. We both stared at the little box between us. I reached for it. "I guess I should say 'thanks' for the Christmas present. Sorry I didn't get you anything." I put the box in my purse.

"That's okay," Jeff said, offhand. "Can we order now?"

"Yeah," I agreed. Now that the marriage pressure was off, I was hungry.

And we had a great New Years' Eve date at a party at Scott's parents' house--for a while anyway. I'd never seen such an opulent home before. The party was around the pool and strayed off to the tennis court. Wow. Scott had invited all the rich kids from UCLA. Jeff knew them, of course, but I was clearly an outsider. There were students from foreign countries that were more at home than I was. The only other outsiders were beautiful girls in bikinis. I don't know where they came from and I never got a chance to find out; they spent most of their time in the pool. I stayed close to Jeff. Scott got really drunk and deliberately fell in the pool a lot. The bathing beauties would dunk him, and he pulled the tops off a couple of them. They didn't seem to mind but I thought it was creepy. The Good Catholic South Dakota girl was staring at Scott and even in his drunken haze it seemed to irritate him.

"Hey, you know what?" he suddenly yelled and pointed to me. "She's from South Dakota." He made it sound like I had lice. I didn't say anything. Neither did anyone else. Scott continued, "I mean, I didn't know you people could even read. Can you?"

"Aw Scott, lay off," said Jeff, slightly contemptuous.

I wasn't contemptuous—well, I was but I was more mad. "I can read," I said quietly.

A couple of the topless girls giggled, and Scott turned to them for approval. "Let's see if she can read, shall we?"

Jeff turned to me and said, "He's drunk. He always has to pick on someone at these parties and he's decided tonight it's you. He won't stop so we might as well leave."

I agreed. As we were walking out, I heard Scott yell, "And did you know her name is Fuchs? It's perfect because that's all she does…"

That made Jeff turn back. "Shut up, Scott, all right? You're drunk and obnoxious. You owe Marianne an apology." He sounded really angry and that seemed to get through to Scott.

"Aww, it was just a joke. Can't she take a joke?"

I turned around and walked out.

On the way back to Jeff's apartment he tried to explain Scott's behavior. "He's mad because I spend more time with you than with him."

"But all those girls at the party—why doesn't he pick one and we could double date?" I asked, even though I wasn't sure I ever wanted to have anything to do with Scott again.

"Those are paid escorts," Jeff explained. When he noticed my puzzled reaction he clarified, "Hookers."

My mouth dropped open. "Prostitutes?" I exclaimed. No wonder they didn't care if Scott took their tops off. They were professional sex workers!

"Well, yeah," Jeff said, uncomfortable. "He has to hire women because he can't seem to get a girlfriend."

"Well, of course he can't if he hangs out with prostitutes," I agreed. "And no woman in her right mind would bother with someone who gets drunk all the time and picks on people just because his dad has money. Why do you live with him? "

"It's close to school and he only charges me a fraction of what the apartment really costs because I help him with his schoolwork. And I feel sorry for him. His parents spoiled him rotten and he doesn't have any other friends. But he can be a good guy."

"Yeah, as long as he gets his way all the time," I said dubiously. "I have to tell you; I didn't appreciate being singled out for his crap tonight."

"Yeah," Jeff agreed. "Look, I'll talk to him, okay?"

"Well, okay," I said, still unsure what to make of the situation or I how I should treat Scott when I saw him again.

We went back to Jeff's apartment and saw the New Year in with a movie and a bottle of cheap wine.

The necklace didn't change anything between Jeff and me except things were more comfortable now. Oh, we still practiced the *Kama Sutra* positions, but we quit referring to the book so much. We were doing just fine with spontaneity.

And Jeff made Scott apologize to me. Scott dug his toe in the carpet and hung his head. "I'm sorry I got out of line at the party. I was drunk, you know," he said as if that excused anything.

I frowned at him. "Maybe you shouldn't drink so much," I offered. I tried not to make it sound too judgmental but there's no really nice way of saying something like that. And frankly, I didn't feel like being particularly nice.

Scott eyed me narrowly and I returned the look. Jeff nudged Scott's arm. "Maybe," Scott said shortly. "Listen, I'd like to make it up to you. Can I take you two out to dinner?"

I was about to coldly refuse—I could buy my own meals, thank you very much; that's what South Dakotans do, along with READING—but I saw the plea in Jeff's eyes. Okay, I'd accept the flag of truce. I was spending a lot of time at Scott's apartment and if I wanted to continue my physical relationship with Jeff—which I did—I'd have to get along with Scott.

Scott took us to a steak place in Santa Monica. The dress code was Hollywood Chic so I could go in jeans. I was glad about that; I was looking pretty damn good in jeans—which is also what South Dakota girls did. And speaking of being from South Dakota, I asked Scott what he had against the place. Had he ever even been there?

"Well, no," he said uncomfortably. "It's something everybody says out here. I don't know why. I guess it was a cheap shot. You want another glass of wine?"

I didn't because I knew he'd get himself another and he was already on his third glass. This guy had a drinking problem. And I didn't think it was the usual college stuff.

I concluded that Scott was jealous. I knew he was. I didn't know why but I wasn't about to give up my time with Jeff to make him happy. Jeff was *mine*.

Oh my God, when did that happen?

I discovered the depth of my changed feelings for Jeff when Scott got into another snarl around Valentine's Day. I'd agreed to spend the night. I sneaked a gym bag with a change of clothes to my car when I left my garret; I'd bought a new dress just for the occasion, but it was too low-cut and daring to wear to work. Jackie had helped me shop so she didn't tease to see it; she wished me well with a twinkle.

"Have a happy Valentine's Day," she smiled.

"You too," I returned. "What are you doing tonight?"

"Dinner in front of the tube," she said dryly. "Not my holiday."

I wondered if she ever got a holiday. That seemed to be the downside to being a mistress—all those holidays by yourself.

Mrs. Friesman was staring out the back window when I left, as usual. You know, if she'd spent one-tenth the time on a stupid painting as she did spying on me she'd've been able to fill a gallery by now. I waved half-heartedly at her, but I knew there'd be dog poop on my step when I got back.

Jeff presented me with flowers and a card when I got to his place. I was touched. This was my first official Valentine's Day date and it was living up to expectations. I didn't know what to do with the flowers, though. Jeff found an old coffee can, put water in it, and my flowers were saved. He seemed to appreciate the rather generic, non-committal card I gave him. Then we both got changed. Jeff whistled when I made my appearance. He'd put on a sport coat and tie. He was taking me someplace with a dress code! Well!

We drove to a seafood place in Malibu. The valet didn't blink at my Ford Tempo. He parked it right next a Mercedes-Benz. Jeff offered me his arm and escorted me inside. The maître d' led us to a table for two next to the window. We had a panoramic view of the Pacific. It was wonderful.

Jeff ordered a bottle of champagne and the swordfish steak. I looked at the prices and swallowed. "Can you afford this?" I whispered behind the menu.

"I saved up for it," Jeff whispered back.

Good enough. I didn't know what to order, walleye wasn't on the menu, so I settled on coconut shrimp. At least I knew what it was. We had a wonderful evening watching the moon dance over the ocean as we finished our champagne.

Jeff drove home slowly. We went to his bedroom where he put on Bolero—it was an idea he'd gotten from a movie--and we made love. And that was wonderful, too. We were getting pretty good at this sex thing. I fell asleep with my head on his shoulder. I woke up once to hear the sound of lovemaking in the other bedroom.

Jeff and I looked at each other and grinned. "Did Scott finally get lucky?" I whispered.

"He probably saved up for a hooker," Jeff whispered back.

I was a little put off by sharing an apartment with a sex worker but as Jeff pointed out, it wasn't my business and at least Scott wasn't bothering us. We both went back to sleep.

Early the next morning a knock on the door woke us. Jeff got up and had an urgent, whispered conversation with Scott. Then he closed the door and started putting on his pants.

"I have to go," Jeff said when he noticed I was sleepily watching him.

"Why? What's going on?" I asked.

"I'll tell you later," Jeff said. He kissed me quickly, grabbed his wallet, my car keys, and put his shirt on as he left. I went back to sleep.

I was out of the shower and getting ready for work when Jeff and Scott came back. Scott was chortling but Jeff looked sheepish.

"What's going on?" I asked, mystified at such early morning amusement.

"Your boyfriend here got my Porsche back," Scott clarified.

"What happened to your car?"

Scott told me the story while Jeff made coffee. Apparently, Scott had brought a prostitute to the apartment last night, which I'd already figured out, and she stole his wallet and car keys when he fell asleep. Then she helped herself to his car. So, he got Jeff to drive him around—in my car!—to the area where he'd picked up the woman. They'd seen a man stopped at a red light in Scott's Porsche, the window down as he tapped his hand along to loud music.

"So, you know what your boyfriend did?" Scott laughed. "He pulls up behind my car, gets out and reaches into the open window of the Porsche. He grabs the keys and turns off the engine before the guy knows what's happening. Then he pulls the keys out of the ignition and walks back to your Tempo. The guy couldn't move! And a cop pulled up then, so I reported the car was stolen. I've got my car back already!" He shoved Jeff playfully as Jeff was putting coffee cups on the table. "I wish I could think that fast. Man didn't say a word, just got out of the Tempo, pulled the Porsche keys out, and walked back. Doesn't say a word! Man, I owe you big time. My father would've killed me if I'd lost another car." And Scott sat there chuckling and saying what a smart guy Jeff was and how he was always thinking on his feet. Jeff shrugged off the praise.

But once I understood what had happened, I was not pleased.

"So, you bring a hooker back here, she rolls you, and Jeff has to get your car back for you? This is what you think is so great?"

"Isn't it?" Scott smirked.

"No, it's not great at all. That was a guy who had your car. He was probably her pimp. What if he'd been armed? Jeff would have been the one shot, not you."

"Oh, I don't think it was that dangerous," Jeff murmured.

I wheeled on Jeff. "How would you know? He could have had a gun and then what would you have done?" I pointed at Scott. "This bozo wouldn't have done anything to help you out. He'd probably have left you to die in the street and wrecked my car." I started snarling directly at Scott. "But I suppose Daddy would have bought you another one and I'd've been out!"

Scott was starting to squirm. Obviously, nobody had spoken to him like this in a long time. Well, it was about damn time someone did.

"You have a problem with me because I'm from South Dakota. Well, you know what South Dakotans don't do? They don't expect other people to put themselves in danger to save their sorry butts. And we don't have to pay people for sex! And we don't have to bribe people to live with us! And we don't get drunk and treat people the way you do!" I was shouting at this point which surprised me. My mother was the shouter in the family, not me.

Jeff started to remonstrate but I shut him up. "No, it's about time somebody told this spoiled brat a few home truths. He could have gotten you killed."

Jeff smiled slightly. "I didn't know you cared."

"Well, I do!" I spat. Then I turned back to Scott. "I ought to charge you for gas. I suppose you two drove my car until it was empty, and I'm supposed to pay for it, right? Because the universe revolves around you, right, Scott? Isn't that what your mommy taught you? Well, it doesn't."

I grabbed my stuff and demanded my keys. I had to leave for work. Scott huddled in his chair. He looked like he was ready to cry.

"And Jeff, don't call me for a day or so. I'm mad at you, too. The next time this obnoxious jerk gets himself in some sort of mess, call the police. Your life isn't worth his car even if he thinks it is."

I swept out.

Of course, Scott got back in the only way he could. He told Jeff to move out. Jeff reported this little fact when I was talking to him again.

"So? Move!" I retorted. "I wish him luck getting another schmuck to room with him."

"It's mid-semester. Where could I go?" Jeff asked.

Oh boy. When you tell off a bully you better not be in his power in any way, manner, or form. "I could ask the Friesmans if you could stay with me for a few months. At least until the semester is over," I offered slowly.

"Nah, it's too far away from school."

"When does Scott want you out?"

"This weekend."

Oh boy. Scott really was a jerk. But I hadn't been working for a lawyer for nothing. "He can't force you out by the weekend, even if you don't have a lease. Tell you what; let me talk to Scott."

"What are you going to do that I can't?"

"Tell him some more truth. You can't without digging your hole deeper. There's nothing Scott can do to me," I replied. I wasn't worried about Scott. Like all bullies he'd never do anything to me head-on, he'd wait until my back was turned. And I didn't intend to turn.

"Don't yell at him," Jeff warned. "You know what he's like."

"Yeah, I know what he's like," I muttered.

I arranged a meeting with Scott at a coffee shop. I explained the law to him—that Jeff was contesting the eviction and we could drag this out for six months and Jeff wouldn't have to pay a dime in rent. That we'd drag his father into the suit and explain why Scott was throwing Jeff out. And that I would personally make a case for Scott stealing my car—they'd taken it without my permission, after all. If Scott wanted to be an asshole, fine. We'd play that game. I didn't yell, I didn't call him any names. I spoke in even, low tones. And Scott backed down.

"Hey, I didn't mean it!" he exclaimed. I raised a skeptical eyebrow and he assured me he'd just been mad. "I didn't like the way you talked to me," he admitted.

That I could believe. I called Jeff and the boys made up. The crisis seemed to be over. Jeff thanked me for going to battle for him then said absently, "This is only until the semester is over.

Then Scott will graduate, and I'll have to find another place to live. But thanks for buying me some time."

I smiled wryly. "I guess we both have problems with our living situations. Mrs. Friesman is still leaving dog poop on my step."

Jeff commiserated with me on my nightmare landlady then said, "You know, we both need new places to live. And we're both on a budget. Maybe we should think about renting a place together. We spend most of our free time together anyway so this would be more convenient." I looked at him, startled. He raised a hand. "This doesn't mean I'm falling in love or expect you to marry me. It's just a solution to a problem we both have. But you don't have to answer now. Sleep on it. We'll talk later."

I didn't really have to take much time thinking about it. I came home to more dog poop. I called Jeff and told him that sharing an apartment was a good idea. Preferably, one where the landlords didn't have poopy little dogs.

CHAPTER 12

Jeff and I Move in Together

Jackie didn't say much when I announced that Jeff and I were going to find a place together.

"At least you'll be out of the rathole you're in," she commented.

"Yeah. Say, how much notice should I give the Friesmans that I'm leaving?" I asked.

Jackie looked judicious. "You're renting month-to-month, right? If they were decent people, I'd give them two months. But they're not decent people. And the dog poop situation seems to be escalating so I'd just give them a month. That's enough to get your deposit back."

I nodded. Mrs. Friesman had been moving the poop deposits up a step a week. I hoped to be gone before the poop reached the landing. God knows what she'd do then.

"I told you not to move there in the first place!" my mother crowed when I reported on the Saturday morning call that I was looking for an apartment. I didn't tell her that I was getting a roommate. And that it was a man. I'd burn that bridge when I got to it.

I was with Jeff when he told Scott he was moving. Scott took the news surprisingly well. "I'm graduating in June, so I'll probably be moving anyway. No big deal." But he slammed the door as he walked out.

Jeff was impressed at Scott's calm reaction. "He usually throws people out. This is the first time, to my knowledge, that anyone moved out first. Maybe he's growing up."

I nodded dubiously. I was getting crank hang-up calls. The calls could have come from Mrs. Friesman although dog poop seemed to be her specialty. I personally suspected Scott. That was the sort of underhanded thing I figured he'd do. I suppose it could have been a random nutball, but I didn't think so. How did a quiet person like me collect so many enemies in so short a time?

The next question was where Jeff and I should move. We both agreed that it should be mid-point between my work and his school. But that covered a lot of territory.

"There's always Palms," Jeff offered.

"Too far west," I objected. "I don't want to fight the 10 freeway every day to get to work."

The San Fernando Valley was inconvenient for both of us. We finally decided on West Hollywood.

"We'll probably be the only straight people there," Jeff remarked. "Do you think they'll even rent to us?"

"We'll see," I returned. We left it at that until Jeff came back from Easter weekend at his parents' place.

"Hey, I ran into an old classmate," Jeff announced. "He's down here trying to make it as an actor and he's managing a building in Hollywood to pay the rent. He says there'll be an opening soon."

"Hollywood? Isn't that dangerous?" I asked skeptically. "I don't think I want to live there."

"It's not that bad," Jeff scoffed.

"Well, there's got to be a better option," I stated firmly. "I won't even go across town to look at it."

We went to check out the apartment the following Saturday. Jeff said he wanted to prepare me before meeting his classmate, Steve. "I don't want you getting freaked out but he's gay," he warned me.

"Why would I get freaked out?" I asked.

"Well, being from South Dakota and all..." he said uncomfortably.

"Why do you Californians think I don't know anything because I'm from South Dakota? We're part of the country, you know," I retorted, irritated. Then I looked at him suspiciously. "And how do you know he's gay?"

Jeff shifted uncomfortably. "Well, he hit on me when I was home. I guess he'd just come out to his parents and figured he could share himself with the world."

"And what did you do?"

"I said no, of course."

"Oh," was all I said. For all my protestations of sophistication, my Catholic South Dakota upbringing was kicking in and I had no points of reference for dealing with this situation. "Were you surprised?" I asked lamely.

"Nah, he's always been an artsy type, but he never hit on anybody or anything. Even when we had a circle jerk in the Boy Scouts, he stayed cool."

Jeff had to explain to me what a circle jerk was. I was horrified. "I thought you made knots and stuff in the Boy Scouts. You mean you sit around the campfire and masturbate on those camping trips?" I was flummoxed. "Oh my God, my brother made Eagle Scout. Does that mean he was better at it than the rest of you?"

Little Suzie Creamcheese was having a hard time digesting all this. When Jeff introduced me to his high school friend, I shook his hand gingerly, surreptitiously looking for traces of semen.

"Marianne, this is Steve Harris, the apartment manager," Jeff announced and gave Steve one of those 'guy' hugs. I watched them suspiciously, but nothing seemed untoward. Steve was medium-height and slim, with dark hair and sharp features. He seemed like a perfectly normal human being; no feather boa, no heels, no extravagant make-up—not what I'd been expecting at all. He was polite and professional as he led us around the one-bedroom apartment that was coming available. The building had been built in the 40s but was still in good condition. The apartment we looked at was on the second floor—the building only had two floors so nobody would be stomping on our heads—and had a good-sized kitchen, a formal dining room, and a back door that led downstairs to the garage. A small pool was in the center of the complex. I liked that. What I didn't like was the green shag carpet that covered every floor except those in the kitchen and bathroom. And the apartment looked like it was being occupied by a hoarder. It even smelled.

"Could I take up the carpet?" I asked, scuffing my toe on the filthy carpet.

"The owner would prefer not," Steve said smoothly. "It keeps the noise down for the downstairs couple."

"Oh," I said, disappointed. I couldn't see me living with this awful carpet for any length of time.

Later, Jeff rhapsodized about the apartment. "It's perfect," he declared. "It's halfway between your work and UCLA. It's close to entertainment so we wouldn't have to drive and pay to park for everything. It's huge even though it's only a one-bedroom, it's got a pool, and we'd each be paying less in rent than we are now because the building is so old. I say we take it."

I absolutely refused. "It's filthy," I objected. "And I think something bit me while we were walking around."

"Steve said that's why we won't be able to move in until June," Jeff explained. "He needs the time to evict the current tenant and clean it up."

We argued all weekend long until we signed a one-year lease the following Monday after work. "Better get it while we can," Jeff said wisely. "Now you can tell Mrs. Friesman to go to hell."

"I'm only giving them thirty days' notice. That way I can get my deposit back without giving Mrs. Friesman any more time to think of awful things to do to me. And maybe she'll stop leaving dog poop once she knows I'm leaving. I mean, that's what she was trying to do, don't you think? Chase me out? Maybe she'll be more pleasant now that she's won. Anyway, that's what Jackie thinks."

"Hope she's right." Jeff murmured.

I did too.

The dog poop was almost to the landing when I gave the Friesmans written notice that I was moving out. Mr. Friesman frowned but the sun came up in Mrs. Friesman's eyes. Even Poopsie seemed delighted.

"Why are you moving?" Mr. Friesman asked.

I was ready with my explanation. "I'm moving into a bigger apartment with a friend. The rent will be cheaper with a roommate and I'm moving closer to work." And that was only partly a lie. Then I added diffidently, "I won't be paying rent since I paid first and last months' rent when I moved in. And I hope there won't be a problem getting my deposit back." I really hoped there wouldn't be, but I'd come prepared with the threat of legal aid from my law firm.

Mrs. Friesman started to puff up and Poopsie snarled but Mr. Friesman waved them off. "I'll have the check ready this weekend." He glared at his wife and she turned on her heel and stomped off.

That seemed to be that. Now all I had to do was wait out the thirty days and pack up my car again. I hadn't added much to the apartment except clothes so it wouldn't take long.

The poop stopped creeping up my steps, so I guess Mrs. Friesman had finally gotten what she wanted. Mr. Friesman made one last visit to my garret when he tiredly trudged up to drop off my check.

"Can I come in?" he asked.

"Sure," I said and stood back from the door so he could enter. He sat in the kitchen chair that he always sat in and I sat across from him, nervously waiting for what he had to say.

He took the check from his pocket and slid it across the table.

"Here it is. Deposit in full," he said and smiled faintly. "I'm sorry things got uncomfortable for you here."

I decided to take the bull by the horns. "Why did Mrs. Friesman hate me so much? What did I do that made her so mad?"

Mr. Friesman sighed wearily. "It wasn't you, really. If it hadn't been you it would have been something else."

"Well, I hope she'll be happier now that I'm leaving. Maybe you should rent to a man next time," I suggested.

"There won't be a next time," Mr. Friesman said forcefully. "She's unhappy; I'm unhappy. I've decided to end it."

I looked at him blankly. "I'm sorry. But really maybe now that I'm going…"

"She claimed I liked being with you more than with her," Mr. Friesman interrupted. "And she was right. But it wasn't like a sex thing," he added when he noticed my alarmed expression. "I liked making closets and going to church…it was like having a little sister from home. My life seemed normal again. And then she'd drink too much and scream that I was keeping her from her art." He slapped his hand on the table. I jumped but he didn't notice. "The only person keeping her from her art is her. And I'm tired of it." He stopped and let his eyes wander around the garret. "At least I can get a good price for the house. I wanted to fix things up the way they were supposed to be. I thought that's what she wanted, too…"

He sounded sad and beaten. I didn't know what to say so I repeated, "I'm sorry."

He shook himself. "Not your problem. And it won't be. I won't tell her my decision until you've moved out. I've put up with her nonsense for years; three more weeks won't kill me. I don't want you to have to worry about any more ugly pranks." My eyebrows climbed. "Yeah, I knew about the crap on the steps, but I couldn't get her to stop." He sighed. "Oh, and you can keep the TV. I hope that will make up for some of the…inconvenience she put you through."

I felt sorry for him. It must be awful to be a decent person married to a psychotic. I hoped he got out before she knifed him in his sleep. She really was unbalanced. I decided I could deal with the awful shag carpet as long as I could lock out the crazies. And I wouldn't have to buy a TV.

June first; the big day had finally arrived. Jeff rented a small stake truck. He actually had furniture and he needed me to help him move it. "Scott says he has back trouble," he explained.

Of course, he did. I couldn't imagine Scott doing any sort of physical work.

Jeff picked me up in the truck on the morning of the move. He'd stowed his motorcycle in the back, so we went to Westwood to load the rest of his stuff. He had a double bed, a dresser, his desk, a sofa ("I thought that was Scott's", "No, it's mine"), his stereo, boxes of books and records, clothes, towels, and bedding...he really had a lot of stuff. The truck was full by the time we got done. But we were done. Or so I thought.

We were bouncing down the road on the way to Hollywood when Jeff slammed on the brakes. "What? What's wrong?" I asked, surprised.

"Do you see that?" Jeff breathed.

"See what?" I demanded, craning my neck around.

"That chair!" Jeff pointed dramatically.

"Chair? What chair?" Then my gaze landed on a poor, forlorn recliner rocker sitting at the curb. "That? You mean that green thing?"

"I've always wanted my own recliner," Jeff sighed.

"Well, you can't have that one," I declared. "That's someone's garbage."

Jeff ignored me. He parked the truck, ran over to the chair, and sat in it. He pushed back and the footrest emerged. "It still works," he yelped, delighted.

"Jeff, it's all ripped and probably has bugs," I objected. "Besides, there's no room in the truck."

"It doesn't have bugs. And if it does, I'll spray it when we get to Hollywood."

"But it's ripped," I pointed out.

"I can tape it," he argued.

"It's garbage!" I repeated.

"One man's garbage is another man's treasure," Jeff returned piously. "People throw perfectly good stuff away all the time. But I like it. And we need furniture."

"We don't need garbage," I muttered but Jeff ignored me. He was busy trying to find space in the truck for the chair.

Jeff rearranged as much as possible, but the truck was full. There was no way to jam the recliner in. Jeff pondered and I sighed pointedly a few times. Then his face lit up. "I've got it. We'll put the recliner on top of everything."

"But won't it blow out? We don't have anything to tie it down with."

"That's okay. You can sit in it and hold on to the side of the truck. Your weight should keep it from blowing out. And I'll drive real slow."

"Jeff, I absolutely refuse to sit in the back of the truck in that stupid recliner!" I spat.

After five minutes of wheedling Jeff and I hoisted that miserable recliner into the truck. Jeff gave me a leg up and I settled myself in it. We began our slow progress to the new apartment.

I got a lot of laughs as we cruised through the West Side, but my humiliation wasn't complete until Jeff got on Sunset Blvd. He stayed in the right lane and drove slowly, but I think I almost caused some accidents. I must have looked like Granny in *The Beverly Hillbillies* sitting in Jeff's recliner rocker in the back of the truck. People would stare and then howl. I finally decided if I couldn't beat 'em, I'd join 'em. I pretended I was the Rose Queen and I waved my hand regally to one and all until we finally got to the apartment.

Steve was outside trimming some hibiscus bushes when we pulled up; I smiled and gave him my royal wave. He waved bemusedly back at me then he started laughing. He was wiping tears from his eyes when Jeff parked but he offered to help unload the heavy stuff. That left me with the boxes of books. With three of us working it only took about half an hour to unload the truck. We thanked Steve for his help.

"Happy to help. I haven't laughed that hard in years," he returned and started snickering again.

I grinned and got into the truck with Jeff. "You owe me," I declared.

"Yeah, I do," he agreed.

"You made me look like an idiot," I stated.

"Yeah, I did. But we got the chair, didn't we? And Steve helped. He wouldn't have done that if he hadn't been so tickled."

"Humph," I replied, unmollified. "Can I stay in the cab now or do I have to get in the back?"

Jeff laughed then started the truck again. He drove around to the back of the building and unloaded his motorcycle. The rest of the day was uneventful. We drove to my apartment and got my few boxes of clothes, books, and dishes. And the TV.

"You really don't have much, do you?" Jeff observed.

"I really don't," I agreed.

It didn't take long to load up my stuff. The only surprise was one last poop—on the landing. I guess Mrs. Friesman had the last word. Or the last poop. Jeff shook his head.

I left the key on the table, got in my car, and followed the truck back to our new apartment. We unloaded and I followed Jeff one more time as he dropped off the truck. I let him drive my Tempo back to our new place. I was tired, sweaty, and hungry.

"Let me take you out to dinner," Jeff offered.

"I can't go like this," I declared and gestured to my disheveled self. Jeff agreed. We found some towels and soap and broke in our new shower—one at a time. Jeff offered to share but I was exhausted and still a little miffed about being forced to play Granny. When I got out of the shower, I discovered that Jeff had taken the time to set up the bed frame. We put the box spring and mattress on top and found the sheets. When we were done Jeff got cleaned up. Then we found a nice Italian restaurant on Sunset. Jeff ordered a whole bottle of wine to go with the meal. We toasted each other and enjoyed a leisurely meal. The maître d' seemed to think we were newly-weds, and we didn't disabuse him. He winked at us when we left and said, "Have a wonderful evening." I smiled but Jeff winked back meaningfully.

Which didn't do him a damn bit of good. I was tired. When we got back to the apartment, he tried to get amorous, but it was useless. I fell asleep the minute I hit the bed.

CHAPTER 13

Housekeeping

I was in the mood for a romp the next day. Just knowing that Mrs. Friesman was out of my life was exhilarating. No more encroaching dog crap! And I loved the spaciousness of the apartment. I had a dining room! And a big kitchen! Jeff brought his coffee maker and I had the few pots and pans my mom had sent with me. We had mis-matched dishes, cutlery, and a toaster. We put the TV on the floor. But it was a start. Now I'd have to get a table and chairs. Jeff and I discussed the logistics of buying furniture as we drank coffee in the living room. Jeff sat in that horrible recliner and I stayed on the couch.

"I've got my deposit so I can start looking for a used table and chairs," I offered.

"It's not fair to ask you to buy stuff for our apartment. We can split the cost," Jeff said.

"Do you think it's smart to pool our money on stuff like furniture?" I hedged. "What if we hate living together? Then we'd have all the hassle of trying to buy each other out. We're splitting the rent; I think we should keep our purchases separate, too."

Jeff didn't seem offended. "But what about the phone and stuff like that?"

"Do you have an account?"

"No."

"Well, I do. I won't have to pay a deposit. The phone company will transfer my number here and we can plug a phone in."

"Great!" Jeff enthused.

"Yes and no," I wavered. "I didn't dare tell my mother that I'm moving in with a guy. So that means you won't be able to answer the phone."

"Oh," Jeff said, disconcerted. "Are you sure you can't talk to your mom? She can't be that scary."

"Yes, she can," I assured him. "I remember Aggie M coming home late one time. Mom met her at the door and hit her all the way to our bedroom. She even slammed her up against the wall. I know because I was watching all this from under the covers. My mother is only five foot two, but she scares the crap out of everybody I know."

Jeff looked alarmed until I assured him I'd buy an answering machine so we could screen calls. Not a perfect solution but it would do for the time being.

And I had an excuse to shop estate sales for furniture. That was Jackie's idea. "Really nice furniture goes for a song when old people die. We'll find something nice and cheap," she said.

But I had to fit antique hunting around softball practice. Our team had been so successful last summer the firm partners paid for another season—and tee shirts. Jeff took over as coach because he was working at the firm again for the summer and we carpooled together. The partners admired his public-spiritedness and we split the gas money. Living together was more convenient than I'd thought possible. Steve the Manager was a delight compared to Mrs. Friesman and Jeff declared that I was a lot easier to live with than Scott.

"I don't miss him at all," he confessed on the way to practice one evening.

"Do you ever hear from him?" I asked cautiously. "I thought you guys were friends."

"More just roommates," Jeff assured me. "He was a taker. Had to have his way all the time. And I let him have it because he paid most of the rent. Saved me a fortune. Nah, he's living his own life now. We'll probably never hear from him again."

I didn't tell Jeff, I didn't want to upset him, but I'd been getting more crank phone calls and I still thought they might have been Scott. I wasn't sure because the caller only breathed on the answering machine; it was just a feeling. I found out for sure when I accidently picked up the phone without waiting for the machine to pick up.

"Yes?" I asked absently.

"I know where you live," husked a barely disguised voice. But I was no longer the scared kid from Brookings. I'd been around a block or two.

"Scott?" I interrupted. "Are you trying to scare me? You should know better. I can find out where you live, too. And come on over if you think you're man enough. I've got a .22; I'll blow off both your balls before I put one right between your eyes. I'm from South Dakota; you know I'll do it."

Click! He hung up! Score one for me. Too bad I didn't really have a gun. Maybe I'd talk to Jeff about getting one--although I wasn't sure where he stood on gun control. I didn't understand a lot about him yet. He seemed easy-going but he was pretty sure he was right about everything and liked getting his way—but then again who doesn't? We hadn't seriously disagreed about anything yet, so I wasn't sure what he'd do when a disagreement finally arose. But I wasn't too worried; he was probably one of the most decent people I'd ever met. Which really surprised me because in my experience good-looking guys didn't have to be decent—they could get away with pretty much anything. I was discovering that he was the best roommate I could ask for—although my only other roommate to this point had been Aggie M and we hadn't gotten along at all.

I liked him. I really did. And the sex thing was pretty good, too.

"I guess all it takes is practice," I murmured, slightly surprised after a particularly satisfactory session.

"Yeah," Jeff grinned. "Just have to practice more."

So, we did.

Summer ended and so did softball. Jeff went back to school and I went back to driving to work alone. But that was okay. I spent more time with Jackie. I even got to know Steve the Manager better. Not only was he an actor, he was a budding screenwriter which I found fascinating. I'd never met anyone trying to make a living that way. I even invited him to go furniture shopping with Jackie and me one Saturday. It was a successful day. He and Jackie seemed to like each other, and I found a slightly banged up mahogany dining room table and six chairs. The problem was getting my purchase home. Thank God we'd brought Steve. He figured out how to strap the table and two of the chairs to the top of my Tempo. He shoehorned the other four chairs in the back seat. Before we left the sale site an auctioneer asked me, "Is this a sorority prank?"

"No, I'm just poor," I replied.

The three of us crowded into the front seat for the trip home. I had to drive slowly so the car wouldn't airplane with the table on top. That gave passersby time to really appreciate the sight. The laughter and pointing didn't bother me—this was nothing compared to playing Granny—but Jackie seemed a bit bemused. And amused. "So, this is what college is like," she commented drily.

"Pretty much," Steve assured her. "Nobody has any money, so we have to make do."

"Nice to know I didn't miss much," Jackie murmured.

"Just poverty," I said.

"I know all about poverty," Jackie retorted. "I never laughed about it. Maybe I should have."

Jeff was home when we arrived so he and Steve man-handled the table upstairs to the apartment and Jackie and I carried chairs. We broke in my new dining set when we ate the pizza I ordered as a reward to everybody for furniture hauling. I was enjoying my new life.

Things got even better when I got a raise! And it was a big one. I was impressed—and grateful.

"You deserve it," Mr. Elliot assured me after I stammered my thanks. "You have a feel for the law. Have you ever thought about going to law school?"

"Not really," I said.

"Well, you should." Mr. Elliot leaned back in his chair and looked up at me seriously. That seemed to bother him. "Sit down," he ordered impatiently. I did. "I don't do this often," he continued when he was more comfortable, "but if you want, I can sponsor you to a local school like UCLA."

"I couldn't afford it," I demurred.

"You're not ready now," Mr. Elliott hurriedly assured me. "But in a year or two, if you keep going the way you are, you can set aside some of that paycheck," he nodded at the check in my hand, "and use it toward law school. If you do well on the LSAT maybe you can get some scholarship money."

I nodded stupidly. Mr. Elliot was not a patient sort and he'd said as much as he was going to. "It's something to consider," he finished and waved me out. I wasn't offended. As I said, he was a piece of cake compared to my mother.

And speaking of my mother, she was shocked by the amount of my raise when I broke the news during our Saturday call.

"You're sure you came by that honestly?" she asked suspiciously.

"Of course, I did!" I returned indignantly. "As a matter of fact, Mr. Elliot suggested that I consider going to law school in a few years. He even offered to sponsor me for UCLA if I don't screw up."

"My goodness," Mom marveled. I'd finally impressed her. Lowly little Marianne, who wasn't cute and popular like her sister. Who'd have to use her brain because she didn't have any looks. *What do you think now, Ma?* I mentally snarled. Of course, I kept the thought out of my tone; I wasn't ready to confront her yet. That would take more than money.

But the raise kept Mom's mind off other things—like my living arrangements. She assumed my new roommate was Jackie and I let her think it. She didn't approve of Jackie, being an older woman and all, but she would have lost her mind over the fact that I was living with a guy. And sharing his bed. And having sex without benefit of marriage. I didn't even mention Steve the Manager much. I didn't know how she felt about gay men but if it was anything like how she felt about lesbians I was pretty sure it wouldn't be positive. It seemed safest to keep most of my life a secret from her. Thank God I could keep her mind focused on my raise. It kept her from prying into anything important. And she seemed happy when I suggested I call her on Sundays instead of our Saturday conversations. She'd save money, she wouldn't have to take time off from work, and I'd be able to let Jeff answer the phone.

So, life went on. Jeff bought a nightstand and I bought a TV stand but we both had to agree on each purchase before we made it. We learned to coordinate with each other.

Instead of softball get-togethers I got invited to all of Jeff's parties at UCLA. I was a hit at the Halloween masquerade party. Jeff wore a mask, but I'd lost so much weight I felt comfortable wearing a black unitard, ears, tail, and cat makeup. It was simple, inexpensive, and every woman glared at me and every guy flirted. For the first time in my life I knew how Aggie M had felt in her wicked youth. I was gorgeous! Who knew? Jeff seemed pleased by my impact and I reveled in my success. I was gaining more confidence all the time. I only had one bad moment when I thought I saw Scott, but it was a false alarm—just some drunken idiot spilling beer on people and making an ass of himself.

"Scott seemed to disappear," Jeff commented when I mentioned that I'd thought I'd seen him. "Nobody's heard anything about him. But I bet he's working for his father so he's probably okay."

"Do you miss him?" I asked sarcastically.

"Nah. You're more fun. Our living arrangement is working out great, isn't it?"

"Well, yeah," I admitted. "This is the best time I've ever had."

And it was. What could go wrong?

And the minute you think everything's great, something happens. Jeff answered the phone without thinking on Thanksgiving Day. And, of course, it was my mother.

I knew something terrible had happened when Jeff called to me, "Marianne, it's your mother!" in half-strangled tones. I turned as white as he was and wiped my hands on a towel as I hurried from the kitchen to take the phone from him. His eyes were pleading apology as I took a deep breath and said, "Hello? Mom?"

"Is that the new boyfriend?" was Mom's first question. Of course, it would be.

"Yeah, that was Jeff. He's here for Thanksgiving dinner," I returned smoothly.

"Why did he answer your phone?" Mom asked suspiciously.

"I asked him to. I was peeling potatoes in the kitchen. Jackie's making a vegetable tray and Steve is setting the table."

"Oh, Jackie, your work friend...and roommate?"

"And Steve's the apartment manager," I added smoothly to avoid the roommate comment. Jeff visibly exhaled and gave me a thumbs up. "Do you have the whole family for dinner today?" I asked to take attention off me and my doings.

"Just your brother's and that's plenty. Aggie M's with her in-laws." We chatted for a few minutes before my mother said, "Well, dinner's almost ready here so I'd better go. I wanted to wish you a happy Thanksgiving. Will you be coming home for Christmas this year? It's strange without you."

I evaded that too with an excuse about work and vacation time and closed with, "But I'll see what I can do." I hung up and sighed explosively.

"I'm sorry I answered the phone," Jeff said nervously. "I was passing when it rang and picked it up without thinking. Did I get you in trouble?"

"No, I'm turning into a terrific liar," I admitted.

"Boy, you sure are," Jeff said with admiration. "You'd make a great lawyer."

We grinned at each other and I said, "That's not something I'd ever thought I'd have to learn. I guess what you need is a healthy dose of fear." I shook myself. "No harm, no foul. But please don't pick up the phone in future. My mother has a sixth sense when she thinks something's wrong."

"Maybe you should tell her about us," Jeff suggested.

"Yeah, maybe I should." I shook myself again. "I better get back to dinner."

I was pleased with my turkey dinner. I'd gotten a tablecloth and napkins and a set of china from another estate sale. I was doing things right. Jackie was amazed at my culinary expertise.

"You made a pie from scratch?" she asked.

"My grandmother taught me," I explained. "My mom was never much into cooking, but my grandmother was great. I used to help her all the time."

"Is she still alive?"

"No, she died when I was in middle school. But I still miss her."

It had never occurred to me before, but Grandma had been my only ally. At least I was important to her when Mom was making sure Aggie M had the right dresses for the various dances she attended. Grandma had liked me.

Steve and Jackie did the dishes. Steve washed and Jackie dried—she didn't want to ruin her manicure. Jeff and I sat and burped as we all watched football although the only person who really enjoyed it was Jeff. Steve and Jackie spent more time talking about movies and fashion. I was glad Jackie had a friendly place to spend Thanksgiving Day. I was beginning to think being a mistress wasn't all it was cracked up to be.

Jeff and I continued to talk about the parent problem. I asked him if he'd told his parents yet and he admitted that he'd told them I was his girlfriend, not that we were living together. So, I wasn't the only one keeping secrets! We both agreed that we'd have to bring everything out into the open—but when? The thought of telling my Catholic conservative mother about Jeff made me sick to my stomach but I knew it had to be done. Jeff said he'd tell his parents when he went home.

He didn't get the chance.

After Thanksgiving, some of us at the office went out for a drink after work. I had to drive my car home. I'd only had two drinks; it wouldn't affect me that much. I thought.

I was a little cavalier when it came to red lights. One thing I'd learned in Los Angeles is: no one stops at yellow lights. You gun it and go. So, I did. I should have been looking for cops. They were sure looking for me.

I wasn't too upset when I heard the siren and saw the lights in my rear-view mirror. I wasn't even bothered when two policemen got out of their patrol car after I pulled over. I rolled down my window, smiled, and asked, "Did I do something wrong?"

The first cop was expressionless as he said, "That light was pretty pink."

"Oh no," I objected, "it was yellow."

The first cop raised a speculative eyebrow. The second cop said, "Have you been drinking, ma'am?"

"Just one," I lied. Damn, lying was becoming a habit. Score one for life in Los Angeles.

"Step out of the car, ma'am," said the first cop. I was being tag teamed.

They had me walk a straight line as passersby pointed and gawked. But I wasn't bothered by that anymore. Apparently, I was the best show in town and had been for months.

"She can walk," said the second cop. Of course, I could; I'd had two drinks over two hours. And I was starting to get a little irritated. I'd seen people blow through red lights—real red lights. What did I do to deserve such special treatment?

I had to rummage around in my purse to pull out my license and registration. As the second cop reviewed my paperwork the first cop said, "Where'd you get this car?" And his tone wasn't admiring.

"My mom gave it to me. It was her old one. And there's nothing wrong with it. It runs just fine," I returned tartly. Then I added parenthetically, "It could have been a Studebaker. Believe me, this is better."

He snorted and the second cop said, "She has South Dakota plates and a California license. If we take her in, she'll spend the rest of the night in jail. What should we do?"

Were they serious? I looked at their faces anxiously. They were. Was I about to be arrested? Oh God, who should I call? Jeff or Mr. Elliot? My alarm was showing on my face.

The first cop said, "I don't think she can get into too much trouble in an old Ford."

My irritation overrode my good sense. "There's nothing wrong with this car! It got me out here from South Dakota and gets me to work every day. It deserves a little respect!" I retorted.

The first copy guffawed. I think he thought I was cute. Is that why they stopped me? Boy, if they thought I was cute now they should have seen me at Halloween!

"Listen, we'll let you go this time, but watch those lights. And register your car."

I promised earnestly that I would. I sincerely thanked them for not citing me—my good sense had finally kicked in—and I promised to be more careful of lights in future.

We all got in our cars and pulled out. I was waving at them to show how nice I was when I went through another rather pink yellow light. They followed me through and shook their heads. But they peeled off and I got home without any other trouble.

Reaction set in when I got home, and I started laughing. I was still laughing when I opened the apartment door and shouted out, "Hey Jeff, I got stopped by two cops as I was leaving the bar and they..." I stopped abruptly when I noticed an older man in the living room with Jeff. They both stood up. Jeff looked slightly sick.

"Marianne, this is my father," he said by way of explanation.

"Dr. Foster? Nice to meet me," I said feebly. What a way to meet a parent.

CHAPTER 14

I Pay the Piper

Dr. Foster was unruffled by my unorthodox entrance. He wasn't even disturbed—or surprised—that Jeff and I were living together. "You're both adults. I can't tell you what to do," he said equitably and took us out to dinner. It was a pleasant evening but that was all the time he had for his son. He was on his way to a conference in San Diego the following day and had to get up early in the morning.

"You can sleep on the couch," Jeff offered.

"Oh no," Dr. Foster returned. "I don't want to be a bother." Then he asked me to tell him more about myself. But he wasn't creepy or judgmental. He seemed like a nice man. Although he didn't look much like Jeff. He was only about 5'10", slightly chubby, balding, and wore glasses. He looked like the professor he was.

"I take after my mom," Jeff explained when I commented on it. "Or maybe my grandma. I've seen pictures of her when she was young. There's a resemblance. And I'm the only tall one of the family. My brothers all take after my dad."

"Not basketball players, huh," I commented.

"Nah. They're not sports people. Well, my oldest brother played softball. Still does, I think. But that's it. I was the only high school athlete."

"Well, if I ever meet your oldest brother, we can talk softball. That's something," I said cheerfully.

"You'll meet him," Jeff assured me. He paused before adding, "And now my family knows about our living arrangement. Are you going to tell your mother about us?" I gawped at him. "You said you would. Unless you're ashamed of me. Is that it? You're embarrassed?"

"No, of course not," I said vehemently. "It's just…well…"

"You know your mother's going to find out someday," Jeff said reasonably. "It'd probably be better if she knew sooner rather than later."

He had me there. For my own protection I knew I should confess and get it over with. Maybe the knot in my stomach would go away. I decided I'd tell her over Christmas. Jeff was going home, and I didn't want to spend another Yule all by myself. And I figured since Christmas was on a Tuesday, I wouldn't waste more than four days of my precious vacation time for a ten-day holiday. First, I had to get the time off from Mr. Elliot—who wasn't happy when I asked.

"You don't give me much notice," he scowled.

"It's kind of spur of the moment," I apologized. "And it's only for four workdays. Nothing much happens Christmas week, you know that. I'll be back at my desk, bright-eyed and bushy-tailed the following Monday."

"But I'll be handling everything alone," he complained. Whined, really. Boy, he really hated any change in his routine. No wonder he wasn't married. He may have been a brilliant lawyer but when it came to interpersonal skills, he was the equivalent of a two-year-old.

"Someone in the steno pool will help you," I soothed him. "And if you really don't feel like working alone maybe you should take some vacation time for yourself. You've been working really hard and a break would probably be good for you."

"Where would I go?" he asked grumpily.

"Oh, I don't know. Hawaii? Maybe that would be nice," I suggested.

He grunted. And sat in his chair, pouting.

"So, can I take the time?" I prodded him.

"I guess," he groused. "But you'll be back the following Monday?"

"Bright and early," I assured him.

"Well, okay then." I was dismissed. Merry Christmas to me.

I called Mom and told her I was coming home for Christmas.

"Well, it's about time," she said, "although I don't know why you didn't make this decision sooner. We're busy at the store and I don't know how I'll find the time to pick you up in Sioux Falls."

That was just like my mother: nag, nag, nag about coming home and when I tell her I'm coming, bitch and moan and complain. First my boss and now my mom. I felt like the only balanced adult in the world.

"I could rent a car," I offered.

"Don't be ridiculous," Mom scoffed. "That's a needless expense. I'll have someone pick you up. When are you coming?"

"I haven't made the plane reservations yet," I said. "I wanted to make sure it was okay."

"Well, of course it's okay," Mom retorted, miffed. "Where did you get the idea it wouldn't be okay?"

"Oh, it was just…never mind. I'll make the reservations and call you back."

That's what I did.

Jackie didn't say much when I told her I was going to South Dakota for Christmas. She smiled and said she hoped I'd have a good time. When I asked Steve to keep an eye on the apartment while Jeff and I were gone he said he'd be happy to; he was staying in Los Angeles over the holidays. I suggested to Jackie that she call Steve if she got bored. She smiled. "I might do that," she said. "I like the kid."

All I had left to do was pack. Jeff and I didn't even bother with a tree. There'd be no one there to water or enjoy it. We did exchange presents. I gave him a sweater and he gave me a ring.

"A ring?" I asked with a raised eyebrow. "Really?"

"Friendship," Jeff said. "That's all. No deep dark plan to sell you into slavery or marriage. It's just a ring." And he put it on my right hand for emphasis.

It was a simple little ring; silver with a dark blue stone. "It's lapis lazuli," Jeff explained. "It's not expensive so don't look so worried."

I relaxed. It's not like he was trying to buy his way into my bed. He was already there. I'd quit looking for hidden meanings.

Jeff drove me to LAX in the Tempo early the Saturday before Christmas. He was flying out of Burbank later that day but would be back the day after Christmas to make sure he and my car were available to pick me up when I returned. We kissed briefly at the curb and wished each other a Merry Christmas before he pulled away. I dragged my suitcase into the terminal, excited and nervous all at once. I hadn't been home in over a year. I wondered if it would feel different. I carried my coat. It was warm and sunny in Los Angeles, but I knew the weather would be freezing when I got to South Dakota. The flight was uneventful. It was about four when I landed in Sioux Falls and was surprised to see Aggie M and her two kids waiting for me. She introduced me as Auntie Marianne. "You can call her Auntie M," she instructed the toddler. I was a little startled to be named after a Wizard of Oz character—and an old one at that—but her car, her rules. The toddler didn't care. Neither did the baby. They were uninterested in me.

"Everybody else is working so Mom said I had to pick you up," Aggie M said waspishly in explanation. She looked me up and down critically. "God, you've really slimmed down," she exclaimed but she didn't sound happy about it. "And your hair looks different."

"No more perms," I said with a grin. "Mom'll probably have a fit."

"Maybe not. It looks good on you," Aggie M conceded grudgingly. "You need help with your luggage? Of course not. Dad always said you were strong as an ox."

Boy, my transformation really seemed to piss Aggie M off. She was jealous of me! Who'd have thought it. Certainly not me. When we were kids Aggie M got the box of 64 crayons—with a sharpener. I got a box of 24. Aggie M got at least three highly starched can cans when she was in the first grade. I got one. And it was limp. I didn't complain. I didn't look good in can cans anyway. But now I was top dog. I'd take all of Aggie M's spleen with pleasure.

I got my luggage and Aggie M directed me to her Cadillac in the parking lot.

"Cadillac?" I asked. "You're coming up in the world."

Aggie M smiled proudly. She was back to being queen. "We've had a good year. The kids will sit in the back seat," she ordered as she opened the trunk. I hoisted my suitcase in while Aggie M belted in the baby and toddler and we all settled in for the trip home.

Home. There was a light layer of snow on the ground. I gazed out the window, appreciating the familiar landscape as I absently answered Aggie M's questions about living in Los Angeles. She knew a lot more about me than I thought she would've. "Mom always filled me in on your news," she confessed. "I guess I should have called."

Funny. I'd never even questioned why we didn't talk on the phone. We'd never been close. You only call a friend and I'd lost track of the few college friends I'd had. When I left for Los Angeles, I left everything behind—including my siblings. Was that odd? Who knew?

"Do you want to go straight to the house, or should I drop you off at the store?" Aggie M asked as we approached Brookings.

"Oh, home I guess," I said, startled out of my reverie. We'd run out of things to say to each other and I'd concentrated on staring at the scenery to discourage my sister from any bitchy comments.

"Nobody'll be there but I think Mom left the door in the garage open," Aggie M offered and that's the last she had to say until we pulled up in front of the house. "You can get your luggage yourself, can't you? You don't need me to get out, do you? Great!" She popped the trunk latch, waited until I'd gotten my stuff, called, "Tell Mom I'll call later", waved, and drove off.

I trudged up the driveway and entered the garage hoping she was right about the door being unlocked. She was. I walked into the empty house and gazed briefly. Absolutely nothing had changed. I walked down to my old room and unpacked my suitcase. Then I sat on the bed in the eerie silence. Nope, nothing had changed. Then I smiled.

Except me.

Mom's Cadillac pulled into the driveway and I went out to greet her.

"I don't have time to cook so we're all going out to dinner tonight," she nattered absently as she took off her coat and started toward me to give me a perfunctory hug. Then she got a good look at me and stopped dead. "My goodness," she exclaimed. "What happened to you?"

"I lost weight," I shrugged.

"You certainly did," Mom agreed. "And what have you done with your hair?"

"Let it grow."

"Oohhh." Mom sounded bewildered. "You don't look like our Marianne anymore."

I was going to crack that that was probably a good thing but remembered in time that Mom had been my stylist. It'd probably hurt her feelings.

Mom shook her head. "We'll talk about it later. Did Aggie M tell you we were going out?"

Maybe Aggie M had mentioned it, but I don't think so. Of course, I'd been doing my best to ignore her....

"You look fine," Mom interrupted my thought. "The store closes at six, so I booked a table at the Pizza King. Jeans are perfect for that." She looked me over again. "My, my, my. You certainly don't look like our little girl anymore. I don't think anyone will recognize you."

Well, Mom was right when we walked into the Pizza King. Nobody recognized me. Brother Matt looked at me blankly and said, "Marianne? Boy, you look like a city girl."

The restaurant was silent as the patrons stared. I felt like a super model. Instead of feeling tall and gangly next to Aggie M's petite neatness I felt svelte and graceful. And then Dad had to ruin it all.

"Under those clothes it's still our little girl. She'll put on a few pounds and we'll all be back to normal." That kept me from eating too much pizza.

But I got the feeling back when one of my high school classmates invited me to a get-together at a local bar. All the guys flirted with me and all the girls either whispered about me behind their hands or asked me where I got my clothes. They didn't recognize any of the names. "Boutique labels," I explained airily with a superior attitude. Damn, no wonder Aggie M liked lording it over people; it felt great!

I felt superior for the first time in my life. I had changed! Mostly for the better. I did have to modify my driving habits. Mom let me drive her Cadillac on my outings and I drove like an Angeleno—if I saw a yellow light, I gunned it. I'd forgotten that most people in Brookings slow down at yellow lights and I almost rear-ended the guy in front of me. I noticed him looking at his rear-view mirror in alarm as I screeched up on him. *I must slow down here*, I cautioned myself. The thought of wrecking my mother's precious Cadillac, the symbol of her success, made me shiver.

I still had to tell her about Jeff, but we never got much chance to talk. Christmas is the big season for retail people and all the Fuchs were busy at the store. Even my dad. I got a pass because I was on vacation, but I took it on myself to make some meals. And I made them to suit me and control the calories. I didn't want to put on any of the weight I'd worked so hard to take off.

Matt and his wife Eileen hosted Christmas dinner which was uneventful. We exchanged gifts—I'd gotten everybody Lakers T-shirts and I got perfume from Matt, earrings from Aggie M, and a check for $100 from Mom and Dad--and everybody sat around and burped. It was rather dull. I wondered what Jackie and Steve were doing in Los Angeles.

I got all the excitement I needed the next day. The Christmas rush was off, Mom had the day to herself, and she spent it interrogating me.

We thoroughly thrashed out the Friesman situation—including the encroaching dog poop.

"Good thing you left when you did. The woman sounds unbalanced," Mom said. "I told you I had a bad feeling about those people, didn't I? Looks like I was right. That place is Sodom. Tell me about the new apartment. Safer, I hope."

"Yes, it's safer," I agreed. "I have a roommate. And the manager is great."

"Do you and Jackie each have your own room? I never approved of a friendship with an older woman like that but maybe it's for the best. She's probably smarter about the world than you are."

I'd left Mom under the impression that I was living with Jackie. Maybe it was time to explain about Jeff.

"About that, Mom," I started brightly. "You remember that guy I was dating? Jeff?"

"Y-e-e-s-s-s," Mom drew the word out.

"Well, we were spending so much time together we figured it was cheaper to move in together," I blurted. I said it so fast it sounded like one word.

Mom stared at me, so I babbled on. "It's even cheaper than what I paid before so I'm saving lots of money. And he knows about cars so I'm doing a better job about taking care of the Tempo. And sometimes we carpool when he works at the firm. Did I tell you about my last raise? It was huge. And I got a big bonus for Christmas. I'm really learning a lot, too..."

My babbling dried up when Mom fixed one gimlet eye on me and started talking. She started out slow and deliberate then rose to a mighty crescendo. "I told you that place was Sodom. You saw what happened to Aggie M and yet you let this...boy!...use you like a whore. Do you think he's going to marry you when he gets you pregnant? Do you think you have any family out there to put pressure on him to do the right thing?"

"Actually, I'm on the Pill," I offered weakly.

"The Church is against the Pill! What do you tell the priest when he asks?"

"Well, I haven't really gone to church in a while..."

"So, you've abandoned your faith, too! What do you think your future is going to be? Do you want to end up like this friend of yours? This Jackie? Do you want to be a middle-aged woman with no family? No children? And what if this Pill doesn't work? Will you damn yourself by having an abortion? Because I doubt this boy will marry you. He'll have had his fun and will walk away from the stupid girl who gave him whatever he wanted. And if he does do right by you, what do think his family will do? Welcome you with open arms? I can promise you they won't. They'll look at you like a piece of trash who trapped their son. Trust me, I know. Nothing good can come of this. How could you be so stupid? How could you hold yourself so cheaply? How can you dishonor your family like this?"

She was ranting and pacing by this time. And I chose then to say, "Don't you think you're being a little melodramatic?" Which was unwise. I'd seen her beat Aggie M; I knew what she was capable of. And she went nuts. She jumped on me and started hitting. I covered my face from her blows and took it, shocked by the violence. I was taller than she was, and she must have gotten tired of hitting up—it wasn't doing much good—so she grabbed my hair and dragged me to the floor. And started kicking me. She was wearing slippers so she didn't do much damage but being kicked was an indignity I'd never experienced.

And that's when I got angry. I'd been brow-beaten by this woman all my life. I'd been insulted and slighted and sneered at. And I'd taken it because I was too afraid to fight back. But I'd been on my own for over a year now. I'd handled all sorts of ugly situations. I'd learned to stand up for myself. So, I stood up for myself. Actually, I leaped up and shoved her. She looked startled by my audacity then snarled and raised a clumsy fist. And that's when I backhanded her. My dad was right; I was a big, strong girl. I hit her so hard she slammed up against the wall. I was afraid I'd broken something. And then I hoped I had. "That's enough!" I snarled at her. "Don't you ever hit me again. Don't you ever talk to me like that again. You don't know anything about me, and you've never treated me right. And that stops now. Do you hear me? It stops now!"

We glared at each other, panting.

"Get out of my house," Mom finally said, then stalked to her bedroom and slammed the door.

I shakily walked to my bedroom and started packing. Shock had set in. I folded my clothes and included the perfume and earrings. I left the check on the dresser. Then I sat on the bed wondering what to do next. My flight wasn't for a few more days. I'd have to change that. And how was I supposed to get to Sioux Falls? I'd gotten to the point where I'd decided to take a cab when I heard a car pull into the driveway. A few minutes later my brother Matt knocked and poked his head in the door.

"Mom called," he said in answer to my questioning look. "You better come with me."

Mom stayed in her room when I left. Matt drove me to his house. "Jesus, Marianne, what did you do?" he asked. "Wait. Tell me when we get home. Eileen will need to hear this."

Matt and Eileen dismissed the kids and I recounted my fight—and the reason for it. Matt looked shocked but Eileen shook her head.

"Maybe you should quit the job and the guy and come home," Matt suggested. "Maybe Mom'll forgive you then."

"No, I'm not coming back here. I can't go back to being little Marianne, the loser daughter who'll take care of her folks in their old age. You told me to make a life and I have!"

"But I didn't think you'd go off the deep end," Matt muttered. "What happens when this guy dumps you?"

"Why does my life have to revolve around a man? Tell me that? What if I dump him? I'm not ready to settle down! I like my life! I don't see what's so bad! It's just sex!"

"Jesus, Marianne," Matt repeated, clearly disapproving. But Eileen surprisingly took my side.

"Matt, I think everybody's over-reacting. Let's let the fight blow over. Your mother will calm down. We can talk about things then."

"You don't know Mom," Matt said.

But Eileen suggested that I spend the rest of my vacation with them. Matt could take me to the airport. I agreed to spend the night because I had to change my flight but decided I'd rather not hang around Brookings any longer than I had to with Mom on the warpath. Matt took me to the airport the next day. He hugged me briefly.

"I hope you know what you're doing," he said.

"I hope so, too," I replied and hugged him back. Boy, was I glad to be on the plane for Los Angeles.

I'd called Jeff so he picked me up at the airport. "How was your vacation?" I asked wryly as he tossed my suitcase in the trunk of my Tempo.

"I was ready to come back," he said with a grin. "So. Telling your mom didn't go so well, huh."

"Not at all," I agreed bleakly. "On the plus side you can now answer the phone."

Jeff smiled uncertainly but I turned and stared out the window. I was still in shock. I'd been disowned. I was truly alone. In Sodom.

I waited until Jeff fell asleep that night to shed a few tears.

CHAPTER 15

Well, I Wanted to be on my Own...

I didn't want to talk about the big fight with anyone. I wanted to forget about it for the time being. The rest of the week was spent going to movies with an increasingly worried Jeff. I went back to work on the following Monday and fended Jackie off.

"It was bad," I told her shortly when she asked how things went with my mother. She raised an eyebrow but dropped the subject. I had enough to deal with. Mr. Elliot was not happy. He hadn't enjoyed his time off and he blamed me.

"Why is it my fault?" I asked in bewilderment.

"You told me to go to Hawaii," he accused.

"It was just a suggestion. You didn't have to go," I returned reasonably. "Besides, it's Hawaii. What could be so bad about Hawaii?"

"It's nothing but water sports," Mr. Elliot fumed. "Look at me—do I look like I enjoy water sports? My skin fries in ten minutes! And it takes ten minutes to paddle out to catch a wave in surfing class. I spent the next two days under strict orders from the hotel doctor to stay out of the sun. And there's nothing to do there that isn't in the sun."

"Oh, there must have been something indoors," I scoffed.

"There's one museum. I saw it. It was nice. And that took one day."

"Oh," I said, nonplussed. "Well, I've never been there. Why'd you listen to me?"

"Because you usually seem to know what you're talking about. You lost a lot of my trust, Marianne. I hope you realize that. I'm very disappointed in you."

He buried his face in a brief and I returned to my desk, convinced that I was surrounded by crazy people. First my mother, now my boss. When did I become the world's biggest screw-up?

On New Year's Eve I gathered my fellow Sodomites— Jackie, the mistress; Steve, the homosexual; and Jeff, the soulless deflowerer of almost-virgins—to confess about my mother's reaction while we drank wine. I started shaking talking about it.

"Wow," said Steve. "My parents didn't act that bad when I told them I was gay. My mom just started bawling and asked me where she'd gone wrong."

"Well, my mom is a naturalized citizen. I don't think she's got American parenting down yet," I said glumly.

Jeff looked stricken. "I had no idea it could be that bad," he stammered. "I wish I hadn't told you to tell her about us."

"It had to come out sooner or later," I said tiredly. "I knew it was going to be bad. I didn't think it would be that bad."

Jackie shook her head in disgust. "I, for one, am glad you stood up for yourself. Nobody has a right to hit you."

"Yeah, but I hit her back," I said and finished my glass of wine.

"And why did you hit her?" Jackie asked rhetorically. "Because she pushed you on the floor and was kicking you! Jesus, Marianne, no normal mother would do that! I hope you broke her jaw!"

Jackie sounded like she was fighting a few old demons of her own. But she had a point. Why did my mother get her way? Because I'd been trained not to fight back. That sure worked for her, didn't it? Jackie's anger seemed to free me to feel something. I'd been numb for a week. Time to shake it off.

"I didn't but now I wish I had," I said daringly. "I've been scared of her all my life. I couldn't buy clothes that she didn't like. I got those stupid perms because she said I should. I couldn't live on campus, I had to stay home because I might do something 'bad'. But anything that she didn't want was bad! I couldn't do anything right, say anything right. It was always 'Marianne has to get an education because she'll always have to support herself. She's not pretty like Aggie M so she better develop her brain!'" I mimicked.

Jeff and Steve exchanged looks. "She thinks you're homely?" Steve asked, amused. "I'm gay and I think you're pretty. Is her eyesight bad or something?"

"No," I retorted. "It's a family thing. My brother Matt was the sports hero, Aggie M was the cheerleader, and I was…last. I've always been last."

"Well, you're not last with me," Jeff declared.

"Thanks," I said and smiled wanly at him, deflating from my burst of anger. "But that stuff sticks with you. She said no decent man would want me after Jeff moves on." Jeff stirred at that but didn't say anything. "I guess I wanted some distance from my mother, but I didn't want…this. And I probably shouldn't have hit her. But how could I lay on the floor and let her kick me? I'm mad. And I'm guilty. And I feel totally alone in the world." The Sodomites all jumped in to assure me that I had friends and I waved them off with a sad smile. "Oh, I know you guys are my friends. But it's different. I've never been without a family before. What's the saying? Home is where you go, and they have to take you in? I guess I don't have a home anymore. And that scares me."

That quieted everybody down until Jackie said, "Well, your parents were going to die eventually. And when they go brothers and sisters usually drift apart. I'm sorry it happened this way, it seems like it's hard on you, but sooner or later we're all on our own. You've proven you can take of yourself. At least you don't have that constant criticism." She smiled and gently rubbed my arm. "You'll make a life that works for you. We all do. It may not make the cover of a family magazine, but it'll be yours. And I'm here for you until you figure it out."

I was touched. "Thanks, Jackie," I said, getting a little tearful.

Even Steve jumped in. "I know we haven't known each other very long but I'm good for helping you move furniture." He smiled brightly.

That made me laugh a little. "Thanks, Steve."

Jeff hadn't said anything but now he jumped in. "I bought a bottle of good champagne for midnight, but I think we should drink it now. Maybe it'll cheer everybody up. And it's better than the rotgut we've been drinking."

He got the champagne and poured everyone a glass. We toasted to growing up and being on our own, and the freedom that brought. Then we picked a movie to watch until midnight. Jackie and Steve played gin rummy and Jeff and I cuddled. He kissed my hair and whispered, "You're not alone, you know. I'm here."

"For now," I replied.

"Yeah, yeah," was all he said but he looked troubled. We saw the New Year in quietly.

Mr. Elliot never seemed to forgive me for his bad holiday. He gave me tiresome little make-work jobs and demanded a lot of overtime. Which wasn't so bad because I got paid time and a half but still...it ate into my personal time. It kept me from worrying about hitting my mother, but I was developing a hatred for lawyers in general and Mr. Elliot in particular.

"Doesn't he know I don't exist to serve him?" I complained to Jeff after another late night. "I don't have time to do my laundry or anything else. This apartment is a mess. I'm so sick of saying 'Yes, Mr. Elliot, No, Mr. Elliot'. Just because he doesn't have a life doesn't mean I shouldn't have one."

Jeff looked startled. "Well, maybe I could see if I can talk to him..." he began.

"You can't do anything!" I yelled. "You're a student! He won't listen to you! And it's my problem!"

"Then why are you asking me to...." Jeff began again.

"I'm not asking you to do anything!" I returned, exasperated. "Well, maybe you could clean the bathroom. It's a real pit. But you can't help with Elliot! You know that!"

"Then why..." Jeff repeated reasonably.

145

"I'm trying to tell you my problems!" I interrupted. "Can't I talk without you trying to take over and fix things? Because you can't." Jeff subsided and I continued my rant. "How come lawyers are all so self-centered? And that's purely rhetorical," I added when Jeff tried to say something. "Elliot keeps trying to talk me into going to law school, but I'll be darned if I end up like him. God, why are you trying to be one? Do you hate people, too?" I waved him off when he tried to speak. "No, don't answer that. I'm going to bed so I can get up bright and early to wait on Lord Elliot." I stomped off. I stomped back to give Jeff a goodnight kiss and caught that thoughtful look on his face again. If I'd had more energy I'd've asked him what it was about.

Mr. Elliot eventually got over his pique and my schedule went back to normal. But then I missed the extra money. And I had time to process the fight with my mother. I was over the shock of the whole thing. And the guilt that I'd hit her was wearing off. But my anger grew. I relived the part where she grabbed me by my hair, dragged me to the ground, and started kicking me. Who does that? Nobody normal, that's for sure. When I lived under her roof, I followed her rules. And I did that, to my detriment in my opinion, for far too long. I missed out on a normal college experience. Me living at home saved her a lot of money but she didn't seem to object to paying for Matt and Aggie M. How come I always came last? Wasn't the baby of the family supposed to be spoiled? I guess Mom hadn't gotten that memo. I'd been shorted by her all my life. When it came to work and sacrifice ol' Marianne was at the head of the line. When it came to anything good, well, "Too bad, Marianne, keep your mouth shut and do what we tell you." And her attitude toward sex was medieval. Maybe in her day a young woman was spoiled by losing her virginity. Well, welcome to the 20th century! I wasn't even sure I was ever getting married and I wasn't going to miss out on sex, as well as dorm living.

Unfortunately, I didn't get a chance to yell my declaration of independence at her because she never called. And that was fine by me. I didn't want to talk to her either.

Jeff kept his head down. I don't think I was very pleasant to be around.

A few more weeks passed. I was congratulating myself to Jeff and Steve over pizza at home one night that I'd finally come to terms with my disownment. "You guys don't have to be afraid to talk to me anymore," I assured them. "It's okay. Life will go back to what it was before...except Jeff can answer the phone without fear. And that's a good thing, right?" I smiled at them brightly.

Jeff smiled back, relieved, I think, but Steve put his pizza on a plate and sat back. "I wasn't sure when it would be a good time to tell you, but I've got some bad news."

Jeff and I exchanged a look. What could it be? Did Steve have some deadly disease? I checked him out. He looked fine to me.

Steve finally lifted his eyes to us and said, "Your lease won't be renewed. Our apartment building sold. It's going to be torn down."

I gaped at Steve. I didn't know what to say. I looked over at Jeff and he seemed as at a loss as I was. I looked back at Steve questioningly.

"It means we all have to move," Steve explained. "We have to get out."

After a pause Jeff asked, "When?"

"I'm not sure. It could be anywhere between six months and a year. I'm going to hand out the notices that the building has been sold tomorrow. They'll let us know when we have to leave. I thought I'd let you guys know now." He hung his head.

Steve acted like we were going to yell at him. Why would we do that? It wasn't his fault. He was only the messenger.

But I wasn't ready for another body blow. I was getting over being disowned. Well, maybe not getting over but adjusting. Now I was going to be homeless. Despair was settling over my shoulders. "I'm not hungry anymore," I said. "I know it's not your fault, Steve, but do you mind if I go to bed? This is something else I need to process."

I didn't wait for an answer. I went to the bedroom, pulled off my clothes, got into bed, and pulled the covers over my head.

It's a good thing I had to go to work, or I probably would have stayed in bed for a week. And the sheets really needed changing. Jeff seemed relieved when I mentioned that we should probably discuss what we were going to do.

"I wanted to talk about this, too. Let me take you out for a burger," he offered. We went to a sit-down place where we could get beer, too. No Burger King tonight.

Jeff started speaking after we'd been served. "Are you planning on staying in Los Angeles for a while?" he asked.

I shrugged. "I guess. I don't have anywhere else to go. And the job isn't driving me too nuts. What are you going to do after you graduate?"

"I'm going to stay in the area. I've had a few job nibbles. I'm going to get serious about interviews."

"Sounds good," I said, chewing.

"So, do you want to find another place together? I mean, as soon as we find out when we have to leave? No point in going until we're thrown out. I'd like to stay together. You're the best roommate I've ever had."

"You're just saying that because I clean the bathroom," I scoffed.

"Well, there's that. But we get along. And I like you." I started looking alarmed, so he hurried to add, "But I'm not serious or anything. Don't look so worried."

I subsided. "Well, I like you, too. And you are a good roommate although I don't have anyone to compare you to except my sister and she was even messier than you are." We both laughed. "Sure, let's find another place together when the time comes."

We relaxed and ate our burgers. We talked of other things than the bad news we'd both gotten. I was finishing my beer when I commented, "I've been thinking: I've been in Los Angeles a year and a half and I've been forced out of two apartments. Is this normal? I didn't think I'd be moving around this much. It's…unsettling. I'm used to staying in one place."

"It's been 'normal' for me," Jeff admitted. "I mean, I was like you; lived in one house all my life until I went to college. Then I moved every year."

"I thought this version of the college experience would be more fun."

Jeff smiled. "You're not having fun?"

I smiled back. "Yeah. I don't think this would have been such a big deal if I hadn't just been disowned." I shrugged. "I'll get over it."

Jeff looked at me intently. He hesitated, like there was something he'd like to say then thought better of it. He grabbed the check. "Let's go home," he said. "I've got work to do."

We talked about what part of the city we'd like to live in— like we had a few months ago. I was getting pretty good at apartment hunting. But anything decent cost a fortune.

"My God, these places cost twice what we're paying now," I grumped after an afternoon of apartment inspections. "I won't be able to save a dime."

"Yeah," Jeff agreed. "And in twenty years we won't have anything to show for all that rent money."

"Oh man, I never thought of that," I breathed.

Jeff got that look on his face again. "Do you have something on your mind?" I asked.

"Yeah, but let me think some more. I'll get back to you."

I was puzzled but let it drop.

The following Saturday I had the paper out, checking apartment rental ads, when Jeff took the paper out of my hands. "I've got an idea and I want you to hear me out without getting all nuts. Okay?"

I nodded.

He took a deep breath and let it out explosively. "Okay, here's my idea. Instead of getting another apartment, how about we buy a house together?"

I blinked at him, so he hurried on. "I was thinking we could get a fixer-upper. Your folks have a hardware store, you must know something about tools and all that." I nodded. "And I used to work on Grandma's ranch so I'm not completely helpless. And really, how tough can it be? If construction people can learn, so can we. We're not stupid."

I was intrigued. "And we sell it in a few years at a profit? You know, that's not a bad idea. At least no one could toss us out whenever they felt like it. It'll be a lot of work but I'm not afraid of work. But how would we go about buying it together?"

"Okay, this is the part where I don't want you to freak out. In order to pool our resources and get a loan we have to a) incorporate or b) get married. And, Marianne, you know how you hate attorneys. You can hardly say Elliot's name without swearing. And getting married will be cheaper than incorporating." He looked at me hopefully.

"Married?" I asked doubtfully.

"It's a legal contract not a life sentence," Jeff said. He hurried to add, "Your decision. I'm not trying to railroad you into anything or tie you down. Just a legality. So, don't get nuts."

"Married," I repeated.

"So we can get a loan," he assured me.

I looked at the ads in the paper. The apartments were expensive and probably temporary. I was tired of moving. I eyed Jeff. I thought he was honest. He wasn't trying to marry me for my money because I didn't have any. Neither did he. We were equals. I was sure he'd keep his end of the bargain. And if he didn't, we could split up. And sell. And I bet dissolving a no-fault divorce was easier and cheaper than dissolving a corporation. Of course, marrying Jeff would make my mother happy; that was a downside. On the other hand, it would probably really piss her off; she hadn't picked him—and he wasn't Catholic! We'd go to a Justice of the Peace and do the deed. Was there a downside? I didn't see it right now.

I stuck my hand out. "Deal," I said, shaking his hand. "Let's get married."

CHAPTER 16

Somebody Needs to Propose

Nobody was happy when I announced that I was going to marry Jeff. When I bounced up to Jackie's desk with my news, tail wagging for her approval, she looked up from her typing and said, "I thought you wanted to keep your freedom."

I explained that it was basically a business arrangement; we were going to pool our resources to buy a house so we couldn't be abused by landlords anymore. "Also, it'll be a good investment," I said importantly. "We're thinking of getting a fixer-upper so we can flip it." I beamed at her. She didn't beam back.

"I think you're walking into a trap," she stated flatly and went back to her typing. "Jeff seems nice enough, but they all do until they've got access to your bank account. Then hell begins."

"I don't have much of a bank account for him to be after," I pointed out.

"Not now you don't. But this house you think you're going to flip—how much will you get out of it?"

"Half, I guess," I shrugged. "California is a community property state."

"Wait'll the judge gets hold of the case," she warned. "You better hope you get a woman. Any male judge will decide in Jeff's favor."

"How is that even possible?" I asked, puzzled.

"It shouldn't be," Jackie retorted. "But you'll be unpleasantly surprised at how things turn out when it comes to a marriage dissolution. The guy'll get the money and you'll get the kids."

"I don't have any kids," I replied.

"Not yet you don't." Jackie said grimly. "But if he can talk you into this marriage, he can talk you into anything."

I was deflated by her response, but I was floored by Mr. Elliot's reaction when he got wind of my decision. "Marriage isn't a good idea if you're planning on going to law school," he stated. "You'll have plenty of time for marriage--if that's really what you want--after you pass the bar."

"But I'm not sure I even want to go to law school," I murmured.

"You have a good logical, legal mind," Mr. Elliot lectured. "You shouldn't waste it. This isn't your idea, is it," he guessed shrewdly.

"Well," I fidgeted, "Jeff brought it up as a good way to combine our resources so we could buy a house."

"You don't need a house," Mr. Elliot retorted. "You need a law license. You can buy all the houses you want after you find a good firm to work for. I might even put in a good word for you here." He turned his chair away and started reading a brief. I wish he'd find a better way to dismiss me. That was just rude.

The only person who was happy for me was Steve. And that's because he wanted to plan a wedding.

"I can see your colors in soft pinks," he suggested happily. "The bridesmaids' dresses could be long with a peplum—like flower petals."

"We're going to the Justice of the Peace," I said firmly. "No big wedding. The point of this marriage is to save money, not spend it."

"Well, that's no fun at all," Steve declared. "Don't you want some sort of party? It's going to be a long time before you ever do something like this again. You should at least make an occasion of it."

He had a point. We'd need some witnesses at the JP's if nothing else. We might as well have a small party; a pre-housewarming, as it were. Jeff had no objections to the party, he thought it was a fine idea. He was a little annoyed when I reported that Jackie thought that he was after my money.

"You don't have any money," he said.

"I told her that," I assured him.

"And I wouldn't try to cheat you," he continued.

"I think she's projecting," I soothed him. "She had a really terrible marriage. I'm guessing the guy hit her and I know he took off with their combined savings."

"Well, I'm not him," Jeff stated firmly. "And I live up to the bargains I make."

"I'm sure you do. And the house will be in both our names so we'll both be protected by contract law," I offered.

"Of course," Jeff agreed stoutly. "I wouldn't have it any other way. We'll both be protected. And you know what? I want Jackie to be one of the witnesses, so she'll be sure that the license is all legal and above-board." He sounded really irritated with Jackie. He didn't like having his honor questioned. I guess I couldn't blame him. He shouldn't be punished for the sins of other men.

Jackie half-heartedly apologized when I told her that Jeff resented having his intentions questioned. "I know he's probably a good guy," she admitted. "Ted, I mean Mr. Brady, thinks the world of him." She paused. "Maybe that's why I was bothered. Ted cheats on his wife with me and doesn't think a thing of it. And I know he's got her over a barrel when it comes to property division. He knows all the attorneys and judges in town. She's stuck." Jackie looked slightly ashamed. "I feel sorry for her sometimes. But I'm not taking anything away from her. If he wasn't cheating with me it'd be with someone else. And I need to live, too." She shook her head. "The world isn't fair to women. I want you to be careful."

I went back to my desk, chastened after that depressing little speech. Thankfully, Mr. Elliot seemed to forget all about my scheme, and I didn't remind him. I appreciated that he was trying to encourage me professionally, not set me up in a condo--and that I didn't have to have sex with him to keep my job. It also reinforced my determination to go through with the property acquisition plan with Jeff. I needed a place to live that nobody could take away from me. I wouldn't have to part with sexual favors to exist. What Jeff and I did together was fun, not payment. I was starting to feel sorry for Jackie.

Well, Steve never let up on wanting to plan our wedding no matter how many times I told him it wasn't a big deal.

"Even if it's to 'pool your resources'," he made air quotes with his fingers, "it's still an occasion. You should treat it as one. I mean, how many people marry for money? You're going with the flow! I don't know why you don't enjoy it anyway."

Steve was starting to convince me. Just because it was a marriage of convenience didn't mean we shouldn't have fun with it. At least I wasn't pregnant.

"And one of you should actually propose," Steve advised. "I know, I know, business deal," he held up a palm when I started to protest, "but you guys have sex, right? Why can't you throw in a little romance? With you two, who knows if you'll ever get the chance again? Honestly, you're taking the fun out of everything and you don't have to. It may not be the sort of marriage you ever imagined but it's still a marriage. Do it up right!"

That was another good point. This had gotten so serious and depressing. It was time to insert a little levity into the situation. Jeff had made his offer and I'd accepted. Maybe it'd be fun to turn the tables; maybe I should propose. That would convince Jackie that I wasn't being steered around like a two-year-old; I was a controlling part of the equation. Too bad it wasn't a Leap Year, that would have been perfect. But it wasn't so I had to make do. I decided I'd take Jeff out to dinner for Valentine's Day. I'd spring a proposal on him then and watch his face drop. Of course, Steve lost his marbles when I confided my plan to him.

"I know where you should take him to dinner!" he enthused.

"I thought I'd take him out for a steak," I said. "The only thing he really seems to like is steak."

"Of course, sweetie," Steve agreed. "And I know just the place. I'll call and make the reservation for you. I know the maître d'. I'll make sure you get a good table and the best service. Leave it up to me."

The place he chose was Rex il Ristorante, an expensive place that I'd always been curious about but wasn't sure I could afford. I still wasn't sure I could afford it, but Steve waved my concerns away. "You only propose once," he breezily assured me. "You have to do it right."

Maybe, I thought dubiously. But wasn't the point of our joint exercise to save money not spend it? Oh well, I'd always wanted to try Rex and if Steve's friend was taking care of us maybe I wouldn't feel out of place.

Unfortunately, we'd waited too long. We couldn't get in on Valentine's Day, they were booked up. Steve got us in on the 13th. Close enough. At least it wasn't a Friday.

But Steve wasn't done yet. He made me get out the outfit I'd wear to see if it met his approval. It didn't.

"I guess we'll have to go shopping," he caroled. "Call Jackie. She has the best taste. Between the two of us Jeff will be knocked out of his socks."

"That's really not the point," I started.

"Oh hush. You don't want to go to Rex looking like a schoolteacher. Let me know when Jackie's free. We don't have much time."

The three of us went shopping the following Saturday. Steve and Jackie had a wonderful time. I felt like a not-very-bright little sister. It was like being out with Aggie M--times two.

They finally decided on something cut low in the back, high in the hem, and spangly in the middle. They put me in four-inch heels ("Good thing Jeff is over six feet tall; you can wear heels," Jackie approved) and sat back to admire their doll.

"My God," Steve breathed. "If you looked like that all the time, I might switch sides."

Jackie smiled approvingly. "I had no idea you had such great legs," she marveled. "You should show them off more often."

"You've seen me in my softball shorts," I pointed out.

"Marianne, it's not the same thing at all," she returned dryly.

I looked down at my long legs in the short skirt. I smiled smugly. She was right; I did look pretty good. I wish my mother could see me now. She'd be lighting candles for my soul in church. As if that was going to help. I was marrying for gain! Who'd have thought it?

I got a nice card for Jeff and told him I was taking him to dinner for Valentine's Day—one day early.

"Let me at least pay half," he offered.

"No, no, this is my party," I waved him off. "You can pay for something else."

Steve told Jeff he had to wear a suit for the occasion, but I put my foot down when he suggested a limousine.

"It's too expensive," I said firmly. "You can hire one when you get engaged."

Steve pouted. "You don't need to be so bitchy. You know I won't be getting engaged any time soon because I'm not even dating anyone seriously. Besides, it's illegal. And I don't appreciate you throwing that in my face."

I apologized for my insensitivity but still refused to hire a limo. Enough was enough.

Well, February 13th finally came. Jeff wore his one suit and was struggling with his tie in the bathroom when I appeared in my spangles to touch up my hair. His jaw literally dropped.

"My God, you look great!" he gasped.

"I do, don't I," I agreed smugly. "Steve and Jackie picked out the dress. I don't know where else I'll ever wear it but it's fun to do it at least once." I eyed my raincoat before I put it on. "I wish I'd gotten a better coat to go with it. Maybe next year."

Steve was waiting outside the apartment door with a camera to take a picture. It was like the prom—except I looked a lot better. And so did my date.

Unfortunately, my car looked like a high school effort which was probably why Steve had urged me to rent a limo. But it was better than the motorcycle and that was our only other option. I was faintly embarrassed when we pulled up to Rex and the valet took the keys to my humble Tempo. Jeff and I looked at each other, shrugged, and grinned. We were obviously not the sort of clients this place catered to. Time to see how the other half lived.

We walked into the restaurant, or ristorante, and stared. Steve had told me that it was an old haberdashery. It was built in the 1920s and was all period wood and glass in two stories. I managed to pull myself together to give my name to the maître d', explaining that Steve had made the reservation for us.

The maître d' looked cold and forbidding until I mentioned Steve. Then he smiled warmly and slightly conspiratorially. "Ah, yes, Miss Fuchs," (he even pronounced it right!) "I have just the table for you. Follow me please." But before I could he imperiously waved at a footman (I don't know what else to call him) who gently helped me out of my coat and took it away. I was tempted to ask where he was taking it but was too intimidated. If it was gone, it was gone. I needed a new one anyway. I noticed heads turned when the other customers saw me in my spangles.

I strode confidently as we followed the maître d' to a table for two right in the middle of the restaurant. He even held my chair for me. I managed to sit down without embarrassing myself and he gently wafted the napkin into my lap. He seated Jeff, napkinned him, and we sat quietly while water ("Tap or bottled." "Is there anything wrong with the tap water?" "Of course not!" "Then we'll have that." Country bumpkin strikes again.) was poured and a breadbasket stuffed with various kinds of bread was brought.

Then the maître d' brought over the sommelier and the wine list. "This is a very special evening," he confided to the sommelier as Jeff looked at me in amazement. "We must make sure everything is perfect." He beamed at me and left me with the sommelier who made suggestions as to main courses and corresponding wines. There were no prices on anything which is never a good sign for someone like me, but I repeated to myself, *It's only once.*

I chose a bottle of wine and the sommelier was replaced by a waiter. Jeff and I made our final choices. We both went with beef and the sommelier returned with a bottle of cabernet. He popped the cork and let me sniff it. After I nodded, he poured some in a tall wine glass, swirled it around, and presented it to me for approval. I cautiously took a sip; it tasted all right to me although I probably wouldn't have known if it was crap. He smiled widely as I nodded my approval and poured for Jeff and me. Then we were left to ourselves for a few minutes.

"I'm completely out of my league," I whispered to Jeff across the table.

"So am I," he whispered back. "But everybody seems nice enough."

And they were nice. Everybody loves a lover.

It was the most spectacular meal I've ever had, before or since. It took two and a half hours from start to finish and I quit being self-conscious after the first glass of wine. Jeff was more relaxed than me. It takes more than a fancy ristorante to make him uncomfortable. The food was delicious, and the service was impeccable. After the main course I whispered to Jeff that I had to pee, and did he know where the bathrooms were? Jeff nodded at the stairway behind me and I put my napkin on the table. Instantly, a footman was pulling my chair out for me. I rose as grandly as I could and picked my way across the room to climb the stairway to the toilet--which was as spectacular as the rest of the ristorante. I could learn to live like this.

When I returned to the table the same footman was there to seat me. I thanked him and whispered to Jeff, "How did they know I was going to the bathroom? Is the table bugged?"

He choked on his wine. "Hope not. Let's eat."

So, we did. And drank. At least I did. Maybe Jeff was staying sober so he could drive home. I wasn't sure what his reason was, and I didn't care. I loved the wine.

We helped ourselves to the dessert table and coffee then sat back to finish the wine. It was time for my big move. I pulled my pre-Valentine's card from my purse and said, "Surprise!"

Jeff wasn't surprised at all. He pulled a card out of his coat pocket and put it in front of me. "Happy Valentine's Day to you, too."

I smiled and opened my card which was sweet and had the word 'love' in it. Jeff thanked me for his card--which did not have the word 'love' in it.

Jeff sat back to finish his coffee and I reached down again in my purse and pulled out a washer I'd gotten at the local hardware store. I hoped it was big enough to fit over his knuckle; I'd had to guess.

I intoned pompously, "Jeff, in the spirit of property co-ownership, will you marry me?"

Jeff's eyebrows went up and he smiled at the washer. "Shouldn't you be on one knee?" he asked.

"I don't know if the footman could get me back up. I've drunk most of the wine," I confided. We both cackled at that.

Jeff took the washer and slid it over his finger. He admired it for entirely too long.

"So, will you?" I interrupted his reverie.

Jeff lifted his wine glass and said, "Give me some more of this and I'll think about it."

I yelped laughter then controlled myself. I started to pull the wine bottle out of the stand but was co-opted by a footman who poured wine for us both, finishing the bottle.

"So?" I asked when the footman left.

Jeff admired his washer and said, "What the hell, sure. Why not." And we clinked glasses.

We were talking desultorily when the check came. The waiter was very discreet about it; he placed it halfway between the two of us. It could have gone either way. Well, it was my party, so I picked it up—and almost choked when I saw the amount. But I was fortified with very expensive wine--I had the bill to prove it--so I pulled out a credit card and grandly paid. I even included a 25% tip. The staff had earned it.

I was full of wine and food and tottered in my four-inch heels out to the lobby where the footman helped me into my coat from wherever it had been. I didn't know if I was supposed to tip him or not and frankly, I was too befuddled to worry about it. I hope Jeff tipped him. I didn't want anybody to get stiffed because I was drunk and inexperienced.

Jeff didn't even ask if he should drive. He took the keys when the valet came and helped me into the passenger seat. Cinderella was back in her pumpkin. Jeff made sure we got home in one piece and helped put me to bed. Which I appreciated. It had been a wonderful evening. Maybe someday we'd get to do it again. I noticed Jeff kept the washer on all night but put it out of my mind. I suppose a normal couple would have made love, but I'd had too much to eat. I didn't want to end a perfect evening by barfing on Jeff.

Well, I was officially engaged. I put that out of my mind, too.

CHAPTER 17

I Meet Jeff's Family

I had a hangover for Valentine's Day, so Jeff and I exchanged one more card each and had soup for dinner. I noticed the washer was gone. I wondered what he'd done with it. The only real souvenir from our lovely evening was a huge credit card bill. Between the clothes and the dinner my bank account had taken a severe hit. I was a bit surly with Steve when he asked for details of the dinner and again offered to plan the wedding.

"Absolutely not," I said shortly. "Do you have any idea what that evening cost me?"

"Oh, you usually only do it once," he scoffed. "You did it right and have a wonderful memory."

"Yeah, I've got a wonderful credit card bill, too."

"We won't spend much money on the wedding," he assured me.

"We won't spend *any* money," I assured him right back. "Jeff and I are going to the JP when the time comes."

That sidetracked Steve. "When will that be? Have you set a date?"

"No," I replied. "Jeff has to get through these last months of school. We'll probably talk about it when we start looking at houses."

And that's where we left it. But I decided that I had to be more vigilant about money. I wouldn't save anything if I kept going out to eat. I announced to a surprised Jeff that we'd be eating from home at least five times a week.

"If we want to buy property, we need to be more conscious of where our money goes," I lectured. "Besides, I can control the calories better. I don't want to gain the weight back that I lost. I can't afford a new wardrobe. And I can't face any more ramen noodles."

I didn't have time to spend an hour on meal preparation on work nights, so I spent a few Saturdays cooking spaghetti sauce, stew, soups, and lasagnas and stocking the freezer. When Easter approached, I suggested to Jeff that we invite Steve and Jackie over. I wanted to make a ham.

Jeff brightened. "I love ham," he said enthusiastically, then sobered. "But I was going to ask if you wanted to come home with me for Easter. My mother and grandmother want to meet you. Maybe we could have the ham when we get back."

"How much is this going to cost me?" I asked suspiciously. It seemed every time we did something normal people did it ended up costing me a fortune.

"Nothing," Jeff said patiently. "I'll even pay for the gas if we take your car. You can stay at our house. Although I'm not sure if we'll be able to share a bedroom. My mom hasn't said anything about our living arrangement so I'm not sure how she feels about it." And he looked at me expectantly.

Oh boy. Meeting the parents. That had never occurred to me. But even if this was just a marriage of convenience, I'd probably have to deal with them one way or another. Might as well start out on the right foot. And maybe it wouldn't be so bad; I'd liked his father--what little I'd seen of him.

"Okay," I agreed. "Do I need to ask for time off from work?"

"Maybe the following Monday," Jeff said. "It's a long drive to and from Davis.

Davis. That's where his father taught. Well, I'd never been to Northern California so it could be interesting.

Mr. Elliot was annoyed when I asked for Easter Monday off. "But you took a week last Christmas!" he protested.

"It was four workdays," I pointed out. "And I still have vacation time coming."

He grumbled but agreed I could have the day.

On Good Friday the firm closed at noon. Jackie told me Mr. Brady, as a Catholic, took Easter seriously. I wondered why he didn't take marriage as seriously but didn't complain about the extra time off. Mr. Elliot couldn't even say a word. Hah!

I have to admit I felt wicked not going to Good Friday service. I'd spent my childhood in church over Easter weekend. All my Protestant friends would play softball on Holy Thursday, Good Friday, and Saturday. I spent all that time in church getting shushed by my mother because I giggled when the drones--the men who sat in front to read the lessons--sang. I called them the drones for a reason; they 'sang' the hymns in individual monotones. But I digress...

Instead I drove home to change clothes, pack my suitcase, and wait for Jeff to show up. When I heard his key in the door, I peed one last time and grabbed a water bottle. Jeff told me this would be a seven-hour drive with no traffic. But this was Friday and traffic was backed up to the Grapevine. I was glad I agreed to let Jeff drive. The beep and creep would have driven me crazy. Jeff suggested I take a nap. So, I did.

We stopped at Buttonwillow to gas up, pee, and have a bite to eat. The selection of restaurants were all chains so we got a sandwich at the least greasy place we could find. The traffic had cleared up, so I drove for the next two hours. I managed to find some radio stations, so I had music to keep me company while Jeff slept. It was a straight shot up the I-5. The crops were different than those in South Dakota. I'd never seen a cotton field before. Or grape vines. Or almond trees. That was interesting for a while but even the novelty of different crops palled after two hours. We stopped at a rest area to pee again and Jeff said he was ready to finish the drive. He'd had a two-hour nap, so I took him at his word and took another nap myself.

It was dark when I woke. I was thirsty, and I had to pee...again. I had my water bottle so that took care of the thirst problem but there were no rest stops coming up. I suffered in silence for about half an hour then said, "Jeff, I really need to pee."

He glanced over at me. "There isn't any place to stop around here. Can't you hold it?"

"I have been," I answered. "I'm starting to gargle."

Jeff looked helpless. "Well, I don't know what to do."

I did. I was a country girl—peeing outside of four walls was nothing new to me. I told Jeff to pull off at the next exit and find an empty field. He looked faintly surprised but obediently pulled off. We drove down a mile trying to find a convenient spot, but apparently other drivers had the same problem I did; about three cars followed us down the road.

"I can't pee in a crowd," I declared so Jeff made a U-turn back to the freeway and drove to the next exit. No one followed us this time, so I got out of the car, walked to a flat spot, de-pantsed, and squatted. Jeff followed and unzipped. He was contentedly peeing when he noticed me doing an ungainly duck walk.

"What in the world are you doing?" he asked.

"Pee splashes. I don't want it to hit my shoes," I explained.

Jeff started laughing. He laughed so hard he almost peed on *his* shoes. I waddled until I air-dried; I didn't want to leave any paper waste behind me, that was too icky. Jeff was zipped up by the time I was ready to get in the car, but he asked for details on why I'd done what I'd done.

"Haven't you ever seen a girl pee outside before?" I asked.

"Of course not. All I've got are brothers and I think my mother would die before she'd pee outside."

"I hope she never goes camping then," I retorted. "She'd probably get kidney failure holding it all the time."

We resumed driving and I mulled over what he'd said. His mother sounded like she wouldn't approve of any earthiness. I told Jeff to keep the peeing story to himself.

The rest of the trip was uneventful. We got to his parents' house by nine. We parked in the driveway of a stucco-sided, two-story home with a curved sidewalk leading to the front door. We were taking suitcases out of the trunk when Jeff's mother opened the door.

"It's just me, Mom," Jeff called out.

"I was hoping it was," she called back. "I didn't recognize the car."

We trudged up the steps and Mrs. Foster hugged Jeff briefly. Jeff turned to me and presented me to his mother, "This is Marianne Fuchs." She held out her hand as he said, "Marianne, this is my mother, Ruth." We shook hands briefly and smiled cautiously at each other. She was an ordinary looking woman— no horns or tail. She was impeccably dressed, she was even wearing pearls, which I thought was odd for sitting at home on Friday night. I noticed her attention on my Coach bag and figured she knew to the penny what it had cost. I was glad I let Jackie talk me into buying it.

"Nice to meet you," I murmured.

"Fuchs? How in the world is that spelled?" she asked, amused.

I spelled it out. "It means 'fox' in German," I explained.

"Hmmmm. Well. You must be hungry," Mrs. Foster said. "I've got lunch meat for sandwiches."

"Great," Jeff said.

Mrs. Foster led the way past the living room where we saw Dr. Foster in his recliner. He put his newspaper in his lap as he looked up.

"Hi, Dr. Foster," I said weakly, remembering my entrance at our first meeting. His eyes twinkled.

"Good to see you two got here safe," he said with a smile and returned to his newspaper.

Mrs. Foster took over. "You can put your suitcases in Jeff's room. You're used to sharing and Brett is coming tomorrow. He'll need his room and the other bedrooms are closed off." She waved us away. "I'll put out the sandwich stuff. You can come down when you're settled."

Jeff led the way up the stairs to his room which contained a single bed and a cot.

Jeff sighed. "I used to have a double bed."

"At least we get to stay in the same room," I commented. "My mother certainly wouldn't have let us do that. Assuming, of course, that she'd let you in the house after de-flowering me."

"I didn't de-flower you," Jeff protested. "And it's not a big deal."

"Not to us it's not. But it's your folks' house. Let's try to make this as easy as possible."

I paused to take in the decorations in Jeff's old room. He had shelves of trophies and awards. He told me the trophies were for sports and the awards were for debate and scholastic achievement.

"You're the kind of guy who wrecked the curve for the rest of us," I joked.

Jeff shrugged. "It made my folks happy. And all this stuff looked good on college applications. I got scholarships which really helped. College professors aren't rich, you know."

"Neither are hardware store owners. Did your brothers get scholarships?"

"Some. They were really smart."

"But you were the golden boy," I concluded.

"Well, I am the only blond," he grinned. "Let's settle in. I'm hungry."

After we unpacked Jeff showed me the bathroom where I got cleaned up. Then we went downstairs.

Mrs. Foster had put out several kinds of lunch meat, cheeses, condiments, and rolls. She flashed a huge diamond ring as she put liter bottles of soda on the counter. "You can make what you like," she said.

Dr. Foster joined us in the kitchen and listened as Mrs. Foster grilled me. Between bites, I related my background, my parents' jobs, my educational attainments, and my secretarial position. She seemed to relax when I finished. She smiled, pleased.

"My family has been in California for four generations. My father was a partner in a Sacramento law firm," she declared proudly. She'd established that her family was grander than mine and she rattled on and on and on about them. "I considered going into law myself," she confided at the end, "but I had the boys. Of course, I would have been a lawyer not a secretary but I'm sure you're doing your best."

I looked at Jeff who rolled his eyes. "Dad, anything new?" he asked, trying to redirect the conversation.

Dr. Foster shook his head. "Not really. Still trying to instill some agricultural or economic knowledge into students. It's a losing battle."

I looked around the kitchen. This didn't look anything like a farmhouse. "How'd you get into agricultural economics?" I asked, puzzled.

"I was raised on a ranch, but I'd rather theorize than practice," he said. "My mother sold the place when Dad died. You'll meet her Sunday. We're going to her place for Easter dinner."

"Does she live here in Davis?" I asked.

"Yes, she still has her own house. It's a lot for a widow but she likes it."

The Fosters talked among themselves as I digested sandwiches and information. Jeff had mentioned his grandmother but hadn't gone into specifics about her. I wondered if she was another version of his mother. How many interrogations did I have to endure for the sake of property? Maybe it would have been easier to incorporate. Oh well, too late now. I'd get through this somehow.

We went to bed early. Jeff volunteered to take the cot and I let him. I needed some comfort after the grilling I'd endured.

Mrs. Foster was already in her pearls when we got up for breakfast the next morning. She probably slept in them. Dr. Foster asked if he could take me on a tour of the UC Davis campus that morning and I thought it was a great idea. Jeff even sounded enthusiastic. Mrs. Foster loudly announced that she wasn't interested in coming along. She seemed oblivious when no one expressed regret.

We took Dr. Foster's Mercedes. "Professors make more money than I thought," I whispered to Jeff.

"It was a gift from Grandma," Jeff whispered back.

UC Davis didn't look much like UCLA. For one thing, there was a river. And lots of trees. "It's a land grant college," Dr. Foster explained. "It was founded in 1908 or 9."

"So's South Dakota State," I exclaimed. "Except South Dakota State was founded in 1881. Who'd have thought my school was older than yours," I teased Jeff. Well, I didn't have to feel quite so inferior to the Fosters.

We toured Dr. Foster's department and office. Then we walked around the campus for an hour. It really did remind me of South Dakota State University. Maybe Jeff and I had more in common that I thought.

Dr. Foster took us out for lunch all by himself, which I appreciated. Then he took us home. Jeff and I took my car to the river where Jeff showed me some of his favorite haunts. We even necked a little at the local Lovers' Lane. We hadn't been able to do that in his room. That cot might as well have been a moat.

We went back to his parents' house at about four. We couldn't think of anything better to do. We watched sports on TV until Mrs. Foster ordered pizza for dinner. She didn't seem to be big on cooking.

Jeff took me out on the town that night to hunt up some of his old friends. I didn't have any memories to share, they didn't seem interested in me, and I probably wouldn't remember any of their names anyway. But they reminded me a lot of South Dakota people, too. I reflected on Mrs. Foster's attitude about my background. Maybe she should travel more. She'd see we were more alike than different.

We didn't stay out very late. I was glad. I wanted to be rested up to meet the Grande Dame of the family.

But first we had to go to church. I'd brought a nice dress, but I was surprised when the Foster clan joined the pew of an erect, white-haired lady who wore a flowery hat and white gloves.

"This is my grandmother, Fiona Foster," Jeff said. "Grandma, this is Marianne."

Grandma looked at me searchingly then murmured, "So nice to meet you."

"I like your hat," I stammered. I really did. I even liked her gloves. She looked fresh and neat for Easter.

No more conversation was possible because the service started. It wasn't very different from what I was used to, but I was amused at the grape juice that was served in place of wine.

"Scots-Irish," Jeff whispered. "It's probably cheaper."

I stifled a giggle.

Halfway through the service a young man pushed his way into our pew. "That's my youngest brother, Brett," Jeff whispered. "He was supposed to be here yesterday."

Mrs. Foster glared at Brett, but he grinned, looked at me with interest, and winked at his brother. He seemed lively. Maybe he'd take the attention off me at dinner.

We had coffee and Easter candy with the Presbyterians after the service. I got a lot of stares and I overheard Mrs. Foster whisper something about a 'fiancée'. The stares became more interested. I didn't feel comfortable with the term 'fiancée'. I know we were getting married, but 'fiancée' implied a relationship that really didn't exist. Did it?

Grandma Foster excused herself early. "I have to put the lamb in the oven. I'm planning dinner at four but come any time after two. I want to have a talk with you, young lady," she finished, looking at me.

Oh boy.

CHAPTER 18

Future In-Law Problems

We all went back to the Dr. Foster house for bagels and orange juice. Mrs. Foster said that was all we'd need since we'd be eating a big dinner soon. She hadn't cooked a meal yet. I thought it was interesting that she didn't do housewifery. My mother didn't excel at it either, but she worked sixty hours a week. And Mrs. Foster didn't. I wondered what she did all day. Oh well, not my concern. But it explained why Jeff was surprised when I started cooking.

We left for Grandma's house at two. We stayed in our church clothes because that's what Grandma Foster would want—anyway, that's what I was told. I got the feeling Grandma usually got her way. Jeff talked about her with a respect he didn't show either of his parents. The dread I felt about the talk she had planned went up a notch.

We drove to a small ranch-style house. It wasn't very big, but the front yard and back garden made it seem luxurious. Grandma Foster had hibiscus, azaleas, rose bushes, lots of potted plants…she even had a magnolia tree in the front yard.

"Wow," I breathed, taking in the beauty of her garden. "Who takes care of all this?"

"She does it herself," Jeff said. "She says the exercise keeps her young."

Dr. Foster knocked on the front door and opened it before we got any acknowledgement. "We're here, Mom," he called as he ushered us in.

Grandma Foster came out of the kitchen with an apron over her church dress. Her ungloved hand sported a simple wedding band, but her pearl necklace and earrings looked real to me—and expensive. Her white hair was curly without her hat. She carried herself regally. She wasn't very big, but she seemed mighty. And she must have been about eighty years old.

Dr. Foster kissed her on the cheek and murmured that she looked great. Mrs. Foster chimed in an agreement.

"Oh, fiddlesticks," Grandma Foster waved them off. She sent 'the boys' into the living room to watch TV. She hesitated for a moment then said, "David and Ruth, you might as well go with them. Marianne can help me in the kitchen. If she doesn't mind," she added.

I shrugged agreement and followed her into the kitchen—which was an extension of her outside garden. Plants covered the windowsill and side tables.

"What would you like me to do?" I asked.

"Nothing. I've got everything under control," she replied. "I wanted to get you away from Ruth so we could have an honest talk."

I nodded, resigned. "What would you like to talk about?"

"What do you think? You. Tell me where you come from." But before I could start, she said, "Wait. Where are my manners? Would you like something to drink? A glass of wine maybe?"

"Not before dinner," I hedged. "I don't think wine on any empty stomach is a good idea."

"I bet your stomach *is* empty," Grandma Foster commiserated. "Ruth isn't much on the home front, is she?" I didn't want to criticize Jeff's mother, so I looked at my hands. Grandma Foster made an amused 'humph'. "Well, how about some coffee? I made fresh."

We sat with cups of coffee and I explained my background: South Dakota, business-owning parents, undergrad degree...She seemed to approve of everything she heard. And then she asked baldly, "You're a good Midwestern girl. Why are you living in sin with my grandson?" She leveled a stern gaze on me.

Maybe she could buffalo her son and grandsons, but I'd been raised by a woman who made Grandma Foster seem gentle. I looked back at her just as levelly. "Because it saves money," I retorted.

"And now you're getting married," she said.

"We want to buy property together," I replied steadily.

Grandma Foster nodded. "That's a better answer than I expected to hear. My son got married because he was in love" (she sneered the word) "and look how that turned out. You must have some Scots in you."

"German and Catholic Irish," I corrected.

She didn't bat an eye at the Catholic reference. "I knew you had to have some Celt in you," she said and patted my hand. "You can call me Fiona. Grandma sounds so...elderly. But it makes the boys comfortable. Let me tell you about the family you're marrying into."

She told me her maiden name had been Campbell and three of Dr. Foster's sons, her grandsons, had been named after men in her family. Except for Jeff. He'd been named for Ruth's father. "Jeff is good-looking and smart, like my side, but tall, like her side. You'll see; his brothers are shorter and stockier. But they're smart like the Campbells, too. My oldest daughter's children take after their father. They're all tall. You'd never guess there was any Campbell in them. You never know how children will turn out, do you?"

She told me she'd been a rancher's wife until her husband died. Then she sold the ranch and moved to Davis to be close to David. "The ranch sale is where the family money comes from. A house developer paid a fortune for it," she finished.

David Jr, his wife Linda, and their two boys, Bruce and William, showed up. Jeff's next older brother, Angus, would not be at dinner. He was an investment banker currently out of the country.

There was desultory conversation, the women set the table, and we finally sat down to a lamb dinner. My mother came from a sheep-eating tradition, but she could never get Dad to like it. I didn't blame Dad one bit; I thought mutton tasted like old socks smelled. But Fiona's lamb was flavored with garlic—a seasoning my mother would never dream of using. And her lamb was rare. My mother believed in cooking everything to a charcoal brown. This lamb was good with spring potatoes, green beans, and biscuits. I got some snickering glances from Brett but other than that dinner was quite pleasant.

Oldest brother David quizzed me on farmland prices in South Dakota. I regretfully told him I didn't know anything about agricultural stuff; my family lived in town. He seemed disappointed.

"I was thinking I'd like to try ranching, but I can't afford land in California. It's all going for housing. I wish I could have bought Grandpa's ranch," he sighed.

"How many acres was it?" I asked.

"About 360," he replied.

I looked at him in surprise. "That's a farm not a ranch," I exclaimed. I knew that much.

"Maybe in South Dakota," David said, amused.

"Do you want to raise cattle or crops?" I continued.

"Both. Either. I'm willing to try anything," he replied.

"You stick with your government job," Fiona called out. "Farming or ranching, whichever you do, it's a hard life. You better check with your wife."

Linda didn't seem fazed. "I'm interested. I'd like to get the boys out of Sacramento. The crime is awful. I just don't know how we'd pay for it. It's a big risk."

"Especially without any practical experience," Fiona agreed.

David looked unhappy but subsided. He was the first city person I'd ever met who wanted to be a country mouse. What a novel concept!

Fiona interrupted my musing. "Ruth, I cooked. Maybe you wouldn't mind bringing out the pie. My feet are tired."

Mrs. Foster looked mutinous at the implied criticism but rose obediently. Dr. Foster quickly followed. "I'll bring the ice cream," he announced in what seemed to be an attempt to smooth his wife's ruffled feathers.

Fiona humphed. There didn't seem to be love lost between the two women.

Mrs. Foster returned with a strawberry/rhubarb pie. Now, I grew up eating my grandmother's pies. When people tasted her pies, they looked like an angel had pissed on their tongues. I knew what good pie tasted like. Fiona's pie wasn't bad.

Jeff and I helped clean up then everybody got ready to leave. Fiona took my hand at the door and said, "I'm looking forward to your wedding."

Jeff looked astonished but she shoved us out the door after giving him a peck on the cheek. "Wow, she likes you," he whispered as we walked to the car.

"People do," I said dryly.

"Yeah, but Grandma doesn't like most people. She can't stand Mom."

Jeff's whisper was louder than he thought. Dr. Foster turned back to say, "Hush now. She loves Ruth." He looked at his wife. "She really does like you," he assured her.

Mrs. Foster made a face, "Umhmm."

No more was said until we got home. We were all tired. I was looking forward to going back to Los Angeles. Meeting Jeff's family had been stressful.

But first I had to get through one more evening at the Foster household. Brett decided to take charge of my entertainment. "Do you play ping-pong? We've got a table in the garage," he suggested.

I used to play ping-pong all the time with my dad--at least until I could beat him, then he didn't want to play anymore. I could beat my brother about half the time, and he was really good, so I said, "Sure, I play some."

Brett beamed and led me to the garage. Jeff had been reading a magazine but called out, "You want me to come?"

Brett yelled back. "No, this shouldn't take long." He sounded supremely confident which irritated me. Did he want to show me up? And if so, why?

"I play at school. You know, UC Berkeley?" Brett explained. "Don't feel bad if you lose big. I beat Jeff all the time."

Ooohhh, so little brother was trying to show up his big brother by proxy! I guess I could see why he felt inferior. He was only 5'10" and stocky compared to Jeff's tall slimness. He also had dark hair like his father—what there was left of it—not an ash blond mop like Jeff. What he hadn't counted on was my serve. I blew the first one past him. Brett wasn't anywhere near as good as my brother. But he was right about one thing; it was a short game. He was chagrined when I beat him 21 to 8.

"Another?" I asked innocently at the end of the game.

"No, that's okay," he returned slowly and put his paddle down. I nodded and started to leave the garage when he piped up, "You want to play Trivial Pursuit?"

He seemed desperate to beat me at something. I must have hurt his masculine pride. Well, now he'd offended my feminine pride. We'd see how smart he was.

Brett set the board up in the kitchen and we enlisted Jeff and Dr. Foster to play with us. I didn't win, Dr. Foster did, but I came in second.

Jeff smiled. "I didn't know you knew so much," he congratulated me.

"I read a lot," I returned modestly.

"No wonder Elliot wants you to go into law," Jeff continued.

Dr. Foster's eyes lit up. "You're going to be a lawyer?" he asked.

"I don't think so," I said. "I'm not really sure what I want to do yet."

"Well, you have time," Jeff's dad said.

Brett had lost to everybody and didn't seem to be in the mood to say anything nice to me. He pouted.

"Buck up, Brett," Dr. Foster teased him. "Maybe you can play your mother. She'll let you win."

Of course, that made Brett feel worse. "Don't feel bad," I offered an olive branch, "we're all older than you. Maybe you should stick to playing with your college friends."

I don't think I made things any better. He scowled at me and walked away. I looked at Jeff helplessly. "Don't worry about it," Jeff said. "He's mad because he thinks you're cute and he wanted to impress you."

That was creepy. "I think I'll turn in early," I said. "We have a lot of driving to do tomorrow. Goodnight, Mrs. Foster," I called out. I got a muffled response. I didn't care. I trudged up to the bathroom, brushed my teeth, and closed the door to the bedroom. I was alone at last, thank God. Keeping up this pretense was wearing me out. I pulled out a book I'd brought.

Jeff came up an hour later and interrupted my reading. "I got gas in your car and checked the tires and fluids. We're ready to take off any time tomorrow," he said as he changed and crawled into his cot.

I put my book down. "I think this charade is going off the rails, don't you?" I asked.

Jeff punched his pillow and plopped down on it. "What charade?"

"This whole marriage thing," I specified.

"The marriage isn't a charade," Jeff pointed out. "We're getting married."

"Yeah, but your parents think it's the usual love match. It's about money. If you were an illegal alien, you'd be getting a green card out of this. It seems dishonest," I argued.

Jeff squirmed in his cot and said, "This thing is awful. I'm glad we're going home," He arranged his covers before responding. "It's not dishonest. In the Middle Ages the whole point to marriage was combining resources. We're not doing anything new. We're probably more traditional than anyone I know."

That was a new way of looking at things. I nodded thoughtfully. "Your grandmother said something like that. She thought marrying for love was stupid. She said to look how your parents' marriage worked out. She really doesn't like your mother, does she?"

"She thinks Mom's lazy. Mom came from an educated family and she likes the country club way of life. But she didn't bring in any money to support it," Jeff said ruefully. "And Grandma really hates that Mom got a housekeeper and yard guy last year. She thinks the least Mom could do is clean her own house. Mom prefers to play golf."

I agreed with the grandmother but thought it best not to say anything.

"Maybe you should turn off the light so we can get some sleep," Jeff advised. "We've got a long drive ahead of us tomorrow."

That sounded like good advice, so I followed it.

We packed quickly the next day. I asked Mrs. Foster what I should do with the dirty sheets. Thank God we'd been separated; I didn't have to worry about any 'dalliance' stains. I found myself thinking in quotes when I thought of sex with Jeff when his mother was remotely involved. Must have been my Catholic upbringing. She told Jeff to show me the laundry chute and clean sheets. We remade the single bed together and Jeff folded up the cot.

Mrs. Foster served left-over bagels and juice for breakfast. Dr. Foster made the coffee before he left for the university.

Mrs. Foster half-heartedly apologized for the left-overs, but Jeff said, "Don't worry about it. We'll eat on the road." He wolfed down a bagel, slurped his juice, and said, "I have to finish packing. Take your time, Marianne. I've got some stuff I want to go through before we leave." He loped out of the room and left me with his mother.

I looked at her warily, but she smiled. "You don't have to worry about me," she declared. "I have no intention of being the kind of mother-in-law I have. It's okay with me that you don't have any money," she said stoutly. Then added, "Although we all thought Jeff would find a young woman more connected. But I certainly don't blame you for grabbing him. He has a wonderful, lucrative future ahead of him. He'll be a real step up for you, won't he?"

She made me sound like a stray cat. Where did this woman ever get the idea that I was anxious to marry advantageously?

Mrs. Foster wasn't finished. "But I see why Jeff picked you. You're very pretty and it sounds like you want to better yourself. As I said, I won't hold your background against you. Which is a far cry from how Fiona treats me. She thinks I should clean my own house. Can you imagine? It would absolutely wreck my nails. And really, who cooks anymore? Fiona has all these medieval ideas about what a wife should be!" And she waved her hands at me so I could admire her fingernails.

"Doesn't that cost a lot of money?" I asked diffidently.

"Oh, money," Mrs. Foster scoffed. "Money is to be spent. And David stands to inherit a lot of it from Fiona. He also has his pension which is quite respectable in California, you know. Really, Fiona could part with more money than she does. She could pay for all the boys' educations if she wanted to."

"Jeff said she pays for part," I said.

"Oh, she contributes. But she wouldn't pay for a fraternity and that's where you make friends...and contacts." She made a slight grimace at me when she said this last. I'm guessing she'd wanted Jeff to bring home some sorority girl instead of plain little old me.

"But that's all water under the bridge, isn't it?" she finished brightly. "You have a good job and that'll be a help. And I'm sure you'll be the best wife you know how to be under the circumstances. I want to assure you that you don't have to worry about any interference from me. As I said, I don't want to be anything like my mother-in-law."

I was speechless. She'd just told me that I was under-educated, socially unacceptable, and a potential gold-digger in one sitting. Who says stuff like that? And where had she gotten these ideas? They came from her own diseased little mind. It was time to set the record straight and tell this woman that she didn't need to worry about me hanging around any longer than it took to flip a house. This was the second California woman who'd trashed me to my face. Mrs. Foster and Mrs. Friesman could have been the same person. And I was starting to rethink this whole 'let's get married; it's cheaper' plan. I opened my mouth to defend myself against her assumptions when Jeff reappeared with some notebooks under his arm and a bag in each hand.

"We better get going before the traffic gets too bad," he announced.

"I think we better have a talk with your mother first," I started.

"I've been telling her that we don't object to her lack of breeding," Mrs. Foster clarified.

Jeff looked at me. "Lack of breeding?" he repeated, mystified.

"Your mom doesn't think I'm good enough for you," I announced with a manic smile.

"Mom, what have you been telling Marianne? Never mind, we have to go. Tell dad thanks for everything and I'll call when I get home."

He gave his mother a brief hug and handed me his notebooks. Then he retrieved our suitcases and led me out the door.

"Do you want to thank my mother?" he suggested.

"I will not," I hissed back. "Did you hear what she said...?"

He threw both suitcases in the trunk of the Tempo. "I'll drive until we get out of town, okay?" he interrupted and held the passenger door open, handed me in, and slammed the door behind me.

"Bye, Mom," he yelled as he opened the driver's door and crawled in beside me. He quickly backed out of the driveway, put the car in gear, and sighed as we pulled away.

"That didn't go so bad, did it?" he asked cheerfully.

I stared at him in astonishment. "You better start looking into incorporating," I announced. "That's how well it went."

CHAPTER 19

Jeff will be a Good Lawyer

For the first two hours of the trip home Jeff listened to me intermittently rant about his mother; how I'd never agree to any relationship with a woman who held people like me and my family in such low regard. I'd yell for a few minutes, stop for a few more, then start yelling again.

"She thinks I'm after money," I spat. "I'm the one with the credit rating, not you. Didn't you tell her that?"

"Oh, Mom doesn't mean any harm. She's always trying to find someone to look down on, probably because Grandma looks down on her. You shouldn't take it seriously," he said.

"Well, I do take it seriously," I returned vehemently.

"Yeah, I can see that," Jeff said thoughtfully. "Maybe we should calm down for a while. We'll both have more perspective if we give this some thought."

"I don't need to calm down!" I howled. "You calm down!"

Jeff nodded but didn't give me any more ammunition. I fumed in silence for a few minutes then said, "I don't blame your grandmother for not liking your mother."

"She thinks Mom's a climber," he admitted.

"Well, she's got that right," I muttered.

"Mom thought Dad had a lot more than he did. She's always trying to keep up with her college girlfriends who married money. I think the house cost more than Dad could really afford. He had to get some money from Grandma to keep from losing it."

"Why didn't your mother get a job?" I asked scathingly.

"She always said us kids took up most of her time. But her friends have cleaning ladies, so Mom wants a cleaning lady. And she likes to eat out. She says she never learned to cook."

"What's stopping her from learning? Can't she read?" I asked sarcastically.

"There's not much point anymore. We're all gone most of the time."

"What does she do with her time?"

"I think she goes to the country club a lot."

"Can your dad afford that?"

"I don't know. I guess so or he wouldn't pay for it," Jeff replied. "I don't really know much about their finances. It's not something I can ask Dad about. It's not my business, you know."

"I suppose he's helping with your education," I said grudgingly. "Brett, too."

"No," Jeff admitted. "I work, there's Grandma, and I have a few loans."

I was marrying a man with outstanding loans? And this is the first I'm hearing about it? I pounced. "You have debt and you want me to marry you? I'd be liable for your debt! Oh no," I said, warming to my argument. "I'm not taking on your mother and your debt. The marriage is off!"

Jeff nodded unhappily and I stared out the car window until we got to Harris Ranch which was two hours outside of Los Angeles. That was a lot of silence, especially with the radio reception going in and out. But Jeff had been preparing arguments. He offered to buy me a steak.

"Will I have to pay for that, too?" I asked snidely.

"No, no," he soothed. "I'm going to tell you everything. And the steaks are good here. Trust me, I can afford to treat."

I looked at him suspiciously but found the idea of a steak appealing. I'd had two days of bagels. And lamb. Some beef

181

protein would be welcome. Jeff even encouraged me to get an expensive glass of wine. He said he wouldn't drink because he was driving. I didn't even feel too guilty about him doing all the driving. It was a punishment for his wretched mother.

I pouted until my wine came then I mellowed a bit. That must have been the plan. We ordered rib-eyes and salad and waited until the waiter was out of earshot. Then Jeff began.

"First of all, I don't have a lot of debt. I told you, I got scholarships for most of my undergrad work. I got a small one for baseball. The rest were for academics," he explained.

"Wow, I didn't know you played baseball that well."

"I don't play much anymore. The law firm plays softball and that's sort of a comedown."

"A comedown?" I repeated. "What's the difference?"

"Well, the ball's a lot bigger," he said with a wry smile. "It's hard to play with weekend warriors when you've played at a high level."

I imagine that was true. "I never got any scholarships," I confessed.

Jeff shrugged. "My dad's a professor. He knows how to play the game. And he's tenured in the UC system. There are perks." I must have started to look unimpressed because he hurried to assure me, "But I got the grades, too. I earned those scholarships. And I had summer jobs to pay for what the scholarships didn't cover."

"Oh." I wasn't sure how to respond. It didn't seem fair to me that these insiders got all the goodies and people like me had to pay. But we'd discuss that topic later.

"What's this debt you're talking about?" I asked, returning to the important subject.

"Well, law school isn't cheap. I didn't get any deals there. But Grandma was so impressed that I got into UCLA that she offered to pay a third. She said she'd take it out of my inheritance. And I work. But I still have some small loans. I figure I can pay those off in a couple years when I get a good job. The amount's really not significant. But I'll show you the figures when we get home."

I was half-way through my glass of wine. "Yes, I'd like to see them," I said calmly.

The waiter brought our salads and we dug in. Neither one of us had much to say for a while. I was foggily pondering what he'd told me, and Jeff shoveled food in—as was his usual practice.

The scholarship part of his confession was impressive. The fact that he'd gotten an undergrad degree mostly on his own was remarkable. And it didn't sound like he'd gone too deeply into debt for law school—although I'd wait to see the figures before I made a judgement.

And I was starting to appreciate my mother for getting me an undergrad degree without a load of debt hanging over my head. It gave me enormous freedom. It was something I'd never realized before.

Jeff interrupted my musing. "Your wine is almost gone. You want another?"

I smiled fuzzily. "Sure. Why not? If you don't mind doing all the driving..."

"Not at all," he assured me and flagged down the waiter.

So, I was wined and dined excellently. I wasn't mad any longer. I wasn't much of anything any longer. Jeff made sure I peed before we left. Then he belted me into the passenger seat, and I dozed until we got home.

Jackie interrogated me about 'meeting the parents' the next day.

"I told Jeff we better start thinking about incorporation," I reported drily.

"That bad?" Jackie asked delicately.

"It's his mother," I said with a shrug. "She's the deal breaker. But I figure, if we incorporate, I won't have to put up with her."

"How about his other relatives?"

"I like Jeff's grandmother. When I told her we were getting married for property, she said that was smart. She said marrying for love is a bad idea."

"Sounds like a practical woman," Jackie commented.

"Well, she's retired from a ranch. I think you have to be practical to run a farm or a ranch. There's not much time for romance."

"If you incorporate, you'll be business partners," Jackie said. "That's practical."

"Yeah," I fervently agreed, thinking about the Catholic Church. I'd been brainwashed all my life to believe that if I got married, it was for life. I'd be stuck. I'd rather sign a contract—with ink, not blood.

"Yeah," I repeated slowly. "I think it would be best if we were just partners."

Unfortunately, Jeff was still under the assumption that we were getting married and seemed surprised when I reiterated that the deal was off; we'd have to incorporate.

"But we agreed," he started.

"We did but I changed my mind," I stated firmly. "Especially considering all the extenuating circumstances."

"Which are?"

"Your mother and your debt," I retorted.

So, Jeff started arguing again. He got out a scratch pad and jotted down figures. He told me how much he owed and demonstrated how he would pay the debt off monthly over two years.

"You know I've been interviewing," he stated. "What you don't know are the amounts I'm being offered." He wrote down some figures on his pad and pushed it toward me. I was astounded at the amounts. "Wow," I said admiringly. "Is that what UCLA grads normally earn?"

"Only the top grads," he replied a little smugly. "So, you can see I won't have a problem paying off my loans in two years if we economize."

Geez, maybe I should *go to law school*, I mused then brought myself back to the problem at hand.

"Why not incorporate?" I argued. "We could probably get a boiler-plate contract someplace."

Jeff shook his head. "A boiler-plate isn't specific enough. We'd need someone who knows what he's doing. And I shouldn't do it because I'm one of the parties involved." He told me how many hours a lawyer would bill us for drawing up the incorporation contracts and how expensive that would be. He outlined the filing fees and the fact that we'd have to go through all the cost again if (and when, I mentally added) we dissolved the partnership. He made a compelling argument. He was going to be an effective lawyer. I nodded agreeably but I have to admit, I got a little distracted when he looked at me with those amazing blue eyes.

We discussed facts and figures and he talked me into marriage again. "We can save until we get evicted. Steve thinks we'll probably have until the end of the year. Between the two of us we should be able to come up with a small down payment."

"Sounds reasonable," I said slowly.

Jeff smiled, pleased. "So, the decision is final? You won't change your mind again?"

"Wel-l-l-l," I hesitated.

"Will you shake on it?" He thrust out his hand.

I looked at his hand doubtfully. I felt like I was being boxed in. But I could see his point; he wanted some certainty.

"Not yet," I evaded. "There's still the matter of your mother."

"Look, I know she can be a pain," Jeff said patiently. "Don't pay any attention to her. None of us do. She has her little...I don't know...quirks. Let her talk about her country club and she'll be happy as a clam. She doesn't pay much attention to David's wife. And vice versa. And they live half an hour apart. I don't seriously see her as a problem. How many times have you seen her down here? But if she does show up, I'll take care of her. See? No big deal."

I looked at his outstretched hand. He had answers to all my objections. And, boy, he was really going to make a lot of money. I shook myself. That wasn't my money, it was his. But it was nice to know that I wouldn't have to do all the work the way my mother had.

I reached across and shook his hand. "It's a deal," I said firmly. The marriage was back on.

Jeff hesitated for a moment then asked diffidently, "Would you like an engagement ring? I don't want you to feel cheated."

I glanced at the page of figures. "No," I returned shortly. "Save the money. We'll need appliances for our house. I'd rather have a refrigerator than a diamond. You can't keep beer cold with a ring."

Jeff chuffed a short laugh. "At least you've got your priorities straight," he grinned.

Jackie looked at me narrowly the next day when I informed her that the marriage was back on. I explained that Jeff had good arguments for all my objections—that the Justice of the Peace was cheaper than a corporate lawyer and the marriage license was still cheaper than all the legal fees we'd pay to incorporate.

"How about the mother?" Jackie asked. "Will she be a problem?"

"Jeff says his family all ignore her--and I should do the same," I retorted loftily.

Jackie winced. "Makes me feel sorry for her," she murmured.

"Yeah," I said uncomfortably. "I guess I wouldn't like it if one of my family talked about me like that. But she is sort of silly—all that one-up-man-ship. And she really irritated me when she went on about how superior Californians were to South Dakotans. What would she know about it anyway? I'm the only South Dakotan she's ever met." I calmed myself down and continued, "And Jeff pointed out that he doesn't see her that often and if she does come down here, he'll take care of her."

"Sounds like Jeff has answers to everything," Jackie said.

"Yeah," I agreed. "I even shook hands on the deal, so I'm stuck now."

Jackie made a face at me. "This isn't the third grade. A handshake doesn't mean much."

"It does to me," I insisted.

"Maybe it's good that you're marrying Jeff," Jackie muttered. "You're still such an innocent." Then she raised her voice. "Make sure you don't go signing a pre-nup or anything without talking to Mr. Elliot or some other lawyer. Will you promise me that?"

"Sure," I said, daunted at the seriousness of her tone. It wasn't that big of a deal. It was only marriage.

So, I forgot about it. I went back to cooking at home. I also started jogging with Steve. We decided we needed more exercise and we kept each other from quitting. Sometimes we picked up Jackie at her high-rise and took tours of old downtown for exercise. Jeff didn't come with us. He preferred running on his own.

Life was quiet for a few weeks. We were watching TV when Jeff cleared his throat.

"I got a phone call from my parents," he started, "when you were out running." He stopped.

"So? Anything new?" I prodded.

Jeff hesitated. Then he said in a rush, "They want to know when the wedding is. Mom wants it to be around my graduation, so they only have to make one trip." He took my gape-mouthed stare as a need for clarification. "You know hotels cost a lot of money. The whole family wants to see me graduate and it would be nice if they could combine the events. And the nephews really want to go to Disneyland."

I shrugged. "They can come with us to the Justice of the Peace if they want. It won't be that big of a deal."

"Wel-l-l..." Jeff hesitated with a wince.

"You told them we going to the Justice of the Peace," I repeated slowly. "Didn't you?"

"Look, my parents don't understand that sort of thing," Jeff said. "They're going to expect a real wedding. Not something impromptu at City Hall."

"That's not what we agreed on," I pointed out.

"Yeah, I know. I'm sorry," Jeff said unhappily. "But even my grandmother wants to come to the wedding. She really likes you."

"That's only because your mother doesn't," I snapped.

"And I don't want to disappoint them. You can understand that, can't you?" Jeff continued.

"I suppose," I said reluctantly. "But what about saving money and all that? Weddings cost money."

"Maybe we can think of something?" Jeff smiled at me winsomely.

Damn. He was talking me around again. I wouldn't be able to face Jackie if I let him talk me into another change. So, I argued right back. We couldn't pay for a wedding and save for a house and the whole point of this exercise was to buy a house.

So, Jeff came up with a new argument. "My grandmother always said she'd probably give me a big chunk of cash when I got married. That could go for the down payment." He saw me wavering. "But she probably wouldn't do it if there weren't a wedding. And you don't want them coming down here twice, do you? Once for my graduation, and again for a wedding? Wouldn't you rather get it done in one swell foop?"

Well, that made me laugh. Then I thought about how much a wedding would cost and sobered.

"You don't expect me to pay for a wedding all by myself, do you?" I asked suspiciously. "It'd be for your family. I don't even have any family out here."

"Maybe we could split it? It doesn't have to be much. Just family and a few friends. And we wouldn't need a big reception or anything. We could have some sandwiches here at the apartment. You know, the small party we talked about?"

"Wel-l-l," I wavered. Dammit, he was doing it to me again. But if his grandmother would part with some much-needed cash maybe it was worth it. We were going to have a graduation party anyway. Might as well make it a two-fer.

My gaze wondered around the apartment as I chewed on the idea. My eye returned to Jeff sitting on that awful recliner rocker covered in duct tape.

I made a counteroffer. "I'll split the cost of a wedding with you if you pay to get that recliner re-covered."

"What's wrong with my chair?" Jeff asked, mystified. But he grabbed at the offer. "Deal," he said. "Shake?"

I shook his hand dubiously. All this handshaking was getting me into a world of expense.

CHAPTER 20

Planning

N ow it's a wedding?" Jackie exclaimed when I told her the new arrangement. "Do you not know how to say 'no'?

I explained how maybe grandma would give us some wedding cash for a down payment on a house. And a wedding probably wouldn't be that expensive.

"When are you supposed to have this wedding?" Jackie asked.

"The same weekend as his graduation. That way his family only has to make one trip," I explained.

"June?! You want to do this in June?! That's only two months away!"

"Well, that's enough time. Isn't it?" I asked ingenuously.

Jackie shook her head. "You better get on it," she advised.

So, over my lunch hour I got out the yellow pages and started calling chapels. I only had one criterion: it couldn't be either Catholic or Presbyterian. If Jeff wanted to get married it was going to be on neutral territory. I was shocked at how much most of the chapels cost. This was not going to be cheap. And then I was shocked to find out that most of the chapels were booked on the date we wanted. I reported my findings to Jeff when I got home that night.

"I think the Justice of the Peace option is back on the table," I said firmly. "But we can still have a combined graduation/wedding reception when your parents come down."

Jeff was thoughtful. "Maybe we should try for a Sunday. I don't think that's such a popular day. And my family can spend Saturday at Disneyland. What do you think?"

"Feel free to try," I said. "I spent my lunch hour making calls. It's your turn."

"I'd do it, but I'm completely swamped with interviews and final projects. I'll pop for pizza tomorrow night to make it up to you," he coaxed.

Why was Jeff always trying to bribe me with food? Because it worked, that's why. I grumpily agreed to make more calls.

I finally found a chapel in a big Methodist church on a declining part of Wilshire Boulevard. They had one opening left on the Sunday required because they'd had a cancellation. *Probably decided to go the JP*, I grumped to myself. But I grabbed the 3 o'clock slot when the coordinator told me the time came with a rehearsal, an organist, and bows on the pews. The minister was optional at extra cost.

I had a date and a time. I could order invitations. I found a print shop close to the office. The proprietor told me that the minimum order was fifty and it would take two weeks to process. When I reported back to Jeff that night, we agreed on the wording and card stock. I spent my lunch hour the next day ordering invitations, RSVP cards, and envelopes. More expense. I sighed but I could forget about the wedding for two weeks.

At least until Steve got wind of what was in the works.

"A wedding, not the JP?!" he rhapsodized. "I've got some ideas…"

"Oh no you don't," I objected. "You planned the proposal dinner and it took me a month to pay that off. This is going to be a small service to make Jeff's family happy. We're supposed to be saving money to buy property."

Steve pooh-poohed that—he really did, I'd never seen a man do that before—and said, "Listen, you only get married a few times in your life no matter the reason. Let's do it right."

"I'm doing it right," I protested. "I've ordered invitations, I've booked a chapel. What else do I need to do?"

"Well, there's the flowers," Steve ticked off his fingers, "and the cake. And the food and drinks. And decorations...."

"No, no, no," I said. "We're having a few people here at the apartment afterward, so it doesn't have to be fancy."

"Who said anything about fancy? I'm just trying to keep you from looking like a charity case. Now, I know a guy who does flowers. Maybe he'll give me a discount..." And Steve was off. I sighed.

It turned out that Steve being involved was a good thing. "Who's your maid of honor?" he demanded a few days later.

"I don't have one," I confessed. "Do I need one?"

Steve frowned at me in pity. "Yes, you do. Get thinking."

Well, there was only one obvious choice. Jackie had been my friend and mentor ever since I'd met her. She was the only friend I would want in that position. But she was so anti-marriage I wasn't sure she'd even do it.

"Ask her," Steve urged. So, I did.

"You want me?" Jackie asked, surprised.

"You're the best friend I've got out here," I said. "Of course, I'll understand if you don't want to..." I hastened to add. I didn't want to put her on the spot.

"No," Jackie returned thoughtfully. "I'd love to be your maid of honor. I've never been one before. Maybe it'll be fun."

"Great!" I said, relieved. "Don't worry about buying a dress or anything. It's going to be small. You know, close friends and Jeff's family."

"Aren't your family coming?" Jackie asked.

"I don't think I'll even invite them," I returned slowly. "The way things are with my mother...I haven't even spoken to her since Christmas. I doubt she'd come. And I'm not sure I want her to. I know my brother and sister wouldn't come if she didn't. And my father does what she says." I shrugged it off.

Jackie looked sympathetic but let the subject drop.

The invitations arrived and Jeff and I spent an hour addressing them, stamping them, and putting them in the mail. I invited Mr. Elliot to be polite and a few girls on the softball team. Jeff invited his family members, of course. We also addressed invitations to Steve and Jackie. We still had a lot of invitations left.

"What a waste," I commented.

"We might need them for something," Jeff said. "Aren't you going to invite your family?" he prodded gently.

I gave him the same story I'd told Jackie. He looked thoughtful when I finished. I noticed he took some invitations without explanation but forgot about it.

Steve started haranguing about cakes again and had suggestions for some pretty fancy—and expensive—wedding extravaganzas.

So, I stopped at a bakery down the street from our house and ordered a small, two-tier cake that would feed about thirty. We'd have cake left over so I ordered a chocolate one with white frosting. I like chocolate cake. I'd make sure not to waste it.

The baker asked me what decorations and colors I'd selected.

"Colors?" I asked blankly.

"It's customary to have the bride's colors on the cake," the baker informed me.

Good lord, this was all too complicated for me. I pulled a color out of thin air.

"Yellow!" Steve screeched when I told him. "With all the lovely pinks and blues to pick from why'd you pick yellow?"

"It matches the stripe down my back," I offered weakly.

"It's going to be hard to make attractive flower arrangements," Steve muttered.

"What flower arrangements?" I asked, bewildered, but he was off.

I still had to get a dress. Surely that would be the last thing I'd have to worry about.

And then Jackie asked, "Where are you registered?"

"Registered?" I repeated bewildered.

"You know, for gifts," Jackie explained patiently. "Mr. Brady would like to send you something. And I know some of the secretaries would like to take up a collection."

"I hadn't even thought of that," I replied blankly. "Do I have to register someplace?"

"It's a good idea," Jackie advised. "Otherwise God knows what sort of presents you'll get. You don't want people to waste their money."

"Maybe I should tell people not to give any gifts," I offered. "It's not like this wedding is that big of a deal. Is it?"

"People like weddings," Jackie advised. "They don't care if your reasons are mercenary. They want to wish you well."

I felt like a fraud. And I was completely out of my depth. "But I'm not even inviting most of these people to the wedding. I don't want them to spend their money," I protested.

"They probably will anyway," Jackie said. "I'll tell Te...Mr. Brady to keep it simple."

She smiled when she said this, but I sensed a little envy in her tone. And it didn't matter that the wedding was going to be small. About twenty paralegals and secretaries organized a party for me. They scheduled it for a Friday after work at a bar a few blocks from the firm. Jeff didn't say much when I told him I'd be home late. "Some of the office women want to have a girls' night out," I explained.

Jeff was under pressure to complete his classwork. "Have fun," he muttered distractedly. "I've got to get these papers done. I can't believe how far behind I've gotten." He propped his head in his hands and groaned. I let him alone. It was the kindest thing I could have done.

That Friday night Jackie and I walked over to the bar and she led me to a room in the back. About twenty of my work friends were whispering excitedly around a table that supported champagne glasses and a small pile of presents.

"Congratulations!" they chorused and attached a cheap paper veil to my hair before pouring me a glass of champagne. They took turns toasting me with the wine then the serious drinking began. I stayed with white wine, but the others ordered interesting mixed drinks with little umbrellas and fruit garnishes.

They had me sit at the head of the table and open the presents. Nobody had spent a lot of money, thank God, but these presents were different than ones I'd expect to get in South Dakota. Back home I'd get kitchen stuff but here in L.A.? I got underwear—most of it brief and lacey. I was bemused by a pair of crotchless panties. I didn't see the point to them, but all the women smiled knowingly at each other. I'd ask Jackie about them later.

But the party was just starting. A young man in a cop's uniform appeared and the girls shrieked. They put a chair in the middle of the room and put me in it. They made sure my veil was in prominent view then turned on some music. The cop started to dance and do a slow strip tease in front of me. I didn't know where to look. The young man was gorgeous, that wasn't the problem, but I'd never had a man, even Jeff, bump and grind in my face. He worked so hard sweat started pouring off him. When he twirled some of it fell on my face and clothes. I wondered how I'd explain the sweat stains to Jeff. I finally excused myself to get another drink when he rubbed up against me. If I couldn't explain sweat stains how would I ever explain a man's cologne on me? Nobody seemed to mind. The girls took turns bumping and grinding with the stripper; they were having a wonderful time. Jackie sat in the back of the room, so I joined her.

"Is this usual?" I asked.

"For Los Angeles it is," she confirmed. She watched the stripper with a professional eye. "He's good. They're getting their money's worth. I should get his card so I can recommend him." I gazed at Jackie in awe. She laughed. "I worked in Vegas, remember? I never worked parties like this but it's good money."

"Wow," I breathed and took a long drink of my wine. "Did you stay in your underwear or did you…you know."

"Strip? No, I just danced. But I was glad Ted came along. It's a business for young bodies. Once you hit thirty your price goes down."

I was watching the stripper avidly. Jackie's discussion of the profession made him a human being, not a party favor. But I don't think I had to worry about his feelings; he seemed to be having a ball.

Jackie watched my reactions with amusement. "Didn't any of your girlfriends hire strippers for bachelorette parties?"

"In Brookings?" I exclaimed. "No! No. We played stupid games and ate cake. Our mothers would have disowned us if we'd done anything like this. And who would we hire? The kid down the street? It's tough when you know everybody in town."

Jackie looked concerned. "Is it too much? We can stop this if you're embarrassed."

"Oh no, it's just...different," I said quickly.

The girls turned up the music and invited some of the men in the front to come on back for dancing. After my fourth glass of wine I found myself dancing with some stranger, my veil wafting as I twirled the crotchless panties over my head. I even danced with the stripper once. His name was Gavin and he wished me well on my wedding. I grinned to myself when I thought of what my mother would do if she ever saw this. Good thing she never would.

The party wound down at eight and I weaved back to the office arm-in-arm with two other secretaries. Jackie had left much earlier, they said. I tottered over to my car, pushed the veil out of my eyes, and unlocked the door before what little sense I had woke up. I couldn't drive like this. If the cops stopped me, they'd throw away the key—I still hadn't registered my car— and I'd probably miss the wedding. I shoved that tempting thought aside. I'd spent too much already. I'd better call Jeff to pick me up. I went up to the silent office to use the phone. Jeff sounded a little testy when I asked if he could come get me, but he agreed I shouldn't drive. He said he'd be right down and to wait for him on the corner. I stashed the underwear presents in my desk drawer, except for the crotchless panties. I wadded them up in my purse; I wanted to show them to Jeff. Then I walked down the block to the specified corner. As I waited my eyes focused on a dress shop across the street that was still open. I didn't want some strange man getting any ideas about why I was loitering, so I wandered in. There was a sale rack in back; I carefully walked over to it, smiling at the clerk as she watched me warily. I didn't want her to think I was drunk. It was a losing battle.

I sorted through some dresses and came upon a white cocktail length dress with a lacy collar, full sleeves, full skirt, and a big bow in the back. And it was my size. I looked at it dubiously. This was the sort of dress Aggie M would have been adorable in, but I was afraid I'd be regressing if I wore it. But it was pretty in a Gibson Girl sort of way. I checked the price tag. It was only $95.

"How come it's so cheap?" I asked the clerk.

"There's a spot in the back," she explained and showed it to me. Well, the stain was nothing. I could probably get that out easily enough.

"Do you think this would work for a wedding?" I asked.

"Only if you're the bride," she replied.

"I am," I confided.

She looked at me skeptically. "You better try it on," she suggested. So, I did. And it was lovely. The bow cinched in my waist and made it look tiny. And the high collar with lace inserts down to the bra line was poetic.

"I didn't think I could wear flounces," I said as I admired myself.

"It'll look better with white heels," the clerk assured me. "But you don't even need jewelry. It looks sweet on you."

It did. So, I bought it. The clerk carefully wrapped it and put it in a box. She showed me some hats to go with it, but the hats cost more than the dress. I reluctantly declined. I'd seen much cheaper hats at discount places. I'd make do with one of those. But at least the dress was bought. One less thing to worry about.

I was on the corner when Jeff roared up on his motorcycle. "What in the world do you have there?" he asked, nodding at the box.

"My wedding dress," I said, grinning goofily.

Jeff looked surprised. "How much have you had to drink?"

"Four...no, five glasses of wine," I replied with exaggerated dignity.

"And you bought a dress like that?" Jeff asked in dismay.

"Yup. It's pretty," I assured him.

He shook his head. "How are you going to ride with that dress box?"

"No problem," I assured him. I hiked up my skirt and climbed on the back of the bike, put on the helmet Jeff had brought, and squashed the dress box between our bodies as I clutched his middle.

Jeff had one last question before we took off. "You're not going to barf, are you?" he asked anxiously.

"I hope not. I like this dress," I retorted. And we roared off.

Fortunately, I didn't barf on the ride home. I waited until I got inside to do that. I came out of the bathroom wiping my mouth. Jeff eyed me with some distaste. "What are those stains on your blouse?"

I goggled down at myself. "Probably from the stripper," I concluded. "The girls hired a male stripper. Isn't that a hoot?"

"Yeah, a real hoot," he agreed without enthusiasm.

"Hey, you want to see one of my presents?" I asked him, knowing the crotchless panties would take his mind off the stripper and my bilious display.

He agreed so I whipped out the crotchless panties.

"Ta da," I sang and slung them at Jeff. Then I peered up at him owlishly. "You want to make love?"

Jeff looked at the panties hanging off his shoulder then back at me. "Maybe some other time," he said quietly. "You better go to bed. I have work to do anyway."

This was the first time he'd ever walked away from a proposition, but I'd never vomited before issuing the invitation before. There was a lesson to be learned here: if you puke, use mouthwash before trying to seduce your boyfriend. I went to bed and left him to his papers.

I guess it's a good thing I couldn't interest Jeff in sex. I'd forgotten to take my Pill. I didn't know if missing one would leave me open to pregnancy, but I didn't want to have to depend on Jeff's tidy-whities keeping his sperm cooked to death for birth control. This marriage was about property, not children.

CHAPTER 21

Fight!

I was hungover that Saturday. I looked at the dress I'd bought with trepidation. What if I hated it? But the dress was still pretty. I think I liked it even better. At least the dress was one less thing to worry about. Except for the spot. I'd have to do something about the spot.

I didn't get much of a worry-free period. Steve showed up with questions about how big the altar centerpiece should be and how many bridesmaids and groomsmen we were having.

"Jackie is the only bridesmaid," I groaned as I sipped Diet Coke. "Can't we talk about this later? I have a headache."

"One bridesmaid?" Steve sniffed.

"It's a small wedding. Remember?" I glowered at him.

"Then how about a groomsman? And ushers?" Steve persisted.

"Talk to Jeff," I growled.

"But he's always busy!" Steve complained.

"Tell me about it," I retorted and went back to bed.

I spent most of the day nursing my headache but resurrected myself in time for dinner. Jeff was churning through his papers when I asked him what he wanted to eat.

"Oh yeah, food," he said distractedly. "Do what you want. Anything is good."

"Scrambled eggs?"

"Whatever," he mumbled and went back to his papers.

First, I took a shower. Then I made scrambled eggs and toast. I was starting to feel human again when I put plates out. "Dinner," I called. Jeff detached himself from his papers and moodily shoveled a forkful of eggs into his mouth.

"Have you talked to Steve lately?" I asked to start a conversation. "He wants to know about groomsmen and flowers."

"Can't you take care of it?" Jeff asked starting to look desperate. "I can't even think about that stuff now. I have work to do and no time left."

"What exactly is the problem?" I asked delicately.

"I put off writing some papers because I was so busy with interviews and stuff. Now I have to get two of them to a typist who'll need a week or two to crank them out. And both papers are due in ten days. So, to save time, I'm trying to combine two different classes worth of material into one paper that I can turn in for both. And it's not working very well."

I chewed thoughtfully. "You know, I need a ride to work because my car's still in the building."

Jeff looked at me narrowly. "So?"

"So, I'm a typist. I work fast and clean. I can take your papers into work and crank them out tomorrow," I offered.

Jeff perked up. "I couldn't ask you to do that."

"I have to get my car anyway. And I owe you for picking me up last night," I said reasonably.

Jeff was starting to look a little less tense. "I'll pay you what I'd pay a regular typist," he offered hopefully.

"Take me some place nice to dinner," I shrugged. "We're friends. Friends help each other out. You helped me; I can help you."

Jeff spent the evening scrabbling through his papers. He produced a wad of yellow sheets covered in his handwriting. Then he gave me a ride on his bike to the office the next day so I could start typing. I spent the afternoon deciphering Jeff's handwriting—which wasn't anywhere near as messy as Mr. Elliot's—then photocopied the end-product before I drove my car home. I plopped both copies in Jeff's lap as he watched TV and said, "You can't turn these in."

"Why? What's wrong?" Jeff asked, bewildered.

"Listen, I've been working for lawyers for a couple of years now. I know the sort of thing they write. And it's obvious you're trying to use one paper for two different classes. If I can pick that up, your professors will, too. And they'll probably flunk you." Jeff was starting to look panicked, so I hurried to reassure him. "But I've got an idea. I've copied the original typed version and you can cut paragraphs apart and paste them in the appropriate paper. All you have to do is write the segues. And I'll take them both in to work and type them on my lunch hour. You'll be able to turn them in on time." I smiled. "See? No problem. And you'll probably get As."

We stayed up late the next few nights cutting and pasting paragraphs on legal pads and Jeff wrote the stuff in between. We worked well together. I typed both papers up--they were very professional looking--and Jeff turned them both in on time.

Which brought us both back to the wedding. We discussed it over the nice steak dinner Jeff treated me to as payment for my flying fingers. For once I didn't worry about expense. He'd have had to pay a typist anyway.

"Has Steve cornered you about a best man?" I asked as I stuffed salad in my mouth.

"Yeah, but I didn't have an answer," Jeff replied. "I thought about my brothers but which one? It'd be sort of strange to pick one and leave the other two out. I'd probably hurt someone's feelings." He chewed moodily.

"Then how about a friend?" I offered, hoping he wouldn't think of Scott. I'd never told him that I'd threatened to shoot Scott months ago. Scott was a dead issue that I wanted to stay that way.

"Actually, I was thinking about asking Steve," Jeff admitted. "He's really been into this wedding. He'd probably be thrilled."

I hesitated. "Well, I was thinking of asking him to walk me down the aisle. I'd feel sort of stupid walking all by myself.

Ooohhh, that's probably weird, too. Although everything about this wedding is weird…"

Now Jeff looked really uncomfortable. "I'm glad you brought that up. I've been wondering how to tell you this but…well, you probably won't need Steve to walk you down the aisle."

My eyes narrowed. "What do you mean?"

"Maybe we better wait until we get home," Jeff equivocated.

"What's wrong with now?"

Jeff looked at me, looked away, and looked back at me. "Nothing. But can we wait until after we eat? The steaks are here," he smiled in relief at the waiter who brought our rib-eyes.

I couldn't start anything with the waiter around, so we talked about safe subjects, like his graduation, as we finished our food. He told me about parties that were scheduled in the next weeks and which ones he felt it was important to have a girlfriend to show off. The party that I agreed to attend without a big argument was the one at the Beverly Hills Hotel. "Isn't that the hotel with the Polo Lounge?" I asked enthusiastically. "I've always wanted to go there."

"I think it's going to be a pool party, but we can certainly have a drink at the bar if you want," Jeff agreed.

I smiled. UCLA parties were a lot ritzier than the ones I'd gone to in South Dakota. At least I had something to look forward to besides that wretched wedding. And speaking of the wedding….

"Who's this aisle-walking candidate you have for me?" I asked abruptly.

Jeff looked cornered. "Maybe you should have another glass of wine," he suggested.

"I won't be able to drive home," I countered.

"I'll drive," he said shortly. "Please. Have another glass of wine. For my sake."

This was making me nervous. But I did as he asked. After the waiter brought my wine, Jeff took an envelope out of his coat pocket and offered it to me.

"What's that?" I asked cautiously.

"It's an RSVP to our wedding," Jeff explained. "You better look at it."

It was from my mother stating that she, my father, and my sister would be attending the wedding. I was shocked. "How did she even get an invitation?" I demanded.

"I sent it to her," Jeff admitted.

"Why?" I asked incredulously after an uncomfortable pause.

Jeff looked determined. "It's your wedding," he stated firmly. "It wasn't right not inviting your family. Or not even telling them about it. And I knew you wouldn't invite them. You won't even talk to them." He took a deep breath. "It wasn't right," he repeated.

I stared at him. "It wasn't your decision to make," I declared.

"Probably not. But somebody had to do it," he retorted.

"No, somebody didn't have to do it," I hissed. I took a long drink of my wine. Now I knew why he waited until we were in a restaurant to tell me about this. He knew I wouldn't pitch a fit in a public place. I probably should have but I wasn't raised that way. The whole world didn't need to watch us fight. We didn't have much to say to each other as I tossed back my wine and Jeff paid the bill. We maintained silence as we left the restaurant. Then Jeff said, "Give me your keys. You know you can't drive now."

I glared at him but tossed him my keys. He opened the door to the passenger side, and I seated myself. Jeff got in and started the car. And I started yelling. I yelled that he'd had no right to go behind my back the way he'd done. That this whole wedding had been his idea, but he hadn't taken any responsibility for any of it except to make my life harder. "She hit me!" I screeched at him. "She threw me out of the house! I've been disowned! How could you do this?" And on and on and on.

Jeff drove, staring stonily ahead. He didn't say anything until we were almost home. "It was the right thing to do," he asserted.

I was beyond outrage. "Stop the car," I ordered. "Stop the car right now!" He did and I jumped out and ran around to the driver's side. I yanked the door open and motioned him out. "I never want to see you again," I announced dramatically.

Jeff nodded, closed the door, and drove away. In my car.

And I stared after him. He was driving away. In my car. I raised one outraged finger in the air like I was going to say,

"Excuse me?" Then I thought of what I must look like, standing in the street, staring after my car. It was so ridiculous I started to laugh. I chuckled as I walked the short way home and let myself into the apartment. I knew Jeff would come back eventually. I had all his stuff.

When Jeff finally came home, I was calm enough to discuss the matter. He still believed he'd done the right thing and I was pretty sure he hadn't. But apparently it was done. Then Jeff produced another letter. It was from my mother telling me to call her. She wanted me to send some invitations to those pesky relatives living in Orange County that I'd managed to forget all about. And she wanted addresses for hotels near our apartment. In the letter she stated that "ordinarily the family would stay with you but since you aren't married it was out of the question so don't even offer." She needn't have worried. I wouldn't have offered.

I put the letter down. "Do you need more wine?" Jeff asked.

"No, no…" I said weakly. "She wants to invite some people I've never met to the wedding."

"The more the merrier?" Jeff offered.

"This wedding is a nightmare," I muttered. "Well, you better get Steve to be your best man. Looks like my father is coming and I imagine he'll want to walk me down the aisle. Although why he should, is beyond me. He's not paying for anything…"

I called my mother two days later. I needed the time to get focused and in control of myself. I hadn't spoken to her in months and I was out of practice.

"I got your RSVP," I started out calmly.

"Listen," she interrupted. "We don't have a lot of time. You should have contacted us sooner, but it's done. How much money do you need?"

"Nothing," I assured here. "Jeff and I are taking care of everything. All you have to do is come…"

"Humph," Mom interrupted again. "Well, you're an adult and I should be glad he's making an honest woman out of you…"

I tried to defend myself. "He's not making 'an honest woman' out of me," I retorted as calmly as possible. "This is a decision we both came to. We intend to buy a house together."

"That's nice," Mom said shortly and changed the subject. "You read in my letter that I need some invitations for those relatives I have in Southern California. I'd like to see them while I'm out there and I can't tell them I'm coming to my daughter's wedding without inviting them."

"But it's a small wedding and I don't even know them," I protested.

"And whose fault is that?" Mom asked rhetorically. I was silent. "Is this Jeff person inviting his family?" Mom added shrewdly.

"Well, yes," I returned hesitantly.

"You don't want to be outnumbered, do you?" Mom asked triumphantly. She had me there. I'd been feeling bad because I wouldn't have anybody on my side of the chapel. Well, Mom was taking care of that. I capitulated and Mom gave me the names and addresses. "Only six of them will probably show up but that's six to the good," Mom assured me.

"I still don't feel comfortable inviting these people. I don't know them," I repeated.

"You knew about them. Remember I told you to look them up when you got out there? They're cousins from the Old Country. They came over a few years before I did and settled out West, but we've exchanged Christmas cards. You must remember those."

I didn't but I promised to send the invitations that day.

"And don't forget," Mom said. "We need the names of some local hotels. Nothing too expensive, of course. Aggie M will be coming with us, but Matt has to stay home and watch the business."

I promised to find some suitable places so she could make arrangements. The rest of the phone call was business-like which was a relief. I still hadn't recovered from the violence of our last meeting but at least this hadn't been too unpleasant. And when she came out, she'd be in a hotel. We'd have room to maneuver around each other.

Jeff was looking at me expectantly when I hung up. "Well?" he prodded. "What are those names you wrote down?"

"Cousins from Orange County my mother wants invited to the wedding," I said.

"How many?"

"Only about six. She says. I'm inviting the adults. If they have children, too bad. I don't know any of them," I reported.

"Oh," Jeff said nonplussed. "I didn't know you had relatives out here."

"I forgot all about them," I admitted. "At least I'll have some people on my side of the chapel."

"Yeah, that's nice," Jeff said doubtfully.

"And I have to get some hotel suggestions to Mom as soon as possible," I added.

"Oh, I hadn't thought about that," Jeff said.

"This wedding is out of control," I fretted. "Now I have to worry about food. My mother will expect something." I thought for a minute. "Listen, are you sure we shouldn't go to the Justice of the Peace?"

"Too late," Jeff pointed out. "Invitations are out. Chapel's booked. We're committed."

"Yeah," I sighed. "Listen, you better call Steve if you want him to be your best man. I have to get this flower situation settled anyway."

Jeff talked to Steve who was delighted to accept. And he was thrilled to do the flowers. "Just give me a budget," he said, rubbing his hands in delight.

"Budget?" I echoed. "I don't know. What do we need? Boutonnieres, corsages, one *small* bouquet..."

"And an altar centerpiece," Steve added. "You can also use it at the food table."

"Yeah, I guess we'll need a centerpiece," I sighed.

"I can probably get something nice for $200," Steve assured me. "Leave it to me."

$200? I should have said 'no' and stuck to my guns when Jeff suggested a wedding. Too late now.

I got a call soon after from the chapel coordinator asking when we could schedule the rehearsal. Jeff suggested we do it after his Friday afternoon graduation. "That way we can have the family at the graduation, do a quick rehearsal, then go to dinner. We'll kill two birds with one stone."

That sounded great to me and the coordinator penciled us in. Then she had another issue. "Do you have a minister?" she asked.

Oh God. I'd forgotten all about that. "No," I admitted.

"The minister at the church will do it," she offered. "But he insists on meeting you both beforehand so he can make sure you two are good candidates."

Oh crap. Well, I didn't have any better ideas, so we scheduled a meeting with the Methodist minister.

"I'm going to hell," I muttered rebelliously to Jeff who scoffed.

Now all I had to do was ask for time off for the minister meeting and the graduation. Mr. Elliot looked at me glumly. "I suppose you're going to want time off for a honeymoon, too," he commented.

A honeymoon? I hadn't even thought about that. "We hadn't planned a honeymoon," I admitted. "Should we?"

"You can have a week if you want it," Mr. Elliot offered grudgingly. "We're coming up on a trial so if you can't go now, I might need you to wait a few months."

I brought up the honeymoon conundrum to Jeff who looked chagrined. "I hadn't thought about it, either," he admitted.

We decided we'd worry about an official honeymoon when we had more time and money. "If we have any left after this stupid wedding," I murmured mutinously.

We met with the minister who was a kind but firm man. He quizzed us on what we expected from marriage. I felt like a fraud when I mentioned financial security...and love, I hurried to add. I had to make him believe we were serious about marriage. I didn't know anybody else who'd perform the service at this late date. Jeff agreed earnestly that love was a priority. I almost believed him myself. The minister listened to us babble about being married then he interrupted. "Are you two living together already?"

I looked at Jeff, not sure what the correct answer would be, but Jeff said simply, "Yes."

The minister nodded. "How long?" he asked.

"About a year," Jeff replied.

The minister threw up his hands. "Then I guess I can't tell you much about marriage," he said. "We won't need any more meetings." I think he felt he was saving us from sin and didn't want to put any impediments in our way. I was glad. I wouldn't have to beg for more time off from Mr. Elliot for bogus marriage counselling.

Jeff took time to pick me up during lunch hour soon after that to apply for the marriage license. We stood in line waiting with the other young hopefuls and I compared us to them. I was comforted because they didn't seem to be any more in love than we were. Maybe this was the way things were done these days. We exchanged pleasantries and the couple in front of us said they were going straight to the Justice of the Peace on another floor as soon as they'd gotten their license. I poked Jeff and suggested, "Maybe we should just get it over with?"

Jeff said, "Absolutely not. You know why."

I subsided. But when we paid the clerk for the license and he asked, "Would you like to be married by a judge right now?" I was tempted to blurt a relieved "Yes!"

But Jeff quickly said, "No thanks. We have our day all planned."

We were committed. The wedding was on.

CHAPTER 22

Families

I concentrated on work until Steve brought up the subject of reception food. "And pictures," he added.

"Pictures?" I groaned in despair. God, how much more was there to do?

But Steve had it all thought out. "I'll get a bunch of those disposable cameras for your guests and hand them out at the chapel. They'll probably think it's fun to take candid shots. And it'll make them feel involved. I'll take the good shots of you at the altar. Maybe the minister can take a picture with the entire bridal party. That way I'll be in it, too. Unless one of your family is a good photographer? No? Well, we'll figure something out. And it won't cost much. Now let's talk about food."

Steve was having the time of his life. And he was so organized! I suggested that he could have a business being a wedding planner while he waited to get a steady acting job or sell a script. He nodded, pleased. "I've thought of it," he said. "Would you give me a good review?"

"Absolutely," I assured him.

"Great! Let's talk about food," he grinned and clapped his hands. Even flattery didn't deter him. We talked about deli platters and champagne. "I'll get a couple of nice bottles for toasting," Steve decided. "We can make do with cheap booze for the rest. I've got some expensive bottles I can funnel cheap stuff into. Most people can't tell the difference. See? Saving you lots of money right there."

I nodded. This 'cheap' wedding had me so addled I didn't even argue anymore. And I was delighted when Steve announced that he'd been talking to Jackie and they'd decided to buy plates, glasses, and napkins as a wedding present. "We both agree that you need help," Steve said sympathetically. "Most brides have mothers who do this stuff but you're on your own. We'll be your family until yours shows up. And we'll get something nice instead of the cheap crap you'd probably buy."

I was touched. And relieved. I still had to go to work every day and get the apartment in shape. I couldn't get anybody (Jeff) to help clean before the impromptu reception. And the place had to be clean. My mother was coming.

Jeff did try to calm my fretting. "Your mother probably won't notice," he scoffed lightly.

"You've never met her," I retorted darkly. He dropped the subject.

I didn't blame Jeff for not helping with the cleaning--much. He had to finish up his school year which meant finishing projects, going to interviews, and attending parties. He went to most of the parties by himself; I was too tired. But I put in an appearance at the big 'do' at the Beverly Hills Hotel the Saturday before the graduation. I finally had an occasion to wear my spangly Valentine's Day dress. It hadn't been a total waste of money.

Jeff treated me to a glass of wine at the Polo Lounge before we went to the pool area. He had something to tell me, he said mysteriously.

"Congratulations on graduating," I said when I had a glass of wine to toast with. "It was a long haul, but you did it."

"I did pretty well, too," Jeff added with a pleased smile. "I guess it's time for my news."

I waited expectantly. "I've taken a job," Jeff announced...and stopped.

"So? Who're you going to work for?" I prodded.

I think Jeff paused for dramatic effect because he suddenly blurted out, "Mr. Brady offered me a job at the firm. We'll still be working together."

He waited eagerly for my reaction. And frankly, I was surprised. "I didn't know they'd even made you an offer," I admitted. "Jackie never said a word."

"I asked her not to," Jeff said. "I didn't want to get your hopes up."

I didn't know I'd had any hopes to get up, but he seemed convinced that my happiness depended on him taking the job. I didn't want to dampen his evening, so I congratulated him again and asked for details. The starting salary would be huge, but it was contingent on him passing the bar as soon as possible. "And since we don't have any money for a honeymoon right now, I can start work on the Tuesday after the wedding!" he finished triumphantly. He had a big grin on his face as he awaited my reaction.

"Great," I said as enthusiastically as possible. Just one thing: "Why are you starting on Tuesday? Why not Monday? We could drive to work together."

"Oh," Jeff stopped and fidgeted uncomfortably. "Mr. Elliot will tell you."

I was mystified but let it drop. We had a lovely time at the last big party of Jeff's class. His classmates were impressed by Jeff's job. I guess it was a big deal. I was surprised that he'd chosen the legal field. I'd been under the impression he wanted to go the business route.

I got an explanation of the 'Elliot' mystery when I went to work the following Monday. Mr. Elliot called me into his office. "Have a seat," he said abruptly. Normally, he didn't invite me to sit so I knew something unusual was going on. "Uh, the wedding this Sunday," he started, then paused. My heart stopped. Was he going to tell me I had to work on my wedding day? "Mr. Brady thinks...and I agree," he added parenthetically, "that you should take this Friday and the following Monday off. We won't even count them as vacation days."

He sat back to enjoy my reaction. And I think I was noticeably relieved. I hadn't gotten around to asking to take

211

Friday afternoon off for Jeff's graduation. I'd had so many other things to think about and I was afraid my boss would be petulant. Well, surprise, surprise. Mr. Elliot wasn't so bad after all.

Things seemed to be falling into place. All I had to worry about now was getting the stain out of my dress. And the fact that my mother was flying in this Thursday. She'd called to tell me she'd booked a room in a motel down on Sunset, about three blocks from the apartment. "We've asked for a cot for Aggie M. She doesn't need her own room," she reported. And she rejected my offer to pick them up at the airport. "We've rented a car," she said. "You'll be busy, and I don't want to be dependent on you or your young man." 'Young man' was said with a sniff. I wondered what she'd make of Jeff when she met him.

Which was going to happen sooner than I'd anticipated. Jeff's family was driving down on Thursday also. And Jeff thought it was a good idea for both families to go to dinner together. "I'd like them to get to know each other before the groom's dinner," he said with a smile. "Hopefully we can iron out any problems."

He'd better have a big iron. But my mother thought it was a fine idea when I suggested it. "We'll come to your apartment" (she didn't say 'den of iniquity' but the tone was there) "and see how you live."

Oh boy.

I'd gotten home from work and finished tidying before Mom, Dad, and Aggie M showed up. I looked at the apartment critically. It looked all right. I even approved of the recliner that Jeff had resurrected from the trash. He'd lived up to his promise to re-cover the chair, but we'd had a set-to about the fabric. He'd wanted to cover it in Naugahyde, but I'd insisted on a knubbly beige fabric. It cost more but it looked better. And maybe it'd meet with my mother's approval. Then I shook myself for even wanting her approval. I still hadn't forgiven her for the brawl at our last meeting.

When the doorbell rang Jeff met my family with a big smile on his face and his hand out. "I'm the fiancé, Jeff Foster," he announced. "I've been looking forward to meeting you, Mr. Fuchs." Dad looked impressed—maybe because Jeff pronounced our last name correctly, bless his heart.

My dad responded to the charm blitz with a big smile of his own. "Marianne mentioned that you accepted a job where she works. Mother always wanted a lawyer in the family," he said jovially.

Then Jeff turned to Mom. And she's impervious to charm—except from my father, I guess.

Mom, tiny little Irishwoman, glared up at Jeff and fixed him with a gimlet eye. "So, you're the one," she accused.

Jeff quailed a little but recovered quickly. "I'm the lucky man who won your daughter, Mrs. Fuchs," he declared and offered his hand.

Mom shook his hand and said, "Humph." I have no idea what that meant.

Jeff turned to Aggie M in relief. She looked up at Jeff with stars in her eyes. "Aggie M," Jeff concluded, his smile recovering. "My new sister-in-law."

Aggie M hung on to Jeff's hand until my mother cleared her throat loudly. I got a pat from my father, a look of envy from Aggie M, and a brief hug and peck on the cheek from Mom which was unusual. Mom wasn't normally demonstrative—unless it was in anger. I returned the hug neutrally.

Jeff offered to get drinks. My mother answered for everybody that all they needed was water. They'd wait for anything else until they got to the restaurant. Mom had spoken. Jeff took Aggie M to get water and I showed Mom and Dad the apartment. It was small so it didn't take much time. Mom looked at the bed and her mouth twitched but she didn't say anything. We all went back to the living room and stiffly talked. Jeff was telling them about the groom's dinner the following evening after his graduation. He even offered to get them some tickets to the graduation although I don't think he could really get any; you had to sign up pretty early to score them. But Mom said that was a celebration for his family. The Fuchs would be happy to attend the groom's dinner. Then Jeff's family showed up. I tensed. I wasn't sure what Mom would do. But she was gracious as introductions were made. I watched Mom and Jeff's grandma size each other up then smile grimly at each other.

Jeff had made reservations at an Italian restaurant that wasn't too far from our place. We all drove in our own cars so "we can go directly to the motel" to quote my mother.

The dinner was pleasant. My mother didn't blow up at me or complain about the food because it had garlic in it. Jeff's mother didn't say anything derogatory; I think she was too full of wine. At the end of the meal I was preparing to grab the check but was beaten by my mother. "This one's on us," she said quickly. I looked at her in surprise, but she didn't explain anything. Was this her way of making up?

When we left the restaurant Mom and I circled each other warily. Dad and Aggie M kept their distance. They didn't want to get in the line of fire. Abruptly Mom said, "So you'll be busy tomorrow afternoon."

"Yes, it's Jeff's graduation," I replied.

"And we won't see you until the rehearsal?" Mom added.

"Probably not," I said slowly. "Do need the address?"

"No, it's on the invitation," Mom said.

We stared at each other briefly. Mom broke the awkward silence. "We'll meet you at the chapel then. Although why you scheduled the graduation and rehearsal on the same day is beyond me."

"Well, we were out of time..." I began testily but Mom raised an imperious hand. "I'm not criticizing." (HA!) "Just as well you don't drag things out," she said.

"Can you find your way around?" I asked cautiously.

"Young lady, I got from Ireland to New York to South Dakota," Mom snorted. "I think I can find my way in a car with a map."

I guess I got told. At least she hadn't taken a swing at me in front of Jeff's family. But I was relieved that our first meeting had ended peacefully. Maybe we could get through this without a brawl.

I slept in the next day. I'd been so stressed for so long I needed the time to relax. I sat in my T-shirt watching Jeff dither over his cap and gown. It was nice not to have to do something—until Jeff asked if I'd lead his family to his graduation.

"Me?" I asked in horror. "They're your family, why can't you show them the way?"

"I have to leave early for some rehearsal. I don't want them to have to sit around for hours waiting on me."

"Well, give them a map," I suggested. "My family has never been to Los Angeles in their lives and they're getting themselves around."

"My folks won't know where to park on campus and you do," Jeff returned patiently. "Please?" he wheedled. "I'll make it up to you somehow."

I growled. I was tired of steak dinners. I did hours of work and he got off with a nice meal. And he got to enjoy the meals as much as I did.

I was keeping track of favors. Just like I was keeping track of money spent on the wedding. And I seemed to be coming up short.

"Please?" Jeff repeated.

"Oh, all right," I capitulated crossly, disgusted with myself. Jackie was right; I couldn't say 'no'.

"Great!" he enthused. "My brother, Brett, and Grandma can ride with you. And David will have his family in his van. Mom and Dad can probably ride with them. I'll take my bike."

He was great at planning everything—except the wretched wedding which was his idea! I scowled but he kissed my forehead. "You're the best. See you at the graduation!"

I resentfully got dressed and picked up his brother and grandmother. My resentment increased when Jeff's mom made a face at my Tempo, but his grandmother said that she appreciated the fact that I would take the time to escort them. And she glared at ol' Ruth. That pleased me and I led the way to UCLA feeling more cheerful. I made sure to sit next to Grandma Foster ("Call me Fiona." "Okay.") and cheered with the Fosters when Jeff got his diploma. We met for pictures after the ceremony. Then we all drove to the chapel for the rehearsal.

And I had a new reason for dread. This would be the first time Mom met Jackie and Steve and I had no idea what she would do. She already thought Jackie was a Scarlet Woman and

I was afraid she'd started ranting about Sodom when she found out Steve was gay. This was turning into a long day.

Mom looked astounded when she found out we were being married in a Methodist chapel, but she recovered quickly. I heard her say aside to Aggie M, "Well, at least she can get a divorce if this doesn't work out. It's not a Catholic service. It doesn't count."

Funny. That was almost exactly what I'd thought.

The rehearsal didn't take too long. There weren't very many of us, so the coordinator quickly gave us our instructions. Jackie walked down the aisle, Steve already knew where he was supposed to be—as a matter of fact, he put Jeff in position—and Dad practiced going down the aisle with me. Mom sat stonily but Aggie M gawked around like she'd never been in a church before.

"Boy, this is a lot smaller than the church I got married in," she crowed.

I glared but Mom shushed her. I guess she wanted to make me miserable all by herself. She didn't need Aggie M tagging in.

The minister finished the rehearsal by asking if we were going to exchange rings. Jeff and I looked at each other. "I could always use the washer," Jeff offered. The minister looked puzzled, but I stifled a giggle and told him I'd switch the ring I was wearing, the one Jeff had given me for Christmas, to the other hand.

Then we all drove to a steak place for the groom's dinner. Dr. Foster took Jeff and me aside and asked that we split side dishes to save money. "David and his family will be splitting dishes. Brett will be sharing with Ruth and me," he said. "I'm sure you understand." I didn't but I only had one glass of wine. I guess the cheap gene had skipped Jeff.

Four tables were put together to accommodate us. Fiona sat at one end surrounded by David's family. Dad sat at the other with Mom next to him. Steve managed to get himself put next to Mom, but she seemed to enjoy talking to him. She didn't even seem to mind Jackie. She looked at her narrowly when they were introduced. I saw Jackie's back stiffen and I almost heard her say to herself, "That's enough!" Mom was pleasant but cool and the moment passed without incident. I sat between Steve and Jeff. Aggie M managed to sit next to Jeff and grinned goofily at him from time to time. Jackie sat across from her and smiled quietly at all the under-currents in the room. Jeff's parents and Brett sat across from us. Ruth looked like something was pinching. And I could feel Mom starting to turn to stone. The mothers would look at each and the temperature in the room dropped ten degrees. I kept waiting for the explosion from Mom, but it didn't come. We all ate our steaks and the toasts began. First, we had to toast Jeff on his graduation.

Dr. Foster rose. "And congratulations are in order; Jeff got hired by the firm he's interned with for the last two years. Let's all toast to the new future partner of Dewey, Beatham, and Howe!"

The Fosters all cheered, and the Fuchs raised our glasses. The moment was spoiled when I heard Ruth murmur, to herself apparently, "He could have married anybody."

I felt like I'd been slapped. My mother heard her, too. She looked daggers at Ruth but didn't say anything. I guess I couldn't expect her to defend me; I knew she felt I'd embarrassed the family. Jackie gave me a sympathetic look, but Fiona raised her voice and her glass.

"Let's toast to the lovely bride who helped Jeff get his degree," she announced and addressed the next comment to me. "Jeff told me you got him through his final projects. He says he couldn't have done it without you. And that's what a marriage is: a partnership. Two equals meeting for a common goal. Would that all marriages were so balanced."

Jeff grinned at me; he'd been oblivious to his mother's remark. And I smiled gratefully at Fiona who nodded. My mother raised her glass and said loudly, "Hear, hear."

Everybody drank to me. I started to relax. The wedding would be on Sunday; only two more days to go. I had my friends with me. It would be all right.

Jeff was exuberant when we got home but all I wanted to do was go to bed. I was exhausted. And constipated. I'd been under so much stress I'd quit crapping—which made me look about three months pregnant. I didn't want Jeff's mother making nasty comments about me gaining weight before the wedding, so I took a laxative. It said on the package that it was safe and gentle. I went to bed hoping for the best.

CHAPTER 23

Interim

Well, the laxative worked—too well. I spent the next morning lying on the bathroom floor, afraid to even go back to bed. I had to stay close to the toilet to catch the explosions. I'd cramp and squirt, cramp and squirt, cramp and squirt. I caught a glimpse of the laxative package on the sink stating that the product was safe and gentle. My ass. I should have eaten a hand grenade and been done. It couldn't have been much worse. Jeff seemed really concerned when he peeked in and saw me curled up on the bathmat with my underwear around my ankles. I didn't dare pull them up; I didn't know if I'd be able to get them down again in time.

"Are you all right?" he asked tentatively…and looking slightly repelled.

"No," I snarled. "I'm sick."

"Is there anything I can do?"

"Just go away." I struggled to my feet as I spoke. "Now!" I ordered. Jeff fled. I sat—just in time.

It was going to be a long day and I still had so much to do. After two hours on the bathroom floor the laxative seemed to have done its job. I was completely cleaned out. Of course, I was weak as a kitten but maybe that would pass, too. I managed to take a shower to remove any signs of illness, but the toilet was a mess. I couldn't worry about that now. I dragged myself to bed. Jeff started hovering. He brought me some water and asked again if there was anything he could do to help. I took him up on his offer this time.

"You can go get the cake," I instructed. "It's supposed to be ready today."

Jeff found the receipt in my stack of wedding papers and trotted off with my car keys. He came back half an hour later absolutely ashen.

"What?" I asked in trepidation.

"The cake wasn't ready," Jeff announced. "The baker forgot all about it."

"Oh my God," I moaned.

"But you shouldn't worry," Jeff hurried to add. "He says he's open on Sunday and we can pick it up tomorrow morning around ten." I stared at Jeff. "He seemed really embarrassed. I think he'll actually get it done," Jeff said comfortingly. I still didn't say anything, so he added, "I threatened him with cancelling the order. He got scared when I demanded the deposit back. I think he needs the money."

I moaned again. Nothing about this stupid wedding was going right. But what could I do? I agreed with Jeff that we'd hope for the best and I dragged myself to the kitchen to make myself some toast and tea. I told Jeff I wouldn't need him again for a while, so he excused himself to spend time with his parents. They wanted to go to the Huntington Museum, and he figured that would only take about two hours. That seemed to be the time limit most people spent at museums. Then my Mom called, and Jeff let the cat out of the bag that I wasn't feeling well. She insisted on coming over.

Jeff made sure I was settled at the dining room table when the doorbell rang. "Your father and Aggie M dropped me off. They're going to Universal Studios," Mom announced after Jeff let her in. "You can go now," she ordered Jeff. "I saw your father parking outside. I told him I'd send you down."

I was going to be left alone with my mother? I looked at Jeff in horror, but Mom took the decision away from him. "I can take care of my daughter," she said firmly and steered him out the door. He looked back but I waved him off in despairing benediction. I was going to have to deal with Mom sooner or later. I wished I felt stronger. If she started another fistfight, I wasn't sure if I could take her this time.

Mom and I stared at each across the table. Finally, she gestured to my cup. "Can I make you more tea?" she asked.

"Sure," I agreed slowly. "Make yourself some, too."

"And more toast," Mom added. "Toast is always good on a tender tummy."

Tender tummy? Mom never talked like that. But I nodded and directed her around my kitchen.

"So," Mom said as she placed a thickly buttered piece of toast in front of me. She sat across from me with her own tea and toast and waited until I'd taken a bite. "How far along are you?"

"What?" I choked, spitting crumbs.

"How far along are you?" Mom repeated. "Have you been to a doctor yet? You have to make sure the baby is healthy."

"Whatever gave you the idea I'm pregnant?" I demanded, bewildered.

"Well, the baby bump," Mom replied calmly. "And the morning sickness."

"I'm not pregnant," I protested indignantly.

Mom looked at me skeptically, so I had to confess that the 'baby bump' had been constipation and I'd taken a laxative. "I had no idea it'd be this bad," I said. "I'll never take another one. It's the laxative that made me sick. But I'm all cleaned out so I should be better by tomorrow. Hope so anyway. I still have a lot to do."

Mom sat back, flummoxed. Then she tried to hide an amused smile. "I thought you had to be pregnant," she said. "That's why this wedding was so hurried."

"Jeff wanted to have it over his graduation weekend so his family wouldn't have to make two trips," I explained.

Mom's eyebrows went up. "And you went along with that," she stated flatly.

"I wanted to go to the Justice of the Peace," I admitted, "but Jeff wanted a church wedding."

"Even though it's not his church," Mom amended.

"Even though it's not his church. His family is Presbyterian."

Mom nodded and sipped her tea, deep in thought. "I still don't understand why you couldn't wait a few months," she finally said. "You could have had a nice wedding at home." I looked at her sardonically and she flushed.

I shrugged. "We want to buy property and need both incomes to qualify for a loan," I told her.

"That still doesn't explain why you're in such a rush," Mom pointed out.

"We're going to be evicted from this apartment at the end of the year and neither one of us wants to waste money on rent anymore. We want to get a fixer-upper so we can make a profit."

Mom nodded. "That makes some sense. At least this young man understands the value of a dollar. I don't think the same can be said of his mother. I have to tell you I'm not too impressed with her."

I immediately wanted to defend Jeff's mother just because Mom didn't like her—except I couldn't. I didn't like her either. But I couldn't admit that to Mom. I said nothing.

"She had some things to say about you last night, but I kept my mouth shut," Mom continued.

I'd noticed that and it wasn't like my mother at all. Normally, if someone said something derogatory about a family member Mom would puff up like a mad cat and the fight was on. I thought Mom kept silent last night because she didn't think much of me either. And that hurt. I stayed silent.

"I didn't say anything," Mom said slowly, "because I thought you were in the family way and it was more important to get this young man to the altar and give the baby a name than defend ours. And now I find you're not even pregnant. That changes things." She had a bite of toast and chewed thoughtfully.

"What changes? I asked cautiously.

"I won't be so careful about what I say to her," Mom said calmly. "It's nice to know you're not in the family way. We had enough of that with Aggie M."

"Maybe you should still keep quiet," I advised. "What if Jeff gets mad and dumps me at the altar? After all this I'd be so embarrassed."

Mom sipped her tea thoughtfully. "No, I don't think that'll happen," she concluded.

"How can you be so sure?"

"He's in love. That's why he's marrying you," Mom explained.

"I don't think so," I argued. "He's never mentioned love in any of our discussions."

Mom looked at me in pity. "I thought you were smarter than that," she said. "He wants to make certain of you. His mother told me what his starting salary is. He doesn't need you for money."

"But he needs me for the down payment and the bank loan," I argued back. "He's never had a full-time job, so he doesn't have much of a work history. The phone is even in my name!"

Mom shook her head. "He'd just work for six months to get a history. And he could probably borrow the down payment from his grandmother. From what she said last night she's expecting him to ask for a loan." She brushed crumbs from her hands and finished her tea. "No, he's marrying you because he wants to. The question is why he couldn't wait a few more months." She picked up her cup and took it to the sink. I stared after her stupidly. Could she possibly be right? I'd have to think about that. But first I wanted to get a few things straight.

"I think you should know it was Jeff's idea to invite you," I said baldly. "I'm still mad that you beat me up and then disowned me. You shouldn't have done that."

Mom leaned against the sink and sighed. "No, I shouldn't have. I have a terrible temper." (No kidding!) "I was tired from the Christmas season, you know how hard retail is in December, and I lost control."

"That's no excuse for such a crazy reaction," I pursued.

"I thought all my fears for you had come true," she said looking past me at the recliner like it had some answers. "I thought you were repeating Aggie M's mistake and wouldn't have a family to make the boy marry you. You knew your father and I had to get married, didn't you?"

I nodded.

"If your father hadn't been decent, I don't know what I would have done. I had no family, no support at all. And then Aggie M did what I did. I hit her, too, when she told me. Did she tell you that?"

I shook my head, dumfounded.

"Aggie M took it," Mom commented. "At least you fought back. I always thought Aggie M was like me because she looked like me. And I thought you were more pliant, like your father, because you favored him." Mom shrugged. "I was wrong on both counts. But I'm sorry I hit you. I shouldn't have done that."

"I suppose I shouldn't have hit you back," I admitted reluctantly.

"You were defending yourself," Mom said. "I never told your father. Will you?"

"Probably not. It's between us," I replied.

"Yes. Well," Mom said and that seemed to be that. It was probably the only apology I would ever get. And, frankly, it was more than I expected. Mom walked back to the table and asked, "What else can I help with?"

I hung my head, embarrassed. "The bathroom needs cleaning. And there's a stain on my dress I don't how to get out."

Mom smiled briefly. "I'll clean the bathroom. Show me the dress; I'll get the stain out. Now you go back to bed."

I took her advice and Mom went to work. She was hanging up the stain-free dress by the time Steve and Jackie showed up with decorations, plates, and cutlery.

I staggered out of the bedroom, not sure how Mom would behave, but she was all smiles even when she shook hands with Jackie. Jackie looked a little surprised but recovered quickly.

"We're here to set up for tomorrow," she said brightly. "I thought Jeff would have the cake by now. Where is it?"

I explained the cake situation. Jackie looked at me sympathetically. "No wonder you look tired."

I was going to explain about the laxative, but Mom jumped in. "She's so stressed out she's making herself sick. I'm going to send her back to bed, so she'll be ready tomorrow. Tell me what you have planned, and I'll help set up."

Jackie looked at me with her eyebrows raised and I shrugged. "Fine," Jackie said. "This won't take very long. You go back to bed."

So, I did. I was feeling much better after the tea and toast, but sleep would sure feel good. It'd been a long couple of months.

Hours later I woke up when I heard Jeff's voice in the living room. He seemed relieved when I made a disheveled yawning appearance.

"Oh, there you are," he said, a little too loudly and a little too cheerfully. "I was explaining to your mother that I'm here to get changed. My brothers want to take me out for a bachelor party."

"And I was telling him," my mother interrupted tartly, "that his future wife shouldn't have been left alone to do everything herself."

Mom was defending me? I felt the resentment I'd felt toward her all my life oozing out a little.

"There wasn't much to do," Jeff murmured. "I knew Steve and Jackie would be over."

"So, you left all the work to them?" Mom asked caustically.

Jeff hung his head. "I suppose that's what it looks like," he admitted.

"That's what it is," Mom said fiercely.

Jeff shrunk down even further. "Well, what would you like me to do?" he finally asked.

"There's nothing you can do," Mom scolded. "You might as well go out with your brothers." I thought she was finished. Apparently, so did Jeff because he started to head toward the bedroom. "But you remember, young man," she threw at his back, "my daughter doesn't owe you a thing. And she's not your maid." Jeff stiffened at that, but Mom continued, "Get dressed and go to your party. I think Marianne's family would like to take her to dinner. She'll have her own party." Jeff nodded and Mom ended her little lecture, "You stay sober, you hear? Steve told me you're in charge of getting the cake and we don't need you dropping it because you're hungover." Jeff was dismissed.

I followed him into the bedroom. "Jeez, what'd I do to deserve that?" he asked plaintively.

"Left me alone to do this wedding—which was your idea—all by myself. As usual," I retorted nastily.

"I know that's the way it sounds," he repeated apologetically.

"That's the way it is!" I paraphrased Mom.

Jeff looked alarmed. "You sound like your mother," he exclaimed.

"You invited her, not me," I retorted. Although I was starting to be glad he had. But I couldn't tell him that.

Jeff decided it wasn't worth arguing about. "I'll be home early," he conceded.

"So will I," I said. He changed into chinos, grabbed a sport coat, kissed in my direction, and left. I heard him say something to Mom as I was pulling on a pair of jeans, but I couldn't tell what it was.

By the time I'd fixed my hair and put on make-up Aggie M had arrived.

"Where's Dad?" I asked. "Isn't he coming?"

"No, he's worn out from Universal Studios," Aggie M said. "He fell asleep as soon as we got back to the room. But he can order something in if he gets hungry later. Where're we going to dinner? I'm starved."

We decided to try a Mexican restaurant that was only a few blocks away against my mother's objections. "Are you sure you can keep it down...or in?" she asked looking at me doubtfully.

I assured her I was fine. Then Mom suggested we walk but Aggie M quickly said, "Oh Mom, nobody walks in L.A."

"It'd probably be good for them if they did," Mom grumbled but didn't argue further. She even said something nice as we got into my Tempo. "I see you've taken care of it," she commented. "I'm glad. I always liked this car."

"I like my Cadillac better," Aggie M crowed.

"Don't gloat, Aggie," Mom said coolly. "Marianne will get a new car sooner than you think. And just so you know, she's not pregnant either. Her first born won't come early. Like yours."

Aggie M looked crestfallen. I was a little surprised. I was the favorite daughter now? There was a time when that would have meant the world to me, but I'd been away from Mom for two years. I was pleased to learn that her approval didn't matter so much anymore. Maybe I'd grown up.

The Mexican restaurant we went to was gringo heaven, but Mom still found it too spicy. "And you be careful what you eat, young lady," she lectured me. "You can't afford to be sick tomorrow."

I repeated I felt fine and dinner was pleasant. Mom told Aggie M how much Jeff's starting salary would be. "He still has to pass the bar," I warned. "If he doesn't it all goes away."

"Then you'll have to help him," Mom said. "Dr. Foster told me how you made sure his final papers were in good shape and handed in on time."

"I just typed..." I started.

"And I'm told your boss wants to help get you into law school. Helping Jeff study for the bar will prepare you if you decide to become a lawyer," Mom continued. "Why didn't you tell me that's why you left home? I wouldn't have tried to stop you, I'd've helped. We have money put away for more schooling if that's what you're worried about. But it's smart to establish residency. It'll cost much less."

"I'm not sure that's what I want to do. First, I want to get a house," I said.

Mom turned to Aggie M triumphantly. "That's why your sister is getting married. They want to invest in property together. That's a reason to get married. Love!" she sneered. "Love doesn't put food on the table. You've yet to learn that."

She sounded like Jeff's grandmother. These Celtic women didn't have a romantic bone in their bodies. I guess that made me a Celtic woman.

Aggie M squirmed so I asked Mom what she thought of Steve and Jackie to change the subject.

"Oh, that Steve," she chuckled. "He's a pistol. And he has such good taste! He's going to make some lucky girl very happy."

"Mom, he's gay," I informed her.

"That he is," she agreed. "Such a happy young fellow."

"No, I mean he's homosexual," I explained. I wasn't throwing Steve under the bus. I knew he'd probably make gay jokes all day tomorrow and I didn't want Mom to be surprised. God knows what she'd do.

"Is he now," Mom said, startled. She mulled for a minute and concluded, "Well, to each his own. The priest would say he's going to hell. But I imagine God likes a good laugh, too."

I thought she'd lose her marbles because he was gay. I guess she just didn't like lesbians. I wondered if there was a story there. "You surprise me," I marveled.

"He probably was a nice boy before he got to Sodom," Mom said wisely. "I bet if you put him in a decent place with a decent girl, he'd be happy enough."

We were back in Sodom again. "I don't think it works that way, Mom. But whatever. What do you think of Jackie?" I asked.

"She's a kept woman, right?" Mom asked. I nodded and she said, "I'm not surprised. She told me a bit about her life. She's done the best she could with what she had. But I pity her. All those lonely times…" She sighed. "I can't pick on her. She's got a tough enough row to hoe. But I'm glad you didn't end up like that."

Wow. I had no idea Mom could be compassionate. What else didn't I know about her?

When I dropped them off at their hotel, I asked Mom if I needed to pick the family up for the wedding. "No, you don't," she said sternly. "We'll pick *you* up. You should be ready by two. We'll escort you to the chapel. Jeff can find his own way."

And on that little grace note she got out of the car and slammed the door.

Aggie M lingered a moment. "Jeff's really cute," she said with a touch of envy. "And I'm glad you're not pregnant. Mom was so embarrassed with me." She hesitated, then asked, "So you and Mom have made up?"

"We both apologized," I said but declined to elaborate. "Good night, Aggie M. See you tomorrow."

"Yeah, I'll see you tomorrow," she said and left.

Jeff was already home when I got in. I looked at him in surprise. "Boy, that was a short bachelor party."

"Brett wanted to go to a strip club," Jeff said. "I knew your mother would scalp me if I went. And David wanted to go home early to help Linda with the kids. It was boring."

I laughed as I walked to the bedroom. He followed and watched me strip down to my T-shirt. "Is everything all right with your mother?"

"We made up but now she doesn't like you," I said, grinning at him. I put my dirty clothes in the hamper and went to the bathroom to brush my teeth. Jeff followed me. "Do you need to brush your teeth?" I asked.

"Already brushed them," he said. "Does that mean she's going to cause trouble tomorrow?"

"Only she knows," I replied cheerfully. He looked downcast so I added, "But I don't think she'll yell at you. She's glad you're marrying me. She thought I was pregnant; did you know that?"

Jeff smiled, relieved. "No, I didn't. But that would explain her attitude."

"I think it's open season now that she knows she doesn't have to be nice to you to get you to marry me."

I enjoyed his discomfort then needed a little clarification of my own. "Mom says you're marrying me because you love me, not for property. Is that true?" I asked as I put toothpaste on my brush.

Jeff looked alarmed. "If I say 'yes' are you going to cancel the wedding?"

"No," I said and gazed at him thoughtfully as I brushed slowly. "You really love me?" I finally asked around my toothbrush.

"Yes," Jeff said simply.

I spat, rinsed, put away my toothbrush and asked, "Why didn't you ever tell me?"

"One of the first things you ever said to me was not to get serious about you. The only way I could get you interested in marriage was to give you a practical reason. And I bet you wouldn't have agreed even then if California weren't a community property state."

I uncomfortably remembered my early speeches. He was right. But... "Why would you want to marry someone if you weren't sure they loved you back?"

"I know you like me," he said with a slight smile. "I'm betting you learn to love me. I wanted to make it hard for you to leave until you figured it out."

Wow. He loved me. And that didn't scare me. As a matter of fact, I was pleased. I smiled.

Jeff looked at me suspiciously. "What?"

"I'm glad you love me. And if you can admit that after seeing me with my underpants around my ankles, I might even love you back."

Jeff laughed. "Good enough. Hey, I missed looking at naked women tonight." He grabbed my hand and led me to the bedroom. "Do you feel well enough to make it up to me?"

"I feel great," I assured him. "But isn't it bad luck to have sex the night before the wedding? Even if it's with your future wife?" I teased.

"It's bad luck to see the dress and I've done that. We're already jinxed. I say we go for it."

I giggled and agreed. My last thought before I fell asleep was: He loved me! And that didn't bother me one bit.

CHAPTER 24

The Big Day!

I woke up early, feeling light and relaxed—probably the result of a laxative and a good lay. I'd remember the double Ls for future stressful times. And speaking of stress, I was proud of myself because I hadn't knuckled under to my mother! A thought occurred to me; would I ever have had the courage to stand up to her if Jeff hadn't come into my life? I was even glad that he'd taken it on himself to invite her to our wedding. I know I wouldn't have. I'd have dug in my heels and resisted to the bitter end. And I probably would have regretted it. Jeff had good instincts.

I got up and found another reason to appreciate Jeff. He'd made coffee and a bagel run already. I lolled around the living room, enjoying my coffee, and thinking about my day. I didn't have to be ready until two so I could go for a run before worrying about getting cleaned up. I was glad I'd gotten a hat, so I didn't have to worry about my hair. All I had to do was make sure the ends were curled. I wandered into the bedroom and admired my stain-free dress. *Mom sure had done wonders with that*, I thought as I sipped my coffee. My reverie was interrupted by a knock on the door. I let Jeff answer it. He had pants on.

I heard some murmured conversation then nothing, so I called out, "Who was that, Jeff?"

"It's Brett," he called back. "He came over for coffee."

Rats. There went my peaceful morning. I put on running clothes, grabbed my keys, and breezed through the living room, saying, "Hi, Brett. I'm off for my run. See you later." I figured I'd wander around for an hour. He'd be gone by the time I got back.

When I returned an hour later, not only had Brett not left, the rest of Jeff's family had appeared. Jeff smiled at me manically, "My family couldn't think of anything to do before the wedding, so they decided to spend the time with us. Isn't that great?"

Yeah, great. Dr. Foster was in the recliner, working on a crossword puzzle. Ruth and Fiona shared the couch and bickered over the TV remote control. Jeff seated himself at the dining room table, so I joined him. I heard Brett rummaging in the refrigerator. "Don't eat anything in there," I called to him. "That stuff is for the reception."

He came out with a wad of lunch meat in his hand. "This? Oh, sorry. Hey, do you have any bread? I might as well make a sandwich."

I stared at him in dismay, so Jeff got up to find some bread and mustard. They both left a mess on the kitchen counter that I hurriedly cleaned up. At noon I decided I'd better get in the bathroom even though I felt self-conscious with his family all around. But Dr. Foster beat me to it. He murmured something about his coffee working and took his puzzle into the bathroom. I took his place on the recliner and twitched. Time passed.

There was another knock on the door. I jumped up to answer and found Steve standing with a case of wine in his arms. Jackie, carrying the box of flowers, peered over his shoulder. He looked at me in horror. "Why are you in sweats? Don't you know what time it is?"

"I can't get into the bathroom yet," I babbled. "Dr. Foster's in there."

Steve walked into the apartment and took in the situation at a glance. "Okay, everybody," he bawled. "If you're not here to work you have to go someplace else. You're taking up space."

That speech was greeted with incredulous silence. Which didn't bother Steve or stop him. "Jeff, haven't you gotten the cake yet? What have you been doing?" He crossed to the bathroom door and rapped authoritatively. "Dr. Foster? You about done? Marianne needs to take a shower. You've got a bathroom in your hotel room, don't you? Better go use it."

The Fosters were all staring at him with their mouths open. Jackie smothered a laugh and retreated to the kitchen. "C'mon people. Chop chop!" Steve clapped his hands. Brett came out of the kitchen with another sandwich. "You can take that with you," Steve ordered. He shooed Brett into the living room and out the door. "I've got a wedding to put on. If you're not here to help, you have to go." He returned his attention to the bathroom door. "Dr. Foster, did you hear me?"

Dr. Foster came self-consciously out of the bathroom. "I didn't mean to keep you waiting," he apologized to me.

I smiled bemusedly but Steve hustled him along. "That's fine. But we'll see you at the chapel." He continued herding Fosters out the door. Mrs. Foster started to get a little huffy, but Steve fixed her with a steely glare. In a few seconds they were all gone. It was like magic.

"If I weren't marrying Jeff, I'd marry you," I told him thankfully.

He smiled briefly. "You get in the shower," he ordered. "I'll clean up the kitchen. Jeff, are you still here? Go get the cake!"

Jeff fled and I had the bathroom all to myself. It was a little smelly, but I suppose when the urge hits you can't fight it. No wonder Dr. Foster was embarrassed. That poor toilet had had a workout the last two days.

I washed my hair and shaved my legs. I came out of the bathroom in a robe, drying my hair with a towel, when I saw my mother and Aggie M sitting where the Foster women had been. Jackie came out from the kitchen, drying her hands. "They came over to help you get ready," she said with a slight smile in their direction.

Steve appeared with a bottle of champagne and glasses for everybody which struck me as a marvelous idea. "You can't do hair and makeup without champagne," he sang. Mom looked at him scandalized but she accepted her glass without comment. She had a sip then said, "You girls start on Marianne's hair. I'll do a quick clean of the bathroom and run the vacuum. We won't have time to do it later."

Jackie, Aggie M, and I retired to the bedroom to dry my hair and plug in the curling iron. Maybe it was the champagne, but I was starting to have fun. I could hear Steve setting up in the dining room and the vacuum whir in the living room. Then Steve was knocking and pushing my mother into the room. "This is where the mother of the bride belongs," he stated. "I've got everything covered out here." He whipped off the towel Mom had pinned on to protect her dress and closed the door behind him.

Mom stood self-consciously until Jackie asked, "What's your specialty? Hair or makeup?"

Mom humphed. "Neither. Can't you tell? But if you need anything sewed, I can do it."

She sat on the bed and Jackie handed her a glass of champagne. "You left the other one outside and I imagine Steve has it cleaned up by now."

"That Steve is going to make someone a wonderful husband," Mom commented.

"Mom, I told you..." I started exasperated.

"I know what you told me," she interrupted. "And I don't care. He's a nice boy. And he's very organized. I wish more men were that organized."

We trashed men for a while. When that subject ran down Aggie M commented as she curled a strand of my hair, "This isn't like my wedding at all."

"I know, it's small," I returned shortly.

"No, I didn't mean that...although it is. I meant it's more relaxed."

"Your in-laws expected a show," Mom pointed out.

"Yeah, but this is nice, isn't it?" Aggie M pursued.

"I'm glad Marianne isn't pregnant," Mom answered and Aggie M flushed. Mom noticed. "I wasn't thinking about you; I was thinking about me."

We all stared at her. "So, you were....?" Jackie prompted.

Mom nodded. "It was the worst time of my life. I was alone in a foreign country. I was young and got carried away by...I guess you'd call it passion." She took a sip of her wine. I think that was the only thing that would have loosened her up enough to discuss her past like this. "I was lucky your father didn't run out on me. I don't know what I would've done. But I paid dearly for it. Your grandmother Fuchs held it over my head every day of my life. 'My son sacrificed his career because you couldn't keep your knees together,'" she mimicked and took another sip of wine. "Marianne, I shouldn't have treated you the way I did. And I shouldn't have thrown you out like that. I know what it's like to be alone in the world." Jackie was looking at her peculiarly. "Your parents didn't help you, did they?" Mom asked her.

Jackie mutely shook her head 'no'.

"And that's why you live the way you do. That married man was the only help available to you, wasn't he?" Mom continued.

Jackie nodded her head 'yes'.

"Is it a life you'd recommend?" Mom pursued.

"It's not for everyone," Jackie said evenly. "I don't think it'd be good for Marianne."

"Well, I have Jeff to thank for keeping her safe. He's doing a better job than I am," Mom admitted.

Aggie M and I exchanged amazed looks.

"But that's not what I need to talk about," Mom said. "I want to discuss marriage with Marianne."

"Mom, I know all about the birds and the bees," I said with an amused look at Jackie.

"No, I want to talk about how difficult marriage is," Mom said firmly. "You need to know that as wonderful as Jeff seems now, he's going to drive you crazy. Isn't that right, Aggie M?" Mom looked to her for confirmation. Aggie M gave a rueful nod.

This was starting to make me nervous. Jeff interrupted. He opened the door abruptly, looked at all us women warily, and said, "You better have another glass of that stuff."

What could have gone wrong? I walked out to the dining room. It was the cake again. Steve was staring at the two-tiered dessert frowningly. I couldn't see anything wrong from the back, so I walked around to join him. On the top tier of the cake were our names "Jeff & Maryanne." The misspelling of my name was bad enough. Then I got to the bottom tier: June 23, 1991. But the decorator had misjudged the spacing, so Ju was written large but the rest of the date sort of petered out and had to be squished together. And all the writing was in Day-Glo pink frosting.

"I knew I should have had a plate of Twinkies," I said. Then I got the giggles. I took Jeff's advice and had another glass of champagne.

Things got surreal from there. Mom kept trying to get me aside to warn me about the difficulties of marriage (Today? She had to wait until today?). Steve kept asking my advice about decorating and then ignoring it. Jeff disappeared into the bathroom, then shooed Aggie M, Jackie, Mom, and me out of the bedroom so he could get changed. I was made up, my hair was done, and I wore my hat and dress. I was basically ready to go. I sat in a modified upright fetal position in the recliner with all the talking and activity going on over my head. I'd have a sip of champagne when it got too onerous.

Two o'clock finally arrived. Dad appeared, Jeff pried the champagne glass out of my hand, and Mom led me to their rental car. I was a bit befuddled to put it mildly but at least I wasn't worried about anything—like how marriage was difficult, and I better prepare myself. Mom really hadn't helped me with those little caveats.

We had a hard time parking. The two o'clock wedding was running late, and their guests were slow to leave. We had to park around the block and walk. But I didn't really care. I let Mom steer me to the chapel. Jeff and his family joined us, and I smiled at them bemusedly. The chapel coordinator directed us to a side room to wait and left to herd the preceding group out. Steve distributed corsages and boutonnieres and handed me my bouquet. That's when we discovered the altar flowers had been left in our apartment.

"I thought you were bringing them," Steve hissed to Jackie.

"I've got the bouquets and boutonnieres," she snapped back. "I told you to grab the altar flowers."

My champagne euphoria was disappearing under their recriminations. Jeff must have noticed the panic beginning to show in my eyes, so he stepped in. "I've got the Tempo; I'll go get them. I can make the drive in half an hour. Just stall the coordinator!" He ran out.

Time passed. And passed. And passed. Jeff didn't appear. The champagne high was completely gone by now. Corsages and boutonnieres had been pinned on. All the relatives were starting to look grave. The coordinator came running into our room.

"Where's the groom?" she demanded. "It's almost time to go!"

"We forgot the altar flowers and he went to get them," Mom explained.

"He's coming back, isn't he?" the coordinator asked, starting to look a little nuts.

That thought hadn't even occurred to me. *Was* he coming back?

"Presumably," I answered, stifling a panic giggle. At least I was giggly, not hysterical. The coordinator rushed off, saying she had to talk to the organist.

"Don't worry, he's coming back," Steve assured me. "Here, I snuck a bottle of champagne in with the flowers. Don't worry, it's the cheap stuff. You better have another drink."

It certainly couldn't hurt. It would anesthetize me if I got jilted at the altar.

I'd taken a big slug from a plastic glass when Jeff rushed in. "I drove up on the sidewalk to get around jams. It's a miracle I didn't get a ticket. But I got the flowers!" He held the flower arrangement up in triumph. It looked slightly disheveled. Jackie grabbed it and ran to find the coordinator.

I finished off my champagne and tossed the glass behind me. "Let's get this show on the road." I burped. "Excuse me."

The coordinator appeared and lined us up then ran off again. I noticed three strangers sitting in the pews. I grabbed Mom's arm and pointed. "Do you know them?" I asked.

"I think those are the cousins from Orange County," she whispered. "I haven't seen them since I was a girl in Ireland, but they have our family look about them, don't they?"

I looked Mom up and down and looked at the strangers again. I agreed that there was an elfin resemblance.

The coordinator was making her hysterical way toward us again, so Mom murmured, "I better sit down before that poor woman has a heart attack." She left me alone with Dad.

I settled in for a quiet wait. Dad and I had never had much to say to each other and I didn't think now would be any different. I was fortified by champagne, so the silence didn't bother me. But Dad surprised me.

"I'm glad I have a minute with you alone," he started. I looked at him in surprise. He smiled quietly and continued. "I wanted to tell you that I've misjudged you."

"Really?" I asked. "How?"

"I always thought you were like me because you looked more like me. I worried that people would take advantage of you because you were quiet and agreeable. The world isn't kind to quiet, agreeable people. I know." He looked toward my little mother who was settling herself like a pleased hen in the front row. "I know my mother always thought I married beneath me because your mother didn't bring any property into the marriage." *Well, that explained Mom's attitude toward property*, I thought fuzzily. "But Mary has been the backbone of the family. I wouldn't have succeeded with the store, I had no interest in it, but she took over and made a wonderful business. She put up with my mother when I avoided her as much as possible and that wasn't fair. My mother was a pill and Mary treated her respectfully. She made sure my mother never wanted for anything." My dad paused, then finished. "What I'm trying to say is: I thought Aggie M was like Mary because they looked alike. But Aggie M doesn't have your spine. You're the one with the drive and backbone. I'm sorry I took so long to see it. So, if your new mother-in-law gives you a hard time you remember: you're your mother's daughter. I know you'll be as big a blessing to Jeff as your mother has been to me." He paused. "And did I tell you how lovely you look? I never realized before that my baby girl was beautiful." Then he ruined the compliment by adding, "Who'd have thought it." He smiled and patted the hand I'd put in the crook of his arm. I gawped so Dad hurried to finish, "That's all I have to say. That crazy woman is waving at us. I think we're about ready to start."

The coordinator was waving all around and the organist took that as her cue to start the wedding march. Dad and I paced gravely down the aisle to the altar which didn't take very long considering how small the chapel was. But it was enough time for the people who'd been given cameras by Steve to take some candid shots. The minister beamed as Jeff took my hand from my father and we both turned toward him. We recited the usual vows--it never occurred to either of us that we should make anything up ourselves--and Jeff put the lapis lazuli ring that he'd bought me on my left hand. Our relatives, friends, and three strangers solemnly witnessed the proceeding.

"I now pronounce you husband and wife," the minister concluded. "You may now kiss the bride," he told Jeff.

Jeff gave me a short kiss then we looked at each other and grinned in relief. "We did it!" we both said at the same time and laughed. Then Jeff gave me a big hug and kiss. I had to hang on to my hat, but I enjoyed the kiss. I think Jeff was genuinely happy that we'd combined our lives. I was glad that the whole wedding thing was almost over. Then we turned and grinned at our audience.

"Ladies and gentlemen," the minister said grandly, "let me present to you for the first time Mr. and Mrs. Foster."

Foster, I mused to myself. At least it was better than Fuchs. I wouldn't have to explain my last name all the time anymore. And the initials would be the same

.

CHAPTER 25

Surprises

W e took a few pictures at the altar then went to the minister's office to finish the paperwork. Jackie wiped her eyes as she witnessed Jeff and me sign the marriage contract. Steve was stoic but left as soon as he'd witnessed the document and posed for some pictures. He said he had to get back to the apartment and open it up for the guests. He took Jackie with him. The minister matter-of-factly said he'd mail the license in and accepted the money Jeff handed over without comment. He wished us well and we all left. Just in time, too. The four o'clock was starting to show up and I didn't want to stress out the coordinator more than she already was.

The guests all got in their respective cars except for Jeff and me. He drove us home in the Tempo—which was good; the day's events and the champagne were catching up to me. I put my head back and closed my eyes for the trip. Neither one of us had anything to say until we arrived. I opened my eyes to see Jeff smiling at me. "Ready for this?" he asked.

I smiled back. "I know I'm not supposed to say this, but I'm glad it's almost over."

"It's been a long day," Jeff agreed. "Just a few hours more."

I nodded, steeled myself, and we went into the apartment together. Steve and Jackie had beat everybody there and were ready with the booze. I had another glass of champagne and admired everything Steve and Jackie had accomplished. The trays of meat and cheese were tastefully displayed on our dining room table under a bower of yellow streamers and white paper bells. The cake was on a separate table with the horrible neon-pink frosting turned to the wall. Steve saw me smiling at the cake and whispered in my ear, "I tried to scrape off the pink, but it made a mess, so I turned it to the wall. I don't think anyone will notice."

"If that's the worst thing that happens today, I'll consider myself lucky," I whispered back.

Steve led me over to the couch and sat me down. "You better take it easy for a minute. I'll manage the guests."

Bless Steve's heart; he made that chapel coordinator look like an amateur. He steered all the guests past the booze and food tables. He brought me a plate of food and placed wedding gifts around my feet. "For pictures later," he explained. I sat like a blob with my plate and glass, accepting congratulations and good wishes. Mom introduced me to the Orange County cousins. Gerald and Noelene—Gerald was the cousin; Noelene was the in-law—had a bar and grill in Huntington Beach. They introduced their grown son, Michael. They thanked me for the invitation, and I thanked them for coming. "It's nice to meet you," I added. "I forgot Mom had relatives in Southern California."

I could see Mom's eyes start to spark when I said that, and I remembered that she'd already scolded me for having forgotten her relatives what with one thing and another. But let's face it, I wasn't thinking clearly at all.

"We'll have you down to the house one of these days," Gerald assured me. "It's a shame it's taken this long to get Mary out here. Say Noelene, what do you say we ask her to spend a few days with us?" He didn't wait for poor Noelene to say anything. He called across the room, "Mary, how about..." He dragged Noelene off to my mother and my attention turned back to my other guests. Everything sort of blurred after that. Steve kept my glass full and the food coming. I noticed Jeff had appeared at my side. I wondered when that had happened. But I didn't care. My job was to sip and smile so that's what I did. Blissfully. With champagne.

Steve interrupted my interlude with the command to cut the cake. Jeff and I rose, grabbed the long knife, and smiled for the camera as Steve took a picture of our hands holding the knife as we cut the cake. Steve wanted a picture of Jeff pushing cake in my mouth, and vice versa, but I nixed it. I'd always hated watching people shoving cake in each other's face. It didn't look loving to me. When I objected Steve said, "It's not supposed to be loving, it's supposed to be a preview of marriage."

"We're not going to be married like that," I retorted. "No cake shoving." Steve accepted my decision with little grace...but he accepted it.

Jeff and I ate our cake and returned to our nest on the couch. Steve announced that the next item on the agenda was opening presents.

"Do we have to do that now?" I protested.

"We have to do something," Steve retorted. "You didn't hire a band."

Jeff and I opened presents and Jackie took down the name of the giver and the gift. That steno training really comes in handy sometimes. We got small, practical things for the most part. Grandma Foster gave us the biggest gift; a duvet. "Jeff said you were getting a queen-size bed, so I got that size," she said as we unwrapped it.

This was wishful thinking on Jeff's part because we had a double bed and no money, but I thanked her prettily. A bigger bed would be nice, I admitted to myself. I was getting scoliosis from curling up in a corner when Jeff stretched his length diagonally.

Aggie M gave us a set of matching glasses. "I've seen your cupboard," she whispered loudly. "You need a matched set."

We did. And I thanked her.

The only gift that gave me pause came from Mom's Irish cousin. I opened a box to find a clay pot filled with plastic mushrooms and fruit. I wasn't the only one having trouble with it. "What in the world is that?" Steve demanded in an appalled voice.

I vamped quickly and said, "It's a...it's a centerpiece! From my cousin Gerald, right there!" I pointed him out and Steve subsided. "Thank you, Gerald. It's very thoughtful."

Gerald grinned and turned to talk to my mother again. I mused over his gift. Where in the world had he found it? And why give it to me? I'd never done anything to him. Jeff and I exchanged glances and snickered. We pulled ourselves together before Gerald noticed.

Dr. Foster handed Jeff an envelope with a flourish and Jeff opened it to find a check for $500. "That'll help buy that new bed," Dr. Foster said with a wink at his son.

That's when Mom stood up, all five foot two of her, and commanded everyone's attention.

"I have a check, too," she announced. "My daughter didn't ask for any financial help with this wedding. Her father and I would have been happy to provide a wedding as lovely, and as expensive," (this was said with a side-long glance at Ruth Foster) "as the one her sister had. But Marianne chose to put her money to better use. She wants to buy property. And I approve of that. Her father and I have decided that we'll give the young people the price of the wedding. I hope this check from Dad and me will help with a down-payment for your new home." And she grandly handed me a folded check.

I opened it as everybody craned their heads trying to get a look at the amount. And I gasped. "It's for $15,000," I wheezed at Jeff.

Jeff took the check from me and stared at it. Then he stared at my mother. And she stared right back, her chin up, proudly smiling.

"I don't know what to say," Jeff stammered. "Thank you, I guess."

"You're welcome," Mom said. "That's what you can save if you're a thrifty, hard-working taxpayer. Not someone who gets their money from the government." She turned and directed this at Ruth Foster. Mom had heard Ruth's little digs. And she didn't have to take them anymore; her daughter was safely married. I think she'd just declared war. From Ruth Foster's expression I think she'd figured that out, too.

I quickly stood up to give Mom and Dad hugs. At least it stopped the two mothers from glaring at each other. Steve passed around more champagne and food and the party returned to normal. It finally petered out at about six.

Jeff announced that we had to leave for our honeymoon, and I rose in relief. We made our thanks and good-byes and trotted to the Tempo, followed by our guests. I stopped when I saw the car. Jeff's little brother had decorated it with tin cans. On the back window he'd written in shaving cream, "Fuchs Off!"

"I'm not going to miss all the dirty jokes about my last name," I said wryly to Jeff.

"It's what guys do at a wedding," Jeff shrugged.

We got in the car and drove off, waving at everybody as we left. I took off my shoes and sighed, "I'm glad that's over. Incorporation would have been a lot less hassle."

Jeff grinned. "But we wouldn't have all that wedding loot!"

I snorted. "I could live without Gerald's centerpiece. And I'm not looking forward to cleaning up when we go back." I sat back and enjoyed the silence for a minute before asking, "Where are we going anyway?"

"We only have tonight and tomorrow off," Jeff said. "I thought we should do something nice."

"Can we afford it?" I asked automatically. Being poor had become a habit with me.

"We've got $15,500," Jeff said with a grin. "Just sit back. It'll be fun."

I sat back with my eyes closed until he stopped at a car wash. People eyed us curiously as we waited in our wedding finery for the Tempo to be cleaned up, but we ignored them. Nothing bothered Jeff much and I was too tired to care what people thought.

When the car was presentable, Jeff drove us over to the Beverly Hills Hotel where he'd reserved a bungalow. The bellman took our overnight bags and led us to our quarters with a twinkle. We accepted his offer of ice and Jeff tipped him handsomely when he returned. And that's the last thing I remember. After the bellman left, I flopped on the bed and died. It's a good thing Jeff had gotten lucky the night before because his wedding night was a bust.

I was still in my dress when I woke up the next morning. Jeff was waiting with a cup of coffee, bless his heart. "I thought maybe you'd like to join me on the terrace?" he asked and gestured outside.

"Let me get showered," I said and jumped up. I felt like a new woman after about twelve hours of sleep.

I ran to the bathroom, dropping my dress and underwear on the way. I wanted my coffee. I scrubbed myself down and put on the hotel robe provided before joining Jeff on the terrace. It was so early we had the area to ourselves. We talked over our wedding day as we sipped. We laughed over the crazy coordinator and Gerry's Cherries. That awful centerpiece had already been officially baptized.

"But we can't laugh about your parent's check," Jeff commented, suddenly sober.

"Well, your parents coughed up $500," I said in the spirit of charity.

"That pales in comparison," Jeff pointed out.

"I think Mom meant it to," I said, amused. "Your mother's digs really pissed her off. And my mother always gets the last word."

"I think that's something you have in common," Jeff observed. He grinned at me then switched his tone abruptly. "Are you awake yet? I want to take advantage of my wedding night before it's over."

I told him I was up for anything—as he obviously was—and we returned to the bedroom. But I had a plan. And I put it into motion before he could kiss me. I hadn't brushed my teeth yet, so my surprise worked better for both of us.

Jeff and I had pretty much mined our 'how-to' sex books for all their secrets. So, I'd asked Steve for some fine points about practices that didn't involve the missionary position—or any parts except my mouth, really. And Steve came through. As did Jeff after a moment's surprise. Afterward, Jeff took a shower and I brushed my teeth and we ordered breakfast. I'd had my protein, but some carbs would be nice. And I don't think Jeff had had anything to eat since last night. He'd need to keep his strength up.

As we waited for room service Jeff asked, "Where'd you learn that? I didn't think our books went into that much detail."

"I asked Steve," I told him. "I figured he'd know what it took to make a man happy. Apparently, this is popular in the gay community."

"It's popular in the guy community," Jeff amended dryly.

"Then it's a good thing he gave me a blow-by-blow description," I said. Jeff choked and started laughing. I grinned at him. "Do you suppose that's where 'blow job' came from?"

Jeff was still chuckling when our breakfast came. He was buttering his toast when I asked casually, "When did you know you loved me?"

"For sure? About twenty minutes ago." He took a bite of toast and chewed. "I remember the first time I saw you," he continued. "You were standing at the bulletin board. You were wearing an odd sort of blouse, but your eyes were incredible. And you seemed so clean. The more I got to know you the better I liked you. I'm not sure when it changed to something deeper. Maybe when you gave Scott hell."

"Which time?" I laughed.

"Didn't matter. You were fearless. I wanted to keep you around."

"I remember that day at the bulletin board," I admitted. "I liked your eyes, too. That's one of the reasons I took the job. That and the fact DB&H had a softball team."

We grinned at each other and finished our breakfasts. As I ate, I reflected that Mom may have thought softball would make me a lesbian but actually it got me a husband. Maybe I'd rub that in someday.

We paddled around the pool for an hour then Jeff asked if I'd mind checking out early. "We're not really getting our money's worth if we leave early," I said. "Did you have anything particular in mind?"

"I'd like to take you back to Disneyland," he announced. "That's where we had our first date and that worked out. I'd like to start our marriage there. Maybe it'll be good luck."

I smiled. Jeff was obviously more sentimental than me. But the idea had appeal. We checked out and drove down to Anaheim. The park was crowded, as usual, but we got there early enough to catch the popular rides before the lines got too long. I even got that damn rat to shake my hand this time. We stayed late to watch the fireworks. I was so rested up from my big sleep my sore feet didn't even bother me much.

What I dreaded was going back to the apartment. I knew the place would be an unholy mess. I'd just have to live with it until after I got off work tomorrow. I guess I should have asked for another day off, but I didn't want to waste vacation time cleaning.

I'd steeled myself to ignore the chaos when we parked the car. I was talking to myself, saying, "The mess can wait, the mess can wait" as we climbed the stairs and Jeff unlocked the door. He picked me up suddenly and carried me over the threshold. I squealed and laughed until Jeff put me down inside. Then I straightened my spine and bravely looked at...a spotless apartment. A note had been prominently left on the dining room table, anchored by Gerry's Cherries, and addressed to me in my mother's handwriting. I opened it and read:

Marianne:

I didn't think you'd want to come home to a mess so that nice boy Steve let Aggie M and me in this morning to clean up. And tell Jeff his grandmother showed up and helped, too. At least one member of his family isn't lazy. ("I think that's a dig at your mom," I commented to Jeff who gave a resigned nod.) *We'll be going down to cousin Gerald's home in Orange County. I've included his phone number. It'd be nice if you and Jeff could come down this Saturday for a barbeque. And tell Jeff we'll be expecting both of you this Christmas.*

Mom

I looked up at Jeff. "I guess we've got our marching orders," I said.

"She doesn't think we're really going to South Dakota for Christmas, does she?" Jeff asked skeptically.

"She really does," I assured him. Jeff looked at me in bafflement. "Hey, don't look at me," I protested. "You were the one who wanted her here. Welcome to my world."

Jeff shrugged. "At least she got the place cleaned up," he said. "And she gave us all that money, too."

"You'll earn every penny of that money," I predicted. But I wasn't really unhappy. I appreciated the money and the cleaning. And it was nice to know I'd have an ally against Jeff's mom if I needed one. I put the note back in the envelope. "Well, I don't know about you but I'm tired. And we have to go to work tomorrow."

Jeff nodded and grinned. "After you, Mrs. Foster," he said and gestured to the bedroom.

Mrs. Foster, I mused. I wondered how long it would take me to get used to that.

CHAPTER 26

The End of the Beginning

So, life went back to normal. Well, at least as normal as it ever got for Jeff and me. We put the money in the bank and carpooled to work. When I got to my desk, I found a card from Mr. Elliot and Mr. Brady. They'd included a gift certificate for a weekend at the Ahwahnee Hotel in Yosemite Park—complete with a pass for a dinner at the hotel dining room. "I've never been to Yosemite," I commented to Jeff.

"It's beautiful," Jeff said. "I hope the hotel gives us leeway on cashing in the gift certificate. We won't have time to use it until next year."

I agreed ruefully but sent nice 'thank you' cards to the attorneys. It was a lovely gesture. And it would give us something to look forward to.

We didn't have to go Cousin Gerald's Orange County home for a barbeque. When I called, Mom said she'd spent enough time in SoCal and wanted to go home. Cousin Gerald promised he'd invite us down at a later date and we left it at that. All the goodbyes were long distance. We were done with relatives for a while.

We went through the pictures from the disposable cameras Steve had provided our guests at the wedding. Jeff looked great but apparently I spent the day in 'deer in headlights' mode. I put the pictures into an album without comment.

Jeff spent his weekends studying for the bar and I played softball. It was so nice not to be worrying about a wedding that I'd forgotten about our potential eviction.

Jeff passed the bar that July on the first try. I was impressed but he was relieved. "Now I know my job is safe," he commented. "And we can start house hunting!"

"So soon?" I asked in dismay.

"We have to get on it," he replied earnestly. "Sometimes it takes months to close."

We talked about what neighborhoods we wanted to live in. "We both work downtown so I don't want to live too far out. I don't want to waste all my time on a commute," he announced. "I drew up a map of the areas that are about ten minutes from the office. I think we should concentrate our search in an area called Echo Park."

"Echo Park?" I asked in alarm. "Isn't that over the hill from the Friesmans? I don't want to be anywhere near the Friesmans."

"They're probably divorced by now," Jeff snorted. "I doubt either of them is still in the area."

"But I heard it was gang hell," I said nervously.

"It can't be that bad," Jeff scoffed.

"Maybe it could. I think we should consider another neighborhood," I stated firmly.

We spent the next month of weekends looking at various properties in Echo Park with real estate agents. The average house price was around $150,000 which Jeff thought was too high for us.

"We only have that $15,000 dollars your folks gave us," he said, scribbling figures on a notepad. "That's a ten percent down payment but I'd like to find something cheaper. We'll need money to fix up a property and I don't want to take out a second mortgage."

"Do you know much about building a house?" I asked doubtfully.

"My grandpa taught me some electrical work on the farm when he was alive. I also took four years of shop in high school," Jeff said confidently. "And you must have learned something working in the hardware store."

"A little," I evaded.

"Can you paint?" Jeff asked impatiently.

"Yeah, but I don't know when I'll have time," I retorted.

"Great! The agent told me about a piece of property that's been on the market for over a year. He says it's pretty bad, but it's got a huge yard with fruit trees and we can make it the way we want it. We can afford it and it's close to work for both of us. I told him we could look at it this weekend."

"Jeff, if it's that bad I'm not even going to look at it," I declared.

We toured it that weekend. It was horrible. It had one bathroom, the kitchen was a greasy shambles, and it was covered in dark green shag carpet—almost identical to the carpet in our apartment; must have been a sale that year--that cats had obviously used as a litter box. And the electrical system was so old the entire house was wired up to one fuse—and a penny.

"We can't live here!" I hissed to Jeff as I pulled him aside while the agent went to another room.

"Sure, we can!" Jeff said enthusiastically. "It'll be like camping. And it's been on the market so long the owners are only asking $80,000 for it. That'll keep our payments low! And when we get it done, we can flip it for a fortune!" Jeff's eyes glowed at the prospect.

"Jeff, it's falling apart, we can't do this!" I declared.

"Sure, we can!" he repeated confidently.

We bought the house the following week.

I'd been so proud that I'd learned to say 'no' to my mother. But apparently Jackie was right; I couldn't say 'no' to Jeff. Or maybe he was deaf.

Oh dear.

Other Books by Barbara Schnell

First Year

Greetings From Casa Cesspoole (with Gordon Johnson)

For reviews and links to Barbara's books, go to:
www.barbaraschnell.com

About the Author

In a career devoted to full-time employment avoidance, Barbara Schnell worked in marketing at an insurance company (now defunct) and was a purchasing agent for a major San Francisco law firm (also now defunct but she claims to have had nothing to do with either failure—really). She restored a 1921 California Bungalow in Los Angeles. She set a cash-winning (at the time) record on *$25,000 Pyramid* and came in last on *Jeopardy*. She sang mezzo and played flute in the St. Paul's Cathedral Choir. With reference to writing credentials, Barbara has had a short story, "Grandma's Straw Hat", published in an anthology. Another short story, "Tracks", was published in *Literary Landscapes*. Six of her flash-fiction stories have won the Southern California Writers' Association "Will Write for Food" contest and have been published in SCWA's collection. She has also written two screenplays—she worked as an actress and is still a member of SAG/AFTRA, it seemed a logical medium to start in—and got lots of compliments but no cash. She got so many raves about her Christmas letter that she and her husband published them as an epistolary memoir called *Greetings from Casa Cesspoole*. Her debut novel was *First Year*. Her second novel, *Marianne Moves On*, won a National Indie Excellence Award. She lives with her patient husband and two cats.

17483683R00144